P9-EEJ-314

I HAVE TWENTY SKILLED ASSASSINS
AT MY DISPOSAL....

Aballister held up a small, bulging bag and shook it once to show the others that its thickness came from many coins—gold, surely. Dorigen understood the bag's significance, understood what it would buy for Aballister, and for Bogo as well. Bogo had come from Westgate, a city hundreds of miles to the northeast, at the mouth of the Lake of Dragons. Westgate was notable as a bustling trade town, and it was known, too, for a band of assassins who were among the cruelest killers in Faerûn.

"Even your Night Masks will have a difficult time striking at our young scholar, whether he's in Shilmista or has returned to the Edificant Library," Dorigen asserted, if for no better reason than to take some of the bite out of Aballister's icy demeanor concerning his son. For all that she hated Cadderly—he had broken her hands and stolen several magical items from her— Dorigen simply couldn't believe Aballister's viciousness toward his own son.

"He is not in Shilmista," Bogo replied with a grin, his brown eyes flashing with excitement, "nor in the library." Dorigen stared at Bogo, and her sudden interest obviously pleased the young wizard. "He is in Carradoon."

"This is pure sword and sorcery reminiscent at times of Fritz Leiber's Fafhrd and the Gray Mouser series."

—Don D'Ammassa on *Promise of the Witch-King*

". . . breathes new life into the stereotypical creatures of the milieu: the motivations of his villains make sense without violating the traditions of the game. His heroes face dilemmas deeper than merely how to slay their foes. Salvatore has long used his dark elf protagonist to reflect on issues of racial prejudice . . . and this novel is no exception."

—Paul Brink, *School Library Journal* on *The Thousand Orcs*

R.A. SALVATORE'S
THE CLERIC QUINTET

BOOK I
Canticle

BOOK II
In Sylvan Shadows

BOOK III
Night Masks

BOOK IV
The Fallen Fortress
August 2009

BOOK V
The Chaos Curse
September 2009

R.A. SALVATORE

FORGOTTEN REALMS®

The Cleric
Quintet
BOOK
III

Night Masks

Cover Art by
DUANE O. MYERS

WIZARDS
OF THE COAST®

WHITE MOUNTAIN LIBRARY
SWEETWATER COUNTY LIBRARY SYS
ROCK SPRINGS, WY

The Cleric Quintet, Book III
NIGHT MASKS

©1992 TSR, Inc.
©2009 Wizards of the Coast LLC

All characters in this book are fictitious. Any resemblance to actual persons, living or dead, is purely coincidental.

This book is protected under the copyright laws of the United States of America. Any reproduction or unauthorized use of the material or artwork contained herein is prohibited without the express written permission of Wizards of the Coast LLC.

Published by Wizards of the Coast LLC

FORGOTTEN REALMS, WIZARDS OF THE COAST, and their respective logos are trademarks of Wizards of the Coast LLC in the U.S.A. and other countries.

Printed in the U.S.A.

The sale of this book without its cover has not been authorized by the publisher. If you purchased this book without a cover, you should be aware that neither the author nor the publisher has received payment for this "stripped book."

First Printing: August 1992
This Edition First Printing: May 2009

9 8 7 6 5 4 3 2

ISBN: 978-0-7869-5327-1
620-23971740-001-EN

U.S., CANADA,   EUROPEAN HEADQUARTERS
ASIA, PACIFIC, & LATIN AMERICA   Hasbro UK Ltd
Wizards of the Coast LLC   Caswell Way
P.O. Box 707   Newport, Gwent NP9 0YH
Renton, WA 98057-0707   GREAT BRITAIN
+1-800-324-6496   Save this address for your records.

Visit our web site at www.wizards.com

To Aunt Terry, who'll never know
how much her support has meant to me.

PROLOGUE

Q

The larger man regarded him warily, beginning to understand, and asked, "You know all in attendance?"

"Of course."

The burly fighter looked back just in time to see the last of the other patrons slip out the door then added, "And they have left at your bidding?"

"Of course."

"Mako sent you . . ."

The weaker man curled his lips in a wicked grin, one that widened as the fighter regarded his skinny arms with obvious disdain.

". . . to kill me," the large man finished, trying to appear calm.

His wringing hands, fingers moving as if seeking something to keep them occupied, revealed his unease. He licked his dry lips and glanced around, not taking his dark eyes from the assassin for more than a heartbeat. He surely noticed that the smaller man wore gloves, one white and one black, and must have silently berated himself for not being more observant.

The thin man replied, "You knew Mako would repay you for his cousin's death."

"His own fault!" the large man retorted. "It was he who struck the first blow. I had no ch—"

"I am neither judge nor jury," the puny man reminded him.

"Just a killer," the fighter replied, "serving whoever gives you the largest sack of gold."

The assassin nodded, not the least bit insulted by that characterization.

The little man noticed his target's hand slipping casually into a hidden pouch in the **V** cut of his tunic, above his right hip.

"Please, do not," the assassin said, and the fighter stopped and eyed him with surprise.

"Of course I know of the knife you keep there," the assassin said. "Do you not understand, dear dead Vaclav? You have no surprises left for me."

Vaclav paused then protested, "Why now?" His ire rose with his frustration.

"Now is the time," replied the assassin. "All things have their time. Should a killing be any different? Besides, I have pressing business in the west and can play the game no longer."

"You have had ample opportunity to finish this business many times before now," Vaclav argued.

In fact, the little man had been hovering around him for tendays, had even gained his trust, to some degree, though Vaclav didn't even know the man's name. The fighter's eyes narrowed with further frustration when he further contemplated that notion and obviously realized that the assassin's frail frame—too frail to be viewed as any threat—had only helped win his trust. If the man, now revealed as an enemy, had appeared more threatening, Vaclav never would have let him get so close.

"I've had more chances than you would believe," the assassin replied with a snicker. The large man had seen him often, but not nearly as often as the killer, in perfect and varied disguises, had seen Vaclav.

"I take pride in my craft," the assassin continued, "unlike so many of the crass killers that walk the Realms. They prefer to keep their distance until the opportunity to strike presents itself, but I"—his beady eyes flickered with pride—"prefer to personalize things. I have been all around you. Several of your friends are dead, and I now know you so well that I can anticipate your every movement."

Vaclav's breathing came in short rasps. The assassin could imagine what was going through the fighter's mind: Several friends dead? And a weakling openly threatening him? He had defeated countless monsters ten times that one's weight, had served honorably in three wars, had even battled a dragon! But he was scared. Vaclav surely had to admit that.

"I am an artist," the slender, sleepy man rambled. "That is why I will never err, why I will survive while so many other hired murderers go to early graves."

"You are a simple killer and nothing more!" the large man cried, his frustration boiling over. He leaped from his seat and drew a huge sword.

Q

A sharp pain slowed Vaclav, and he found himself somehow sitting again. He blinked, trying to make sense of it all. He saw himself at the empty bar, was, in fact, staring at his own face! He stood gawking as he—as his own body—slid the heavy sword back into its scabbard.

"So crude," Vaclav heard his own body say.

He looked down at the figure he had come to wear, the killer's weak form.

"And so messy," the assassin continued.

"How . . . ?"

"I have not the time to explain, I fear," the assassin replied.

"What is your name?" Vaclav cried, desperate for any diversion.

"Ghost," answered the assassin.

Ghost lurched over, plainly confident that the seemingly androgynous form, one he knew so well, could hardly muster the speed to escape him or the strength to fend him off. Vaclav felt himself being lifted from the floor, felt the huge hands slipping around his neck.

"The . . . ghost . . . of who?" managed the desperate man. He kicked as hard as his new body would allow, so pitiful an attempt against the burly, powerful form his enemy possessed. Then his breath would not come.

Vaclav heard the snap of bone, and it was the last sound he would ever hear.

$$C$$

"Not '*the* ghost,' " the victorious assassin replied to the dead form, "just 'Ghost.' "

He sat then to finish his drink, thinking how perfect the job had been, how easily Vaclav had been coaxed into so vulnerable a position.

"An artist," Ghost said, lifting his cup in a toast to

himself. His more familiar body would be magically repaired before the dawn, and he could take it back then, leaving the empty shell of Vaclav's corpse behind.

Ghost had not lied when he mentioned pressing business in the west. A wizard had contacted the assassin's guild, promising exorbitant payments for a minor execution.

The price must have been high indeed, Ghost knew, for his superiors had requested that he take on the task. The wizard apparently wanted the best.

The wizard wanted an artist.

ONE

PLACID FIELDS

Cadderly walked slowly from the single stone tower, across the fields, toward the lakeside town of Carradoon. Autumn had come to the Southern Heartlands and the few tress along Cadderly's path, red maples mostly, shone brilliantly in their fall wardrobe. The sun was bright and warm, in contrast with the chilly breezes blowing down from the nearby Snowflake Mountains, gusting strong enough to float Cadderly's silken blue cape out behind him as he walked, and bend the wide brim of his similarly blue hat.

The troubled young scholar noticed nothing.

Cadderly pushed his sand-brown locks from his gray eyes then grew frustrated as the unkempt hair, much longer than he had ever worn it, defiantly dropped back down. He pushed it away again, and again, and finally tucked it tightly under the brim of his hat.

Carradoon came within sight a short while later, on the banks of Impresk Lake, surrounded by hedge-lined fields dotted with sheep, cattle, and crops. The city proper was walled, as were most cities of Faerûn, with many buildings huddled inside against ever-present peril. A long bridge connected Carradoon to a nearby island, the section of the town reserved for the more well-to-do merchants and governing officials.

As always when he came by that route, Cadderly looked at the town with mixed and uncertain feelings. He had been born in Carradoon, but didn't remember that early part of his life. His gaze drifted west past the walled city to the towering Snowflakes then to the passes that led high into the mountains, where lay the Edificant Library.

That had been Cadderly's home, though he realized that that was no longer true, and thus he felt he could not return there. He was not a poor man. The wizard in the tower he had recently left had paid him a huge sum for transcribing a lost spellbook—and he had the means to support himself in relative comfort for a time.

But all the gold in the world could not have provided a home for Cadderly, nor could it have released his troubled spirit from its turmoil.

Cadderly had grown up, had learned the truth of his violent, imperfect world—all too suddenly. The young scholar had been thrust into situations beyond his experience, forced into the role of hero-warrior when all he really wanted was to read of adventures in books of legend. Cadderly had killed a man, and had fought in a war that had blasted, torn, and ultimately tainted a once-pristine sylvan forest.

He had found no answers, only questions.

Cadderly thought of his room at the Dragon's Codpiece, where *The Tome of Universal Harmony*, the most prized scriptures of the god Deneir, sat open on his small table. It had been given to Cadderly by Pertelope, a high-ranking priestess of his order, with the promise that within its thick bindings Cadderly would find his answers.

But Cadderly wasn't sure he believed that.

The young scholar sat on a grassy rise overlooking the town, scratched at his stubbly beard, and wondered again about his true calling. He removed his wide-brimmed hat and stared at the porcelain insignia attached to its red band: an eye and a single candle, the holy symbol of Deneir, a deity dedicated to literature and the arts.

Cadderly had served Deneir since his earliest recollections, though he had never really been certain of what that service entailed, or of the real purpose in dedicating his life to any god. He was a scholar and an inventor and believed wholeheartedly in the powers of knowledge and creation, two very important tenets for his Deneirrath sect.

Only recently had Cadderly begun to feel that the god was something more than a symbol, more than a fabricated ideal for scholars to emulate. In the elven forest Cadderly had felt the birth of powers he could not begin to understand. He had magically healed a friend's wound that otherwise would have proved fatal. He had gained supernatural insight into the history of the elves, not just their recorded events, but the feelings, the eldritch aura, that had given the ancient People their identity. He had watched in amazement as the spirit of a noble horse rose from its broken body and walked solemnly away. He had seen a dryad disappear into a tree and had commanded the tree to push the elusive creature back out—and the tree had heeded his command.

There could be no doubt for young Cadderly: mighty magic was within him, granting him terrifying powers. His peers called that magic the Grace of Deneir, saw it as a blessing, but in light of what he had done, of what he had become, and the horrors he had witnessed, Cadderly was not certain he wanted that power within him.

He got up from the grassy rise and continued his journey to the walled town, to the Dragon's Codpiece, and to *The Tome of Universal Harmony*, where he could only pray that he would find some answers and some peace.

C

He flipped the page, his eyes desperately trying to scan the newest material in the scant heartbeat it took him to turn the page again. It was impossible. Cadderly simply could not keep up with his desire, his insatiable hunger, to turn the pages.

He was finished with *The Tome of Universal Harmony*, a work of nearly two thousand pages, in mere moments. Cadderly slammed the book shut, frustrated and fearful, and tried to rise from his small desk, thinking that perhaps he should go for a walk, or go to find Brennan, the innkeeper's teenaged son who had become a close friend.

The tome grabbed at him before he could get out of his seat. With a defiant but impotent snarl, the young scholar flipped the book back over and began his frantic scan once more. The pages flipped at a wild pace. Cadderly couldn't begin to read more than a single word or two on any one page, and yet, the *song* of the book, the special meanings behind the simple words, rang clearly in his mind. It seemed as though all the mysteries of the multiverse were embedded in the sweet and melancholy melody, a song of living and dying, of salvation and damnation, of eternal energy and finite matter.

He heard voices as well—ancient accents and reverent tones sang in the deepest corners of his mind—but he couldn't make out any of the written words on the pages of the book. Cadderly could see them, could feel their meanings, but the actual lettering slipped away.

Cadderly felt his strength quickly draining as he continued to press on. His eyes ached, but he couldn't close them. His mind raced in too many directions, unlocking secrets, then storing them back into his subconscious in a more organized fashion. In those brief transitions from one page to another, Cadderly managed to wonder if he would go insane, or if the work would actually consume him.

He understood something else then, and the thought finally gave to him the strength to slam the book shut. Several of the higher ranking Deneirrath priests at the Edificant Library had been found dead, lying across that very book. Always the deaths had been ruled having been the result of natural causes—all of those priests had been much older than Cadderly—but Cadderly's insight told him differently.

They had tried to hear the song of Deneir, the song of universal mysteries, but they had not been strong enough to control the effects of that strange and beautiful music. They had been consumed.

Cadderly frowned at the black cover of the closed tome as though it were a demonic thing. But it was not, he reminded himself, and before his fears could argue back, he opened the book once more, from the beginning, and again began his frantic scan.

Melancholy assaulted him, and the doors blocking revelations swung wide, their truths finding a place in the receptacle of young Cadderly's mind.

Gradually the young scholar's eyes drooped from sheer exhaustion, but still the song played on, the music of the heavenly spheres, of sunrise and sunset and all the details that played eternally in between.

It played on and on, a song without end, and Cadderly felt himself falling toward it, becoming no more than a passing note among an infinite number of passing notes.

On and on . . .

"Cadderly?"

The call came from far away, as if from another world. Cadderly felt a hand grasp his shoulder, tangible and chill, and felt himself turned gently around. He opened a sleepy eye and saw young Brennan's curly black mop and beaming face.

"Are you all right?"

Cadderly managed a weak nod and rubbed his bleary eyes. He sat up in his chair and felt a dozen aches in various parts of his stiff body. How long had he been asleep?

It was not sleep, the young scholar realized then, to his mounting horror. The weariness that had taken him from consciousness was too profound to be cured by simple sleep. What, then?

It was a journey, he sensed. He felt as though he had been on a journey. But to where?

"What were you reading?" Brennan asked, leaning past him to regard the open book.

The question shook Cadderly from his reflections. Terrified, he shoved Brennan aside and slammed the book.

"Do not look at it!" he replied harshly.

Brennan seemed at a loss. "I . . . I'm sorry," he apologized, obviously confused, his green eyes downcast. "I didn't mean—"

"No," Cadderly interrupted, forcing a disarming smile to his face. He hadn't intended to wound the young lad who had been so kind to him over the last few tendays. "You did nothing wrong. But promise me that you'll never look inside this book—not unless I'm here to guide you."

Brennan took a step away from the desk, eyeing the closed tome with fear.

"It's magical," Cadderly acknowledged, "and it could cause harm to one who does not know how to read it properly. I'm not angry with you—truly. You just startled me."

Brennan nodded weakly, seeming unconvinced.

"I brought your food," he explained, pointing to a tray he had placed on the night table beside Cadderly's small bed.

Cadderly smiled at the sight. Dependable Brennan. When he had come to the Dragon's Codpiece, Cadderly had desired solitude and had arranged with Fredegar Harriman, the innkeeper, to have his meals delivered outside his door. That arrangement had quickly changed, though, as Cadderly had come to know and like Brennan. The young man felt free to enter Cadderly's room and deliver the plates of food—always more than the price had called for—personally. Cadderly, for all his stubbornness and the icy demeanor he had developed after the horrors of Shilmista's war, had soon found that he couldn't resist the youth's unthreatening companionship.

Cadderly eyed the plate of supper for a long while. He noticed a few specks of crumbs on the floor, some from a biscuit and some darker—the crust of the midday bread, he realized. The curtains over his small window had been drawn and his lamp had been turned down, and turned back up.

"You couldn't wake me the last three times you came in here?" he asked.

Brennan sputtered, surprised. "Th-three times?"

"To deliver breakfast and my midday meal," Cadderly reasoned, and he paused, realizing that he shouldn't know what he knew. "Then once more to check on me, when you turned the lamp back up and drew the curtains."

Cadderly looked back to Brennan and was surprised again. He almost called out in alarm, but quickly realized that the images he saw dancing on the young man's shoulders—shadowy forms of scantily clad dancing girls and disembodied breasts—were of his own making, an interpretation from his own mind.

Cadderly turned away and snapped his eyes shut. An interpretation of what?

He heard the song again, distantly. The chant was clearer, the same phrases repeated over and over, though Cadderly still couldn't make out the exact words, except for one: *aura*.

"Are you all right?" Brennan asked again.

Cadderly nodded and looked back, not so startled by the dancing shadows. "I am," he replied sincerely. "And I have kept you here longer than you wished."

Brennan's face screwed up with curiosity.

"You be careful at the Moth Closet," Cadderly warned, referring to the seedy private festhall at the end of Lakeview Street, on the eastern side of Carradoon, near where Impresk Lake spilled into the Shalane River. "How does a boy your age even get into that place?"

"H-how . . . ?" Brennan stuttered, his pimpled face blushing to deep crimson.

Cadderly waved him away, a wide smile on his face. The dancing shadow breasts atop Brennan's shoulder disappeared in a burst of splotchy black dots. Apparently Cadderly's guesses had knocked out the teenager's hormonal urgings.

Temporarily, Cadderly realized as Brennan headed for the door, for the shadows already began to form anew. Cadderly's laugh turned Brennan back around.

"You will not tell my father?" he pleaded.

Cadderly waved him away, stifling the urge to burst out in laughter. Brennan hesitated, perplexed, but he relaxed almost immediately, surely reminding himself that Cadderly was his friend. A smile found his face, and a dancing girl found a perch on his shoulder. He snapped his fingers and swiftly disappeared from the room.

Cadderly stared long and hard at the closed door, and at the telltale crumbs on the floor beside his night table.

Things had seemed so very obvious to him, both of what had transpired in his room while he was asleep, and of Brennan's intentions for a night of mischief. So obvious, and yet, Cadderly knew they should not have been.

" 'Aura'?" he whispered, searching for significance.

The young priest looked back to the tome. Would he find his answer there?

He had to force himself to eat, to remind himself that he would need all his strength for the time ahead. Soon after, one hunger sated and another tearing at him, Cadderly dived back into *The Tome of Universal Harmony*.

The pages began to flip, and the song played on and on.

TWO

MOPPING UP

Q

Danica blew a lock of her strawberry-blond hair from in front of her exotic, almond-shaped brown eyes and peered intently down the forest path, searching for some sign of the approaching enemy. She shifted her compact, hundred-pound frame from foot to foot, always keeping perfect balance, her finely toned muscles tense in anticipation of what was to come.

"Are the dwarves in position?" Elbereth, the new king of Shilmista's elves, asked her. His silver eyes kept more to the trees surrounding the path than to the trail itself.

Two other elves, one a golden-haired maiden, the other with black hair as striking as Elbereth's, joined them.

"I would expect the dwarves to be ready in time," Danica assured the elf king. "Ivan and Pikel have never let us down."

The three elves nodded, and Elbereth couldn't help but smile. He remembered when he'd first encountered the gruff dwarves. Ivan, the tougher of the pair, had

WHITE MOUNTAIN LIBRARY
SWEETWATER COUNTY LIBRARY SYS
ROCK SPRINGS, WY

found him bound and helpless, a prisoner of their enemy. Never would the elf have believed he would come to trust the bearded brothers so implicitly.

"The dryad has returned," the black-haired elf wizard, Tintagel, said to Elbereth. He led the elf king's gaze to a nearby tree, where Elbereth managed to make out Hammadeen, the elusive dryad. Her tan-skinned, green-haired form peeked from around the tree trunk.

"She brings news that the enemy will soon arrive," remarked Shayleigh, the elf maiden. The anxious tone of her voice and the sudden sparkle that came into her violet eyes reminded them all of the fiery maiden's lust for battle. They had seen Shayleigh "at play" with both sword and bow, and had to agree with Ivan Bouldershoulder's proclamation that he was glad Shayleigh was on their side.

Tintagel motioned for the others to follow him to where the rest of the gathered elves, some two score of Elbereth's people, almost half of the remaining elves in Shilmista, waited. The wizard considered the landscape for a moment, then began positioning the elves along both sides of the path, trying to properly distribute those better in hand-to-hand combat and those more skilled with their great longbows. He called Danica to his side and began his spellcasting chant, walking along the elven lines and sprinkling white birch bark chips.

As he neared the end of the spell, Tintagel took up his own position, Danica moving to her customary spot beside him, and sprinkled chips upon himself and his human escort.

Then it was completed, and where Danica and forty elf warriors had been standing, stood only unremarkable birch trees.

Q

Danica looked out from her new disguise to the forest around her, which seemed vague and foggy to her, more like a feeling than mundane vision. She focused on the path, knowing that she and Tintagel must remain aware of their surroundings, must be ready to come out of the shapechanging spell as soon as Ivan and Pikel began the assault.

She wondered what she looked like as a tree, and thought, as she always thought when Tintagel performed that spell, that she might like to spend some quiet time as a tree, viewing the forest around her, feeling its strength in her feet-become-roots.

But that would have to wait. There was killing to do.

Q

"Oo," moaned Pikel Bouldershoulder, a round-shouldered dwarf with a green-dyed beard braided halfway down his back and open-toed sandals on his gnarly feet. He watched the distant spectacle of Tintagel's spell. His longing gaze was plain to see, and Pikel almost toppled out of the tree in which he sat.

"No, ye don't!" his brother whispered from across the way, disdaining Pikel's druidic tendencies.

Ivan tucked his yellow beard into his wide belt, shifted his mithral-hard buttocks on the tree branch, and adjusted his deer-antlered helmet on his head, trying to find a comfortable position in a very un-dwarven perch. In one hand he held a club made from the thick trunk of a dead tree. He'd tied a heavy rope around his waist that looped up over a branch halfway across the trail.

Ivan had accepted the high seat, knowing what fun it would bring, but he drew the line at being turned into a tree—above his would-be druid brother's whining protests. Ivan had offered a compromise, enquiring of Tintagel about a variation of his mighty spell, but the elf wizard had declined, explaining that he had not the power to turn dwarves into rocks.

Across the path, in a perch opposite Ivan, Pikel seemed much more comfortable, both with his tree seat and tree-trunk club. He, too, sported a rope around his waist, the other end of Ivan's. Pikel's comfort with the perch couldn't defeat his frown, though, a frown brought on by his longing to be with the elves, to be a tree in Shilmista's soil.

Guttural goblin grumbling down the path alerted the dwarves of the enemy's approach.

"Sneaksters," Ivan whispered with a wide smile, trying to brighten his brother's surly mood. Ivan didn't want Pikel pouting at such a critical moment.

Both dwarves tightened their grip on their clubs.

Soon the enemy band passed directly under them, spindle-armed, ugly goblins mixed in with pig-faced orcs and larger orogs. Ivan had to force himself not to spit on the wretched throng, had to remind himself that more fun would be had if he and his brother could hold their positions just a short while longer.

Then, as the dryad Hammadeen had told them it would, a giant came into view, plodding slowly down the path, seemingly oblivious to its surroundings. By the dryad's words it was the last giant remaining in Shilmista, and Ivan wasn't about to let the thing go lumbering back to its mountain home.

"Sneaksters," Ivan whispered again, the title he had chosen for him and his brother, a title he knew that the giant, above all others, would appreciate in just another moment.

The huge head bobbed steadily closer. One goblin stopped and sniffed the air.

Too late.

Ivan and Pikel leveled their clubs and with a nod to each other, hopped off their high perches, swinging down at the path. Their timing proved perfect and the oblivious giant stepped between them, its gaze straight ahead, its head bobbing at just the right height.

Pikel connected just a heartbeat before Ivan, the heavy dwarves sandwiching the monster's head in a tremendous slam. Ivan dropped his bloodied club and tore out his favored double-bladed axe.

On the path below, the smaller monsters went into a frenzy, pushing and shoving, diving to the dirt, and running in all directions. They had lost many companions in the last few tendays, and they knew what was to come.

The wizard, Tintagel, cried out the dispelling syllable, and Danica and forty elves behind her reverted to their original forms. The elves drew back their bowstrings, or charged with gleaming swords waving high.

The dazed giant wobbled, but stubbornly, stupidly, held its balance. Ivan and Pikel, dangling nearly twenty feet above the forest path, went to work.

Ivan's axe took off an ear, and Pikel's club splattered the monster's nose all over its cheek. Again and again they smacked at the beast. They knew they were vulnerable up there, knew that if the giant managed to get even a single hit in, it would probably knock one of them halfway back to the Edificant Library. But the brothers didn't think of that grim fact just then.

They were having too much fun.

Below the hanging dwarves came the sound of elven bows loosing hail after hail of arrows deep into goblin, orc, and orog flesh.

Creatures died by the score, others cried in agony and terror, and the merciless elves came on, swords in hand, hacking at the squirming forms of the vile invaders, the monsters that had so tainted the precious home of the People.

Danica spotted one group of monsters slipping away through the trees to the side. She called to Tintagel and sped off in pursuit, taking up her crystal-bladed daggers, one with a golden pommel carved into the likeness of a tiger, the other, with a hilt of silver, carved into a dragon.

Q

Pikel's club knocked the giant's head backward so brutally that the dwarves heard the sharp crack of the huge monster's neck breaking. The giant somehow held its balance for just a moment longer, dazed, confused, then it died. It rolled up on the balls of its huge feet and toppled forward like a chopped tree.

Ivan surveyed the path ahead of the falling beast.

"Two!" the dwarf yelled, and the giant's body buried an unfortunate pair of goblins as it landed.

"Ye owe me a gold piece!" Ivan roared, and Pikel nodded happily, more than willing to pay the bet. "Ye ready for more?"

"Oo oi!" Pikel replied with enthusiasm.

Without a word of warning to his brother, the would-be druid grabbed a tree branch and quickly pulled the loop around his waist, freeing his end of the rope.

Ivan managed to open his eyes wide, but the inevitable curses aimed at his brother would have to wait as he took a more direct descent to the ground. To Pikel's credit, the plummeting Ivan did clobber a goblin beneath him.

The yellow-bearded dwarf hopped back to his feet, spitting dirt and curses. He casually dropped his heavy axe onto the back of the wounded goblin's head, ending its complaints, and looked back up to his brother, who was making his way down the tree in a more conventional fashion.

Pikel shrugged and smiled meekly. "Oops," he offered, and Ivan silently mouthed the word at the same instant Pikel spoke it, fully expecting the all-too-common apology.

"When ye get down here . . ." Ivan began to threaten, but goblins closed in around the vulnerable dwarf.

Ivan howled with glee and forgot any anger harbored against his brother. After all, how could he possibly stay mad at someone who had dropped him right in the middle of so much fun?

Q

The fleeing band's lead goblin scrambled through the thick underbrush, desperate to leave the slaughter behind. The monster hooked one ankle on one of many crisscrossing roots in that overgrown space, and stubbornly pulled itself free. Then it got hooked again, and the brush's renewed grasp was not so easily broken.

The goblin squealed and pulled then looked back to see, not a root, but a woman, smiling wickedly and holding fast to its ankle.

Danica twisted her arm in a sudden jerk and

charged up and ahead from her low concealment, tripping the unfortunate creature. She was atop the thing in an instant, her free hand pushing away the frantic beast's futile slaps while her other hand, holding the golden-hilted dagger, came slashing in for a single, vicious strike.

Danica rarely needed more than one.

The young woman pulled herself up from the slain creature, openly facing its surprised comrades, who weaved in and out of the trees behind and to the sides. The band eyed her curiously and looked around, not really knowing what to make of the seemingly lone human woman. Where had she come from, and why was she alone? Not another leaf or bush in the area moved, though fighting continued back on the trail.

Apparently with that thought in mind, an orog cried for a charge, eager to claim at least one victim to balance the loss of the giant. The monstrous band came crashing in at Danica from three sides, through the bush and brambles, gaining confidence and resolve with every step.

Elbereth dropped from a tree limb above Danica, his gleaming sword and shining armor revealing his prominent stature among the elven clan. Some of the monsters halted, and the others slowed, looking back and forth curiously from the elf and woman to their less brave comrades.

A short distance to the side, Shayleigh appeared from behind a tree and set her bow to work, dropping the creature closest to her companions.

The orogs cried out a retreat, a command goblins were always ready to follow. Elbereth and Danica moved first, though, catching the nearest goblins in a furious rush, while Shayleigh concentrated her fire on the orogs.

Those monsters not engaged ran wildly, picking their escape routes through the thick trees and brush.

When a wall of mist rolled up before them, terrified goblins skidded to a stop. The orogs prodded them from behind, knowing that to halt was to die.

An arrow thudded into the back of an orog, and another bolt followed its flight just a heartbeat later. The remaining two orogs shoved the lead goblin into the fog.

Watching from the boughs above, Tintagel launched another spell, throwing his voice into the mist through a rolled-up cone of parchment. His fog wall itself was harmless, but the cries of agony the wizard caused to emanate from within made the hesitant creatures think otherwise.

Three arrows took down the second orog. The remaining brute scrambled, seeking cover behind its goblin fodder. It came out the side of the group, thinking to circle around the fog wall . . . but it found Elbereth—and Elbereth's sword—instead.

Q

"It's about time ye got here!" Ivan growled when Pikel finally made his way down the towering tree to come to his side. Yards from the host of elves, and with many monsters between them, Ivan had been sorely pressed. Still, the tough dwarf had managed to escape any serious injury, for the bulk of the monsters were more interested in escaping than in fighting.

And it had quickly become obvious to the goblins that any who ventured near Ivan's furious axe would not long survive.

Back to back, the dwarf brothers elevated the battle to new heights of slaughter. They overwhelmed the nearby monsters in moments then shuffled up the path to overwhelm another group.

The elves cut in just as fiercely, swordsmen driving the monstrous throng every which way, and archers, just a short distance behind, making short work of those creatures that broke out of the pack. The goblinoids had nowhere to run and nowhere to hide. Already, more monsters lay dead than those standing to continue the fight, and that ratio came to favor the elves more and more with every passing heartbeat.

Q

Tintagel watched as the first goblin that had been pushed into the wall emerged from the other side unharmed. The elf wizard resisted the urge to blast the thing down. His role was to contain the monsters so that Elbereth, Shayleigh, and Danica could finish them. He pulled more dried peas from his pouch and tossed them to the ground, perpendicular to the mist wall. Uttering the proper chant, the wizard summoned a second fog wall to box the monsters in.

Danica followed Shayleigh's next three arrows into the confused horde. She whipped her daggers into the nearest targets, killing one goblin and dropping a second in screaming pain, and came in with a fury that her enemies couldn't hope to match.

Nor could the remaining orog match Elbereth's skill. The creature parried the elf's initial, testing swing then brought its heavy club across wickedly. Elbereth easily sidestepped the blow and waded in behind, jabbing his fine sword repeatedly into the slower beast's chest.

The creature blinked as though it was trying to focus through eyes that no longer saw clearly. Elbereth couldn't wait for it to decide its next move. He whipped his shield arm around, slamming the shield—which had belonged to his father not so long ago—against the orog's head. The monster dropped, star-shaped welts from the embossed heraldry of Shilmista crossing the side of its porcine face.

Shayleigh, sword in hand, came up beside the elf king and together they waded confidently into the goblins.

With no options left them, the trapped goblins began to fight back. Three surrounded Danica, hacking wildly with their short swords. They couldn't keep up with her darting movements, dips, and dodges, though, and weren't really coming very close to connecting.

Danica bided her time. One frustrated creature whipped its sword across in a harmlessly wide arc. Before the goblin could recover from its overbalanced swing, Danica's foot snapped straight up, connected under its chin, and drove its jaw up under its nose. The goblin promptly disappeared under the brush.

A second beast rushed at the distracted woman's back.

Bolts of magical energy flashed down from the tree above, burning into its head and neck. The goblin howled and grabbed at the wound, and Danica spun a half-circle, one foot flying wide, and circle-kicked it across the face. Its head looking too far back over one shoulder, the goblin joined its dead companion on the ground.

Danica managed to nod her thanks to Tintagel as she waded into the lone goblin facing her, her hands and feet flying in from all sides, finding opening after opening in the pitiful creature's defenses. One kick knocked its sword away and before it could cry out a surrender, Danica's stiffened fingers rifled into its throat, tearing out its windpipe.

Then it was over, with no more monsters to hit. The four companions, three of them covered in the blood of their enemies, stood solemn and grim, surveying their bestial but necessary handiwork.

Q

"Ye know, elf," Ivan said when Elbereth and the others came back to the group on the trail, "this is getting too easy."

The dwarf spat in both hands and grasped his axe handle, the blade of his weapon buried deeply into an orog's thick head. With a sickening crack, Ivan pulled the mighty weapon free.

"First fight in a tenday," Ivan continued, "and this group seemed more keen on running than fighting!"

Elbereth couldn't deny the dwarf's observations, but he was far from upset at what the goblins' retreat indicated.

"If we are fortunate, it will be another tenday before we find the need to fight again," he replied.

Ivan balked, and drove his gore-stained blade into the earth to clean it.

As Elbereth moved away, the dwarf muttered to his brother, "Spoken like a true elf."

THREE

HEARTFELT

Q

Y ou sit here and wait while all of our dreams—all of the dreams Talona herself gave you—fall to pieces!" Dorigen Kel Lamond, second most powerful wizard in all of Castle Trinity, sat back in her chair, somewhat surprised by her own uncharacteristic outburst. Her amber eyes looked away from Aballister, her mentor and superior.

The hollow-featured, older wizard seemed to take no offense. He rocked back in his comfortable chair, his sticklike fingers tap-tapping in front of him and an amused expression upon his gaunt face.

"Pieces?" he asked after a silence designed to increase Dorigen's discomfort. "Shilmista has been, or soon will be, reclaimed by the elves, that much is true," he admitted. "But by all reports their insignificant number has been halved—less than a hundred of them remain to defend the forest."

"*We* lost more than a thousand," Dorigen snapped. "And thousands more have fled our dominion, gone back to their mountain holes."

"Where we can reclaim them," Aballister assured her, "when the time is right."

Dorigen fumed but remained silent. She brushed a bead of sweat from her crooked nose and again looked away. Sporting two broken hands, the woman felt vulnerable with both unpredictable Aballister and upstart Bogo Rath in the private room, to say nothing of Druzil, Aballister's pet imp. That was one of the problems with working beside such devilish men, Dorigen reminded herself. She could never be certain when Aballister might decide he was better off without her.

"We still have three thousand soldiers—mostly human—at our immediate disposal," Aballister went on. "The goblinoids will be brought back when we need them—after the winter, perhaps, when the season is favorable for an invasion.

"How many will we need?" he asked, more of Bogo than Dorigen. "Shilmista has but a shadow of its previous strength, and the Edificant Library, too, has been severely wounded. That leaves only Carradoon." The tone of Aballister's voice showed clearly how he felt about the farmers and fishermen of the small community on the banks of Impresk Lake.

"I'll not deny that the library has been wounded," Dorigen replied, "but we really don't know to what extent. You seem to have underestimated Shilmista as well. Must I remind you of our most recent defeat?"

"And must I remind you that it was you, not I, who presided over that defeat?" the older wizard growled, his dark-eyed gaze boring into Dorigen. "That it was you who fled the forest at the most critical stages of the battle?"

Seeing her cowed, Aballister again rocked back in his chair and calmed.

"I sympathize with your pain," he said. "You have lost Tiennek. That must have been a terrible blow."

Dorigen winced. She had expected the remark, but it stung her nonetheless. Tiennek, a barbarian warrior she had plucked from the northland and trained to serve as her consort, had replaced Aballister as her lover. Dorigen didn't doubt for a moment the older wizard's satisfaction upon hearing that the great warrior had been killed. A woman nearly two feet shorter than Tiennek and barely a third of his weight had done the deed. In reporting the incident, the imp Druzil had purposely downplayed the young woman's prowess, Dorigen knew, just to fan the flames that had risen between the two wizards.

Dorigen wanted to fight back, wanted to shout in the wizard's face that he could never understand the power of that young woman, Danica, the monk escort of Cadderly, and of all the enemies she had met in Shilmista. She looked at Druzil, who had been there beside her, but the imp covered his canine face with his leathery wings and made no move to support her.

"Wretched, cowardly creature," Dorigen muttered. Since their return to Castle Trinity, Druzil had avoided contact with Dorigen. He held no loyalty to Aballister, she knew, except that Aballister was in control, and the prudent imp always preferred to be on the winning side.

"Enough of this bantering," Aballister said. "Our plans have been delayed by some unexpected problems."

"Like your own son," Dorigen had to put in.

Aballister's smile hinted that Dorigen might have overstepped her bounds. "My son," the wizard echoed, "dear young Cadderly . . . Yes, Dorigen, he has proved the most unexpected and severe of our problems. Do you agree, Boygo?"

Dorigen looked to the youngest of Castle Trinity's wizards, Bogo Rath, whom she and her mentor routinely called "Boygo."

The young man narrowed his eyes at the insult, not that he hadn't expected it. He was so very different from his two peers, and so often the butt of their jokes. He jerked his head back and forth, flipping his long, stringy brown hair over one ear, away from the side of his head that he kept shaved.

Dorigen, tiring of Bogo's outrageous actions, almost growled at his ridiculous haircut.

"Your son has indeed proved to be quite a problem," Bogo replied. "What else might we expect from the offspring of mighty Aballister? If young Cadderly must fight on the other side, then we would be wise to pay attention to him."

"Young Cadderly," Dorigen mumbled, her face locked in an expression of disgust. "Young Cadderly" had to be at least two or three years older than that upstart Bogo!

Aballister held up a small, bulging bag and shook it once to show the others that its thickness came from many coins—gold, surely. Dorigen understood the bag's significance, understood what it would buy for Aballister, and for Bogo as well. Bogo had come from Westgate, a city hundreds of miles to the northeast, at the mouth of the Lake of Dragons. Westgate was notable as a bustling trade town, and it was known, too, for a band of assassins who were among the cruelest killers in Faerûn.

"Even your Night Masks will have a difficult time striking at our young scholar, whether he's in Shilmista or has returned to the Edificant Library," Dorigen asserted, if for no better reason than to take some of the bite out of Aballister's icy demeanor concerning his son. For all that she hated Cadderly—he had broken her hands and stolen several magical items from her—Dorigen simply couldn't believe Aballister's viciousness toward his own son.

"He is not in Shilmista," Bogo replied with a grin, his brown eyes flashing with excitement, "nor in the library." Dorigen stared at Bogo, and her sudden interest obviously pleased the young wizard. "He is in Carradoon."

"Rousing the garrison, no doubt," Aballister added.

"How can you be certain?" Dorigen asked Bogo.

Bogo looked at Aballister, who shook the bag of gold once more. Its tinkling coins sent a shiver along Dorigen's spine. Bogo's connections in Westgate, his one claim to any prestige in Castle Trinity, were already on the scholar-priest's trail.

Even though her hands continued to throb, Dorigen felt a twinge of pity for the young scholar.

"One problem at a time, dear Dorigen," Aballister said, a thought he had iterated before, when he'd first told Dorigen of his plans for his son. Again the older wizard shook the bag of gold, and again a shiver coursed along Dorigen's spine.

Q

Elbereth and Danica sat atop Deny Ridge, a defensible position that the elves had taken as their base. Few of the People were about in the starry night, and there was no longer any danger demanding an alert garrison. Indeed, according to Hammadeen—and the dryad's information had proven accurate since Cadderly had pressed her into service tendays earlier—no monsters were within ten miles of the ridge. It was peaceful and quiet, not the ring of swords or the cries of the dying to be heard.

"The wind grows chill," Elbereth commented, offering Danica his traveling cloak. She accepted it and lay in the thick grass beside the elf, looking up to the countless stars and the few black forms of meandering clouds.

Elbereth's soft chuckle led her to sit up once more. She followed the elf's gaze to the base of the sloping hill. Squinting, she could just make out three forms—one elf and the other two obviously dwarves—darting in and out of the shadows along the tree line.

"Shayleigh?" Danica asked.

Elbereth nodded. "She and the dwarves have become great friends in the last couple tendays," he noted. "Shayleigh admires their courage and is not ungrateful that they have remained to aid in our fight."

"And you?" Danica asked.

Elbereth smiled as he recalled his first meeting with the dwarves, how he had come close to trading blows with Ivan. How long ago that seemed! Elbereth had been just a prince then, in disfavor with his father at a time when the forest was in grave peril.

"I, too, am not ungrateful," he replied. "I will never forget the debt I owe those dwarves . . . and you." He locked stares with Danica then, his silver eyes catching the woman's rich brown orbs in an unblinking gaze.

Their faces lingered, barely an inch apart.

Danica cleared her throat and turned away. "The fighting nears its end," she remarked, stealing the romance from the moment. Elbereth knew at once where her comment would lead, for she had been hinting at her plans for several days.

"We will be ridding Shilmista of the goblin vermin for the rest of the season," the elf king said. "And I fear that a new attack might begin in the spring, after the mountain trails are clear."

"Hopefully by then Carradoon and the library will be roused," Danica offered.

"Will you help with that?"

Danica looked back down the grassy slope. The three shadowy forms steadily approached.

"Never did care much for trees," they heard Ivan complain as he rubbed at his nose.

"I would have thought that one as short as a dwarf would be able to avoid low-hanging branches," Shayleigh replied with a melodic laugh.

"Hee hee hee," added Pikel, prudently swerving out of Ivan's backhanded reach.

"The time has come for Ivan and Pikel and I to depart," Danica blurted, hating the words but having to say them.

Elbereth's smile was gone in an instant. He looked long and hard at the woman but did not respond.

"Perhaps we should have left for the library with Avery and Rufo," Danica went on.

"Or perhaps you should trust them to handle affairs at the library, and in Carradoon," Elbereth put in. "You could remain here, all three of you. The invitation is open, and I assure you that Shilmista takes on an entirely new beauty under winter's white blanket."

"I don't doubt that," Danica replied, "but I fear I must go. There's—"

"Cadderly," Elbereth interrupted, smiling despite his disappointment.

Danica didn't reply, wasn't even sure how she felt.

She looked back to the slope and watched Ivan and Pikel tried to make their way to where Shayleigh waited. They almost made it, but Ivan must have muttered something that offended his brother, for Pikel sprang upon him and the two rolled down once more. The elf maiden threw up her hands in surrender and sprinted the rest of the way to Danica and Elbereth.

As soon as she joined the two, her smile was replaced by a curious expression. She studied Danica's face for a moment then said, "You are leaving."

Danica could hardly look her in the face.

"When?" Shayleigh asked, her tone still calm and composed.

"Soon—perhaps tomorrow," Danica replied.

Shayleigh spent a long moment considering the bittersweet news. Danica was leaving after the victory, with the forest secured. She could return, or the elves could go to her, freely, with little threat from goblins and orcs.

"I applaud your choice," Shayleigh said, and Danica turned to regard her, caught off guard by the elf's approval.

"The fight here is won, at least for now," the elf maiden continued, gaily spinning a turn in the clean, crisp evening air. "You have many duties to attend to, and of course, you have your studies back at the Edificant Library."

"I expect that Ivan and Pikel will accompany me," Danica replied. "They also have duties at the library."

Shayleigh nodded and looked back to the slope, where the brothers were trying a third time to get all the way up. At that angle, in the clear starlight, Danica could see the sincere admiration in the elf maiden's violet eyes. Danica understood that Shayleigh had put on her carefree attitude because she believed Danica's decision was the right one, not because she was pleased that Danica and the dwarves would soon depart.

"If the fight begins anew in the spring . . ." Shayleigh started to say.

"We will be back," Danica assured her.

"Back where?" Ivan finally came up, shook from his yellow beard the twigs and leaves that had gotten caught up in it from his two rolls down the hill, and tucked it into his wide belt.

"Back to Shilmista," Shayleigh explained. "If the fighting begins anew."

"We going somewhere?" Ivan asked Danica.

"Uh-oh," moaned Pikel, beginning to understand.

"Winter will be upon us soon," Danica replied. "The passes through the Snowflakes will become impassable."

"Uh-oh," Pikel said again.

"Ye're right," Ivan said after thinking things over for a moment. "Things're settling here—not much left to hit. Me and me brother'd get bored soon enough. And besides, them priests at the library probably ain't had a good-cooked meal since we left!"

Shayleigh slapped Ivan on the side of the head. Ivan turned to stare incredulously into her wistful smile, and even the gruff dwarf could recognize the pain hidden beneath the fair maiden's delicate features.

"You still owe me a fight," Shayleigh explained.

Ivan snorted and cleared his throat, sneakily moving his shirt sleeve high enough to wipe the moisture from his eyes as he ran his sleeve across his nose. Danica was amazed by the obvious chink in the dwarf's callous demeanor.

"Bah!" Ivan growled. "What fight? Ye're just like the

other one!" He waggled an accusing finger at Elbereth, whom he had battled to a draw in a similar challenge just a couple tendays before. "Ye'd dance all about and run in circles until we both fell down tired!"

"Do you think I would release you from the insult you gave my people?" Shayleigh snarled, hands on hips, and moved over to tower above the dwarf.

"Ye think I'd let ye?" Ivan retorted, poking a stubby finger into Shayleigh's belly. "Bah!" Ivan snorted, and he turned and stormed away.

"Bah!" Shayleigh mimicked, her voice too melodic to properly copy the dwarf's grating tone.

Ivan spun back and glowered at her then motioned for Pikel to follow him away. "Well, ye got yer forest back, elf," Ivan said to Elbereth. "Ye're welcome!"

"Farewell to you, too, Ivan Bouldershoulder," Elbereth replied. "Our thanks to you and your splendid brother. Know that Shilmista will be open to either of you if you choose to pass this way again."

Ivan smiled Pikel's way. "As if that one could stop us anyhow!" he roared, and he slapped Shayleigh across the rump and darted away before she recovered enough to respond.

"I must go as well," Danica said to Elbereth. "I have many preparations to make before dawn."

Elbereth nodded but could not reply past the lump in his throat. As soon as Danica was gone, skipping down the slope to catch up with the dwarves, Shayleigh took a seat beside the silver-eyed elf king.

"You love her," the elf maiden remarked after a few silent moments.

Elbereth sat quietly for a while then admitted, "With all my heart."

"And she loves Cadderly," said Shayleigh.

"With all her heart," Elbereth replied.

Shayleigh managed a weak grin, trying to bolster her friend's resolve.

"Never would I have believed that an elf king of Shilmista would fall in love with a human!" Shayleigh spouted, nudging Elbereth in the shoulder.

The elf turned his silver-eyed gaze upon her and smiled wryly. "Nor I that an elf maiden would be enchanted by a yellow-bearded dwarf," he replied.

Shayleigh's initial reaction came out as an incredulous burst of laughter. Certainly Shayleigh had come to know Ivan and Pikel as friends, and trusted allies, but to hint at anything more than that was simply ridiculous. Still, the maiden quieted considerably when she looked down the empty slope.

Empty indeed did it seem with the Bouldershoulder brothers gone from view.

FOUR

A LONG TIME TO DAWN

Q

Bogo Rath knocked on the door of the small conference room. The knock was tentative, stuttering. He was never secure in his dealings with the dreaded Night Masks. A score of assassins had accompanied the two Night Mask leaders into Castle Trinity that morning, many more trained killers than Bogo had anticipated for such a seemingly simple murder.

Two sentries searched the young wizard before he was allowed entry. The pair was unremarkable enough, Bogo noted, probably new to the dark band. They wore the customary dress of Westgate's assassins guild, nondescript yeoman's clothes and silver-edged black eye masks. One sentry's tusky grin told Bogo his heritage was likely more orc than human—common enough among the Night Masks—and that thought sent a shudder along the young wizard's spine.

Even if the pair were human, Bogo would have been no less uncomfortable. He knew that while the assassins openly displayed no weapons, each of them

41

carried many and were trained to kill with their bare hands as well.

The guards led the young wizard into the room then stepped back to the door, standing impassively on either side of the portal.

Bogo forgot about them as soon as they were behind him, for the young wizard found the two men inside the comfortable room much more interesting. Closest to him sat a puny man—if it was a man—effeminate and obviously weak, issuing a steady stream of phlegm-filled coughs. The man showed no beard at all, not even stubble. His face was too clean and soft-looking to be an adult's. His heavy eyelids drooped lazily, and his lips, too thick and too full, seemed almost a child-like caricature.

Across the way sat the man's opposite, a thick-muscled, robust specimen with a full, thick beard and shock of hair, both flaming red, and arms that could surely snap Bogo in half. Still, this powerful man seemed even more out of place, from what Bogo knew of the Night Masks, than did the weakling. He brandished a huge sword on his girdle and bore the scars of many battles. His dress, too, was far from that preferred by assassins. Wide, studded bracers, glittering with dozens of small jewels, adorned the man's wrists, and his snow-white traveling cloak had been cut from the back of a northern bear, albeit a small one.

"You are Bogo Rath?" the large man asked in a smooth baritone, with an articulation that was sharper and more sophisticated than Bogo had expected.

The wizard nodded. "Well met, fellow Night Mask," the young wizard replied with a low bow.

The red-haired man gave him a curious look.

"I was not told you retained any connection to the guild," he said. "I was informed that you left by mutual consent."

Bogo shifted nervously from foot to foot. He had paid a huge sum to be allowed out of the Night Masks, three years earlier, and even with the bribe if it hadn't been for the fact that his father was an influential merchant in Westgate—one with political associations and ties to the dark guild—Bogo would have been given the customary send-off for one who could not meet the Night Masks' standards: death.

"It's unusual to see a person who can claim that he once belonged to our beloved brotherhood," the red-haired man teased, his cultured voice dripping with sarcasm.

Again Bogo shifted, and he had to remind himself that he was still in Castle Trinity, his home, and that Aballister and Dorigen, for all their taunts, would look out for him.

"It was an unusual circumstance," the young wizard replied, revealing his nervousness with an uneasy flip of his stringy brown hair. "I had another calling, one that took me far from Westgate. As you can see, my departure has done us both some good. I have attained a level of power that you cannot comprehend, and you shall be paid well for doing me this one small task."

The huge man grinned, seeming to mock Bogo's claims of power, and looked at his puny companion, who seemed none too pleased.

"Do sit with us," the large man bade Bogo. "I am Vander, the taskmaster for this small bit of business of which you speak. My associate is Ghost, a most unusual and talented man."

Bogo took a seat between the two, alternating his gaze to try to determine how far he could trust the assassins.

"Is there a problem?" Vander asked after studying Bogo for a moment.

"No," Bogo blurted. He forced himself to calm down. "I am just surprised that so many have been sent for so simple an execution."

Vander laughed aloud, but stopped abruptly, a curious expression crossing his face. His glower fell over Ghost as his body went into a series of convulsions, and to Bogo's amazement, Vander and his possessions began to grow.

The sword, huge to begin with, took on gigantic proportions, and the northern bear that comprised the fine cloak no longer seemed a cub. Because Vander was seated, Bogo couldn't tell just exactly how large the man became—at least ten feet tall, he guessed.

"Firbolg?" he asked, recognizing the giant for what it was. Bogo was at a loss. A huge, red-haired man, so easily distinguishable, in the Night Masks was stunning enough, but a firbolg?

Vander's angry glare did not relent. His dark eyes peered at Ghost from under his bushy brows. He regained his composure quickly, though, and rested back in his seat.

"Forgive me," he said to Bogo. "I am indeed of the race of giant-kin, though I do not openly reveal my more-than-human stature."

"Then why—?" Bogo began to ask.

"An indiscretion," Vander quickly interrupted, the tone of his deep voice indicating that he did not wish to continue.

Bogo wasn't about to argue with an eight-hundred-pound giant. He crossed his hands defensively over his lap and tried hard to appear relaxed.

"You question our number?" Vander asked, going back to the wizard's original inquiry.

"I did not expect so many," Bogo reiterated.

"The Night Masks take no chances," Vander replied. "Often executions appearing so simple prove the most difficult. We do not make mistakes. That is why we are so well rewarded for our efforts." He cocked his giant head to one side—a curiously ungiantlike action, Bogo thought—and looked to the pouch on Bogo's rope belt.

Taking the cue, the young wizard pulled the bag of gold from his belt and handed it to Vander. "Half payment," he explained, "as was agreed to by your superiors."

"And by yours," Vander was quick to remark, not willing to give Bogo the upper hand, "a wizard named Aballister, I believe."

Bogo neither confirmed nor denied the claim.

"And you will accompany us, as a representative of Castle Trinity, in this matter?" Vander stated as much as asked. "Another unusual circumstance."

"That, too, was agreed upon," Bogo replied. The way he continually moved his fingers defeated the conviction in his tone. "By both parties," he prudently added, "most likely because I was once a member of your guild and understand your ways."

Vander stifled an obvious urge to deflate the pretentious young man's swelling ego. The giant surely knew that Aballister had paid a considerable amount of extra gold to get Bogo included, and that the young wizard's assignment had nothing to do with Bogo's past employment with the guild.

"I will journey to Carradoon beside you," Bogo continued, "to offer a full report to my sup—associates."

Vander smiled widely, catching the slip. "Whatever role you might play in the death of Cadderly does not change the sum owed the Night Masks," he said.

Bogo nodded. "My role will be as observer, nothing more. Unless, of course, you, as taskmaster, decide otherwise," he agreed. "Might I enquire of your own role?" Bogo paused. He knew he might be overstepping his bounds, but he couldn't let Vander have such an obvious advantage in their dealings. "It seems unlikely that a firbolg could parade through the streets of Carradoon. And what of the Ghost?"

"He is called Ghost, not '*the* Ghost,'" Vander snapped. "You would do well to remember that. My own role," he continued, mellowing a bit, "is none of your concern."

It struck Bogo as more than a little curious that Vander took more offense at his concerns for Ghost than for himself, particularly since Bogo had directly questioned the firbolg's value.

"Ghost will lead the way in, gather information, and prepare the target," Vander went on. "I have twenty skilled assassins at my disposal, so we will need to secure a base near, but not within, the walls of Carradoon."

Bogo nodded at the simple logic.

"We will leave in the morning, then," Vander continued. "Are you prepared?"

"Of course."

"Then our meeting is concluded," Vander stated,

motioning to the door. The sentries moved to either side of Bogo to escort him from the room.

Bogo looked back at the door many times as he made his way slowly down the corridor. A firbolg and a weakling? It seemed unusual, but then Bogo had been in the Night Masks only a day more than a month before he had begged to leave, and he had to admit, at least to himself, that he knew very little about the band's methods.

Bogo soon dismissed all thoughts of Vander and Ghost, concentrating instead on another meeting he had planned. At Aballister's request, Bogo would meet with Druzil to learn all he could about Cadderly and his cohorts. The imp had dealt with Cadderly on two occasions—both disastrous for Castle Trinity—and knew as much about him as anyone.

Bogo desperately wanted that knowledge. He was a bit dismayed that so many Night Masks had been assigned to the task, not because he wanted Cadderly to have a chance to escape, but because he wanted to be in on the action. More than anything else, Bogo Rath wanted to play a vital role in the kill, wanted to gain the respect of Aballister, and particularly Dorigen.

He was tired of the taunts, of being referred to as "Boygo." How would mighty Dorigen, who returned from Shilmista stripped of her valuable possessions and with her hands broken and swollen, feel when Bogo delivered the head of Aballister's troublesome son? Cadderly, after all, had been the source of Dorigen's humiliation.

Bogo dared to dream that he might ascend within Castle Trinity's hierarchy to become Aballister's second. Dorigen's hands were slow to heal; the fortress's clerics doubted that many of her fingers would ever straighten. Given that precise movements played a vital role in spell casting, who could guess the implications to Dorigen's power?

Bogo rubbed his soft hands together eagerly and sped off for the meeting room, to where Druzil, his guide to a better life, waited.

Q

"How dare you do that to me!" the firbolg growled at his companion as soon as Bogo had gone. A nod from him sent the two guards scrambling from the room. The giant leaped from his seat and advanced a step.

"I did not know that my . . . that your . . . body's size would return to normal," the little man protested, trying to sink deeper into the cushions of his soft chair. "I believed the enchantment would last longer, at least through the meeting."

The firbolg grabbed the little man by the collar and hoisted him into the air.

"Ah, Vander," the giant purred, his face suddenly calm, "dear Vander."

Then the firbolg's face contorted in rage again and he punched the little man in the face, destroying his nose. A backhand slap raised a welt on one cheek, and a second slap did likewise on the other. Then, with an evil grin, the firbolg grabbed the little man by one forearm and snapped his bone so severely that the man's fingers brushed against his elbow.

The beating went on for some time, and finally the firbolg dropped the barely conscious man back into his seat.

"If you ever deceive me so again . . ." the red-haired

giant warned. "If ever again you humiliate me in front of one such as Bogo Rath, I will beat you until you beg for death!"

The smaller man, the real Vander, curled up in a fetal position, cradling his shattered arm, feeling terribly vulnerable and afraid trapped inside the puny body of the weakling Ghost.

"I want my body back," Ghost said suddenly, tugging uncomfortably at his firbolg trappings. "You are so hairy and itchy!"

Vander sat up and nodded, eager to be back in his own form.

"Not now," Ghost growled at him. "Not until the wounds heal. I would not accept my body back in less than perfect condition," he said wryly. "As it was when I gave it to you."

Vander slumped back. The game had grown old over the last few years, but what options lay before him? He couldn't escape Ghost's evil clutches, couldn't resist the demands of Ghost's magic. Vander wanted nothing more than to get back into his firbolg form and pound the little man, but he knew that Ghost would simply initiate a switch back, and Vander would feel the pain of his own attacks. Ghost would continue the beating, Vander knew, for the better part of a day sometimes, until poor Vander broke and wept, begging his master to stop.

The trapped firbolg put a hand to his broken human nose. Already it was on the mend. The pain had faded and the bleeding had stopped. The broken forearm had straightened again and Vander could feel a warm tingling as the bone knitted back together. Just a few more moments, he thought to comfort himself, and I will have my body back, my own strong body.

"I will be leaving presently," Ghost said to him. He pointed a threatening finger Vander's way. "Remember that you are my spirit-mate," he warned. "I can come back for you, just for you, Vander, from any distance, at any time."

Vander averted his eyes, unable to deny the threat. Once he had tried to flee the nightmare his life had become, had gotten all the way home to the Spine of the World, but Ghost, thousands of miles away, had found him and forced a body switch. Merely to show Vander the folly of his actions, Ghost had mercilessly slaughtered several of Vander's fellow firbolgs, including his brother, on a little-used mountain trail east of Mirabar. Vander vividly remembered the terrible moment when Ghost had given him back his body, holding his oldest son's left arm in his gigantic hand.

Vander had killed Ghost when he returned to Westgate, had nearly torn the little man's head from his shoulders, but a tenday later, Ghost had walked into Vander's camp, smiling.

Vander came out of his contemplations and regarded his hated companion. Ghost towered above him, a black glove on one hand, a white one on the other, and wearing a familiar golden-edged mirror hanging on a golden chain around his neck.

At the clap of the firbolg's hands, Vander felt himself floating. His noncorporeal spirit looked back at the weak, drowsy form on the floor with contempt then looked ahead to the giant receptacle. There came a flash of burning pain as Vander entered his firbolg body. His spirit twisted and shifted to reconfigure itself to the proper form, to reorient Vander to his new coil.

Ghost had come out of the spirit-walk faster than Vander, as always, and was sitting comfortably in a chair, watching the firbolg intently as Vander came back to consciousness. The puny body wore the gloves and mirror—the magic device always transferred with its master. As soon as it became obvious that Vander wouldn't attack him, Ghost clenched his hands and closed his eyes. The gloves and mirror disappeared, but Vander knew from bitter and painful experience that they were well within immediate recall.

"You will depart as planned with the band and the young wizard," Ghost instructed.

"What of this Bogo Rath?" Vander asked. "I don't trust him."

"That is of no consequence," Ghost replied. "After all, you do not trust me, either, but I know you are enamored of my warm personality."

Vander wanted to smash the smug smile off Ghost's sleepy-eyed face.

"The wizard is to accompany us," Ghost instructed. "Aballister paid us handsomely to take Rath along, a fine cache of gold for so minor an inconvenience."

"To what purpose?" Vander had to ask, always amazed at the webs of seemingly pointless intrigue created by less than honorable men.

"Aballister believes that sending an emissary will keep him informed," Ghost replied. "The wizard has a weakness for knowledge. He cannot tolerate the occurrence of anything that affects him, directly or even indirectly, without his knowledge."

Vander did not disagree. He had met Aballister only once, and Ghost had spoken with the hollow-featured wizard no more than three times. But the firbolg didn't doubt Ghost's perceptions. The little man possessed an uncanny understanding of character, particularly of character flaws, and always found a way to use that to his advantage.

Q

The young scholar blinked at the morning brightness shining across Impresk Lake and through the windows of his room's balcony doors. Breakfast sat on the table next to Cadderly—extra portions, he noted with a smile. They were a bribe, Brennan's way of saying thank you for Cadderly's continued discretion. Fredegar wouldn't be happy with his son if he knew where Brennan had spent the evening.

Cadderly was indeed hungry, and the food looked good, but when the young scholar noticed *The Tome of Universal Harmony* sitting open on his desk by the window, he realized a more profound and demanding hunger. He took a single biscuit with him as he went to the desk.

Like so many times before, Cadderly devoured the pages, the blurred words, faster than his eyes could follow. He was through the tome in a matter of minutes, then turned it back over and began again, rushing, almost desperately, to keep the mysterious song flowing uninterrupted. How many times Cadderly went through the work that day, he couldn't know. When Brennan came in with his lunch, then his supper, he didn't look up.

The daylight waned, and still Cadderly pored on. His first thought, when the room became too dark to read in, was to go and light his lamp, but he hated to waste the time that action would take. Hardly considering his actions, Cadderly recalled a page in the tome, a particular melody, and uttered a few simple words. The room filled with light.

The stream of the song was broken. Cadderly sat blinking in amazement at what he had done. He retraced his mental steps, recalled that same page, its image clear in his mind. He uttered the chant again, changing his inflections and alternating two of the words.

The light went out.

Shaking, Cadderly slipped out of his chair and over to his bed. He threw an arm across his eyes as though that act might hide the confusing memory of what had just occurred.

"I'll see the wizard in the morning," he whispered aloud. "He will understand."

Cadderly didn't believe a word of it, but he refused to listen to the truth.

"In the morning," he whispered again, as he sought the serenity of sleep.

The morning was many hours and many dreams away for the troubled young man.

Q

Percival hopped up to the room's window—no, not the window, but the terrace doors. Cadderly considered the strange sight, for the squirrel's sheer size made the doors look more like a tiny window. It was Percival, Cadderly knew, but why was the squirrel six feet tall?

The white squirrel entered the room and moved beside him. Cadderly extended his hand to pat the beast, but Percival recoiled then rushed back in, his not-so-tiny paws ripping tears in the pouches on Cadderly's belt. Cadderly began to protest, but one of the pouches broke open, spilling a continual stream of cacasa nuts onto the floor.

Hundreds of cacasa nuts! Thousands of cacasa nuts!

The gigantic squirrel eagerly stuffed them into his bulging mouth by the score and soon the floor was clear again.

"Where are you going?" Cadderly heard himself ask as the squirrel bounded away. The doors were closed again somehow, but the squirrel ran right through them, knocking them from their hinges. Then Percival hopped over the balcony railing and was gone.

Cadderly sat up in his bed—but it was not his bed, for he was not in his room. Rather, he lay in the inn's common room. It was very late, he knew, and very quiet.

Cadderly was not alone. He felt a ghostly presence behind him. Mustering his courage, he spun around.

He cried out, the scream torn from his lungs by sheer desperation. There lay Headmaster Avery, Cadderly's mentor, his surrogate father, spread across one of the room's small circular tables, his chest opened wide.

Cadderly didn't have to examine the man to know he was dead. His heart had been torn out.

Q

Cadderly sat up in his bed—and it was indeed his bed. His room was quiet, except for the occasional rattling of the balcony doors, shivering in the night wind. A full moon was up, its silvery light dancing through the window, splaying shadows across the floor.

The serenity seemed hardly enough to chase away the dreams. Cadderly tried to recall that page in the tome again, tried to remember the chant, the spell, to bathe the room in light. He was weary and troubled and had not eaten all that day, and hardly at all the day before. The image of the page would not come, so he lay still, terrified, in the dim light.

There was only the quiet light of the moon.

Dawn was a long while away.

FIVE

HOME AGAIN

A steady stream of shouts led the way for Danica and the Bouldershoulder brothers as they walked the halls in the southern section of the Edificant Library's second floor. All three companions knew the source of the ruckus was Headmaster Avery even before they approached his office, and they knew, too, from whispers that had greeted them on their arrival, that Kierkan Rufo bore the brunt of the verbal assault.

"It is good that you have returned," came a voice to the side. Headmistress Pertelope strode toward the three. She smiled warmly and wore, as had become her norm, a full-length, long-sleeved gown and black gloves. Not an inch of skin peeked out below her neck, and between the dark robes and the tightly cropped salt-and-pepper hair, her face seemed almost detached, floating in an empty background. "I'd feared you had lost your hearts to Shilmista—which would have been perfectly reasonable," the headmistress said, with no hint of judgment in her calm tone.

"Ye're bats!" Ivan snorted, shaking his head vigorously. "An elfish place, and not for me liking."

Pikel kicked him in the shin, and the brothers glared long and hard at each other.

"Shilmista was wonderful," Danica admitted. "Especially when we sent the monsters in full flight. Already it seems as if the shadows have lightened in the elven wood."

Pertelope nodded and flashed her warm smile once more. "You're going to see Avery?" she stated as much as asked.

"It is our duty," Danica replied, "but he doesn't seem to be in a very good mood."

"Rufo'd spoil anyone's day, by me reckoning," Ivan put in.

Again Pertelope nodded, and she managed a somewhat strained smile. "Kierkan Rufo's actions in the forest will not be easily forgotten," she explained. "The priest has much to prove if he wishes to regain the favor of the headmasters, particularly Headmaster Avery."

"Good enough for him!" Ivan snorted.

"Oo oi!" Pikel added.

"I've heard that Rufo has already received some punishment," Pertelope continued wryly, looking pointedly at Danica's fist.

Danica unconsciously slipped her guilty hands behind her back. She couldn't deny that she had slugged Rufo, back in the forest when he complained about his companions' deficiencies. She also couldn't deny how much she had enjoyed dropping the blustering fool. Her actions had been rash, though, and probably not without consequence.

Pertelope sensed the young woman's discomfort and quickly moved on to a different subject. "When you're done talking with Headmaster Avery," she said, "do come and see me. We have much to discuss."

Danica knew that Pertelope was speaking of Cadderly, and she wanted to ask a hundred questions of the headmistress then and there. She only nodded, though, and remained silent, conscientious of her duty and knowing that her desires would have to wait.

The perceptive headmistress smiled knowingly and said, "Later," then gave the young woman a wink and walked on.

Danica watched her go, a thousand thoughts of Cadderly following kind Pertelope's every step. Ivan's tapping boot reminded her that she had other considerations, and she reluctantly turned back to the dwarves. "Are you two ready to face Avery?"

Ivan chuckled wickedly. "Not to worry," the dwarf assured her, grabbing her by the arm and leading her to the portly headmaster's office. "If the fat one gets outta line with ye, I'll threaten him with smaller portions at the dinner table. There's a measure of power from being a place's cook!"

Danica couldn't disagree, but that offered little comfort as she neared the door and heard more clearly the level of Avery's rage.

"Excuses!" the headmaster roared. "Always excuses! Why do you refuse to take responsibility for your actions?"

"I did not—" they heard Rufo begin meekly, but Avery promptly cut him off.

"You did!" the headmaster cried. "You betrayed them to that wretched imp—and more than once!"

There came a pause then Avery's voice sounded again, more composed. "Your actions after that were somewhat courageous, I will admit," he said, "but they do not excuse you. Don't presume for a moment that you're forgiven. Now, go to your tasks with the knowledge that any transgression, however minor, will cost you dearly."

The door swung open and a haggard Rufo rushed out, seeming displeased to see Danica and the dwarves.

"Surprised?" Ivan asked him with a wide grin.

The man, tilting slightly, ran his fingers through his matted black hair. His dark eyes darted about as if in search of escape. With nowhere to go, Rufo shoved his way between Danica and Pikel and scurried away, obviously embarrassed.

"Yer day just got better, eh?" Ivan called after him, enjoying the tall man's torment.

"It took you a while to find your way to me," came a surly call from the room, turning the companions back to Avery.

"Uh-oh," muttered Pikel, but Ivan merely snorted and strode into the room, right up to Avery's desk. Danica and Pikel came in a bit more hesitantly.

Avery's bluster seemed to have played itself out. The chubby man pulled a handkerchief from his pocket and rubbed it across his sweaty, blotchy face.

"I didn't believe you would come back," he said, huffing with labored breath. He alternated his glance from Ivan to Pikel. "I had even suggested to Dean Thobicus that we begin to search for new cooks."

"Not to worry," Ivan assured him with a bow that swept the dwarf's yellow beard across the floor. "The masters of yer belly have returned."

Pikel piped up in hearty agreement, but Avery's renewed glare showed how little he enjoyed the boisterous dwarf's smug attitude.

"We will, of course, need a full report of your time in Shilmista—a written report," he said, shuffling some papers around on his large desk.

"I don't write," Ivan teased, "but I can cook ye a goblin ear stew. That'll fairly sum up me time in the wood."

Even Danica couldn't bite back a chuckle at that.

"Lady Maupoissant will help you then," Avery said, articulating each word slowly to show them he was not amused.

"When will you need this?" Danica asked, hoping he would give her the whole winter. Her thoughts were on Carradoon, on Cadderly, and she was beginning to suspect that perhaps she should have continued through the mountains and gone straight to him.

"You are scheduled to meet with Dean Thobicus in three days," Avery informed her. "That should give you ample time—"

"Impossible," Danica said to him. "I will meet with the dean today, or in the morning, perhaps, but—"

"Three days," Avery repeated. "The dean's schedule is not for you to decide, Lady Maupoissant." Again he used her surname, and Danica knew it was to emphasize his anger.

Danica felt trapped. "I am not of your order," she reminded the portly man. "I'm under no obligation—"

Again Avery cut her short. "You will do as you are told," he said. "Do not think your own actions in Shilmista have been forgotten or forgiven."

Danica fell back a step. Ivan, as angry as he was confused, hopped to his toes and glowered at Avery.

"Huh?" was all that stunned Pikel could mutter.

"As I said," Avery declared, slamming a heavy fist on the desk. "You all played the role of hero, both in Shilmista and before that, when the Talonite priest and his insidious curse fell over the library, but that does not excuse your actions, Lady Maupoissant."

Danica wanted to scream "What actions?" but she couldn't get a sound past the mounting rage in her throat.

"You struck him," Avery finally explained. "You attacked Rufo, a priest of Deneir, a host of the Edificant Library, without provocation."

"He had it comin'," Ivan retorted.

Avery managed a bit of a smile. "I don't doubt that," he agreed, for a moment seeming his old, likable self. "Yet there are rules concerning such behavior." He looked straight into Danica's brown eyes. "You might well be banned from the library for life if I were to pursue Rufo's charges.

"Think of it," Avery continued after giving Danica and the dwarves a moment to absorb his meaning. "All of your texts are here, all of the known works of Grandmaster Penpahg D'Ahn. I know how dear your studies are to you."

"Then why do you threaten me like this?" Danica snapped. She flipped a lock of her unkempt hair from in front of her face and crossed her arms before her. "If I erred in striking Rufo then so be it, but if the same situation was repeated—if, after so many trials and so much killing, I had to listen to his endless whining and berating of me and my friends—I can't honestly say I wouldn't punch him again."

"Oo oi!" Pikel readily agreed.

"Had it comin'," Ivan said again.

Avery waved his hand in a patting motion to try to calm the three. "Agreed," he said, "and I assure you I have no intention of letting Rufo's accusations go beyond this point. But in exchange, I demand that you give me these few things for which I have asked. Prepare the report and meet with Thobicus in three days, as he desires. On my word, Rufo's accusations will never again be mentioned, to you or to anyone else."

Danica blew the stubborn strand of hair away from her face, an action she knew Avery understood as a resigned sigh.

"I'm sure you'll be pleased to hear that Cadderly is well, by all reports," the headmaster said, obviously happy to change the subject.

Danica winced. Hearing the name aloud revived lingering fears and painful recollections.

"He stays at the Dragon's Codpiece, a fine inn," Avery went on. "Fredegar, the innkeeper, is a friend, and he has looked after Cadderly, though that has not been difficult since our young man rarely leaves his room."

The portly headmaster's obvious concern for Cadderly reminded Danica that Avery was no enemy— for her or for her love. She understood, too, that most of Avery's surly behavior could be attributed to the same fact that had been gnawing away at her: Cadderly had remained at the library only as long as it took to retrieve his possessions. Cadderly had not, and might not ever, come home.

"I leave for Carradoon this afternoon," Avery announced. "There is much business to be handled between the headmasters and the town's leaders. With this threat of war hanging over us and . . . well, worry not about it. You three have earned at least a few days of peace."

Again Danica understood the implication of the portly headmaster's words. Certainly there was business between the library and the town, but Danica thought it unlikely that Avery, whose duties were to preside over and guide the younger priests, would be chosen as the library's representative in town matters. Avery had volunteered to go, had insisted, Danica knew, and not because of any threat to either the town or the library. His business in Carradoon was an excuse to look in on Cadderly, the young man whom he loved as dearly as he would his own son.

With polite words Danica and the dwarves took their leave, the brothers protectively flanking Danica as they exited the room.

"Not to worry," Ivan said to Danica. "Me and me brother'll have to go to town soon anyway, to stock up for the winter. Get yer business and yer meeting done and we'll set off right after. It's not a long road to Carradoon, but 'tis better, in these times, that ye don't go down it alone."

Pikel nodded his agreement and they parted, the dwarves heading down the stairs for the kitchen and Danica to her room. Ivan and Pikel missed Cadderly, too, the young woman realized. She gave a flip of her strawberry-blond hair, which hung several inches below her shoulders, as though that symbolic act would allow her to put her troubles behind her for the moment. Like the stubborn hair that inevitably found its way back around to her face, though, Danica's fears did not stay away long.

She desperately wanted to see Cadderly, to hold him and kiss him, but at the same time she feared that meeting. If the young scholar rejected her again, as he had in Shilmista, her life, even her dedication to her studies, may well lose all meaning.

Q

"I didn't see much," Danica admitted, adjusting her position on the edge of Headmistress Pertelope's cushioned bed. "I was guarding against the approaching battle. I knew Cadderly and Elbereth would be vulnerable while they cast their summons to the trees."

"But you're convinced that Cadderly played a role in that summoning?" Pertelope pressed, repeating the question for perhaps the fifth time. Pertelope sat near Danica and was clad in her usual modest garments. "It wasn't the elf prince alone?"

Danica shook her head. "I heard Cadderly chanting," she tried to explain. "There was something more to it, some underlying power . . ." She struggled to find the words, but how could she? What had happened back in Shilmista, when Cadderly and Elbereth had awakened the great oaks, was simply miraculous. And miracles, by definition, defied explanation.

"Cadderly told me he had played a role," a flustered Danica responded at last. "There was more to the summons than simply repeating the ancient words. He spoke of gathering energy, of a mindset that brought him into the trees' world before awakening them and coaxing them into ours."

Pertelope nodded slowly as she digested the words. She held no doubts about Danica's honesty, or about Cadderly's mysterious, budding power.

"And the elf wizard's wound?" she prompted.

"By Elbereth's description, the spear had gone a foot or more into Tintagel's side," Danica replied. "So very much blood covered his clothing—I saw that much for myself—and Elbereth hadn't expected him to survive for more than a few moments longer. Yet when I saw him, not long at all after he was wounded, he was nearly fully healed and casting spells at our enemies once more."

"You have seen spells of healing performed here at the library," Pertelope said, trying to hide her excitement. "When that Oghmanyte priest broke his arm wrestling you, for example."

"Minor compared to the healing Cadderly performed on Tintagel," Danica assured her. "By Elbereth's word, he held the wizard's belly in while the skin mended around his fingers."

Pertelope nodded again and remained quiet for a long while. There was no need to go over it all again. Danica's recounting had been consistent and Pertelope knew her to be honest. The headmistress's hazel eyes stared into emptiness for a time before she focused again on Danica.

The young monk sat quietly and very still, lost in her own contemplations. To Pertelope's eyes, a shadow appeared on Danica's shoulder, a silhouette of a tiny female, trembling and glancing around nervously. Extraordinary heat emanated from the young monk's body, and her breathing, steady to the casual observer, reflected her anxieties to Pertelope's probing gaze.

The headmistress knew that Danica was full of passion, yet full of fear. Merely thinking of Cadderly stirred a boiling turmoil within her.

Pertelope shook the insightful visions away, ended the distant song that played in the recesses of her mind, and put a comforting hand on Danica's shoulder. "Thank you for coming to sit with me," she said. "You have been a great help to me—and to Cadderly, do not doubt."

A confused look came over Danica. Pertelope hated that she had to be cryptic with someone so obviously attached to Cadderly, but she knew Danica wouldn't understand the powers at work on the young priest. Those same powers had been with Pertelope for nearly a score of years, and Pertelope wasn't certain even she understood them.

The bed creaked as Danica stood. "I have to go now," she explained, looking back to the small room's door. "If you wish, I can come back, and—"

"No need," the headmistress answered, offering a warm smile. "Unless you feel you'd like to talk," she quickly added. Pertelope intensified her gaze again and bade the song begin, searching for that insightful, supernatural level of perception. The trembling shadow remained upon Danica's shoulder, but it had grown more calm, and the young monk's breathing had steadied.

The heat was still there, though, the vital energy of anticipated passion. Even after Danica departed, the door handle glowed softly from her touch.

Pertelope blew out a long sigh. She slipped one of her arm-length gloves off to scratch at the shark skin it hid and tried to recall her own trials when Deneir had selected her—had cursed her, she often believed.

Pertelope smiled at the dark thought. "No, not a curse," she said aloud, lifting her eyes toward the ceiling as though she addressed a higher presence. She played the song more strongly in her mind, the universal harmony that she had heard a thousand times in the turning pages of the tome she'd given to Cadderly. She fell into the song and followed its notes, gaining communion with her god.

"So, you have chosen Cadderly," she whispered.

She received no answer, and had expected none.

"He could not otherwise have accomplished all of those 'miracles' in the elven wood," Pertelope went on, speaking aloud her conclusions to bolster her suspicions. "I pity him, and yet I envy him, for he is young and strong, stronger than I ever was. How powerful will he become?"

Again, except for the continuing melody in Pertelope's head, there came no response.

That was why the headmistress often felt as though she had been cursed. There never were any answers granted. She had always had to discover them for herself.

And so, too, she knew, would Cadderly.

SIX

A BEGGAR, A THIEF

Cadderly purposely avoided looking at the guardsman as he moved through the short tunnel and under the raised portcullis leading out of the lakeside town. All along his route to the western gate the young scholar had observed people of every station and every demeanor, and the variety of shadowy images he had seen leaping from their shoulders had nearly overwhelmed him. Again the song of Deneir played in his thoughts, as though he had subconsciously summoned it, and again, *aura* remained the only identifiable term. Cadderly couldn't make sense of it all, and he feared his new insightfulness would drive him mad.

He grew more at ease when he had put the bustle of Carradoon behind him and walked along the hedge- and tree-lined road with nothing more to attract his attention than the chatter of birds and the rustle of squirrels gathering their winter stores.

"Is mine the curse of the hermits?" he asked himself

aloud. "That it is!" he proclaimed loudly, startling a nearby squirrel that had frozen in place on the camouflaging gray bark of a tree. The rising volume of Cadderly's voice sent the critter hop-skipping up the tree, where it froze again, not even its bushy tail twitching.

"Well, it is," Cadderly cried to the rodent in feigned exasperation. "All those poor, wretched, solitary souls, so frowned upon by the rest of us. They are not hermits by choice. They possess the same vision that haunts me, and it drives them mad, drives them to where they cannot bear the sight of another intelligent thing."

Cadderly moved to the base of the tree to better view the beast.

"I see no shadows leaping from your shoulders, Mr. Gray," he called. "You have no hidden desires, no cravings beyond those you obviously seek to fill."

"Unless there be a lady squirrel about!" came a cry from down the path.

Cadderly nearly leaped out of his boots. He spun to see a large, dirty man dressed in ragged, ill-fitting clothes and boots, the toes of which had long ago worn away.

"A lady squirrel would turn his mind away from those nuts," the stubble-faced man continued, advancing easily down the road.

Cadderly unconsciously brought his ram-headed walking stick up in front of him. Thieves were common on the roads close to the town, especially with winter fast approaching.

"But then . . ." the large man continued, putting a finger on his lower lip in a contemplative gesture. Cadderly noted that he wore mismatched, fingerless gloves, one black, one brown leather. "If the lady was about, the squirrel would still have no 'hidden desires,' since the unabashed beast would seek to fill whatever his heart deemed necessary, the call of his belly or the call of his loins.

"I'd be one to choose the loins, eh?" the man said with a lascivious wink.

Cadderly blushed and nearly laughed aloud, though he still hadn't figured out what to make of that well-spoken vagabond. He peered closer, trying to find a revealing shadow on the man's shoulders. But Cadderly's surprise had stolen the song fully, and nothing rested there, except the badly worn folds of an old woolen scarf.

"It's a fine day to be about, talking to the beasts," the man went on, seeing no response forthcoming from Cadderly. "A pity, then, that I must get myself inside the gates of Carradoon, in the realm of smells less pleasant, where high buildings hide the pan-orama of beauty so easily taken for granted on this most lovely of country roads."

"You will not easily pass by the guards," Cadderly remarked, knowing how carefully the city militiamen protected their home, especially with rumors of war brewing.

The vagabond opened a small pouch on the side of his rope belt and produced a single silver coin.

"A bribe?" Cadderly asked.

"Admission," the beggar corrected. "'One must spend gold'—or silver, as the case may be—'to make gold,' goes the old saying. I will accept the lore as true, since I know I will indeed secure some gold once I am within the town's wall."

Cadderly studied the man more closely. He wore no insignia of any lawful guild, showed no signs of any craft whatsoever. "A thief," the scholar stated flatly.

"Never," the man asserted.

"A beggar?" Cadderly asked, the word coming out with the same venom.

The larger man clutched his chest and staggered back several steps, as though Cadderly had launched a dagger into his heart.

Cadderly did notice some shadows then. He caught the flicker of a pained look beneath the man's sarcastic, playful facade. He saw a woman on one shoulder, holding a small child, and an older child on the man's other shoulder. The images were gone in an instant, and Cadderly noticed for the first time that the man had a slight limp and a blue-green bruise on his wrist just above the edge of the brown glove.

Waves of nausea nearly overwhelmed the young scholar. As he focused his senses, he felt the emanations of the disease clearly and knew beyond doubt why that intelligent, articulate man had sunk to such a lowly station.

He was a leper.

"M-my pardon," Cadderly stammered. "I-I didn't know . . ."

"Does anyone . . . ever?" the large man asked in a snarling voice. "I do not appreciate your pity, young priest of Deneir, but I'll gladly accept your pittance."

Cadderly clenched his walking stick tightly, mistaking the remark as a threat.

"You know of what I speak," the beggar said. "The coins you inevitably will throw my way to alleviate your guilt?"

Cadderly winced at the biting remark. He was surprised, too, that the beggar had discerned his order, even though he wore his holy symbol prominently on the front of his wide-brimmed hat. The large man studied Cadderly intently as the tumult of emotions rolled through the young priest.

"Pig," the man said with a sneer, to Cadderly's surprise. "How terrible that one such as I should have sunk to the level of a street beggar!"

Cadderly bit his lip in the face of such dramatics.

"To wallow in the mud beside the wretches," the man continued, throwing one arm out wide, the other still clutching at his mock-wounded chest.

He stopped suddenly in that pose and turned a confused expression Cadderly's way. "Wretches?" he asked. "What do you know of them, arrogant priest? You, who are so intelligent—that is the weal of your order, is it not?

"Intelligence." The beggar spat with distaste. "An excuse, I say, for those such as you. It is what separates you, what elevates you." He eyed Cadderly dangerously and finished, deliberately, "It is what blinds you."

"I do not deserve this!" Cadderly declared.

The man threw his hands above his head and blurted a mocking, incredulous shout. "Deserve?" he cried. He jerked the sleeve up on one arm, revealing a row of rotting, bruised skin.

"Deserve?" he asked again. "What, pray tell me, young priest who is so wise, do those kneeling before, and crawling from the alleys of Carradoon deserve?"

Cadderly thought he would burst apart. He felt an angry energy building within him, gathering explosive strength. He remembered when he had awakened the trees in Shilmista, and when he had healed Tintagel, had held the elf wizard's guts in while a similar energy had mended the garish wound. A page from *The Tome of Universal Harmony* flashed in Cadderly's head as clearly as if he held the open book before him, and he knew then the object of his rage. He eyed the bruises on the large man's arm, and filled his nostrils with the stench of the disease that had so tormented the man's soul.

"Pieta pieta, dominus . . ." Cadderly began, reciting the chant as he read the words from the clear image in his mind.

"No!" the large man cried, charging ahead. Cadderly halted the chant and tried to throw up his arms to block, but the man was surprisingly fast and balanced for one so tall. He caught hold of Cadderly's clothing and shook the young priest.

Cadderly saw an opening, could have jammed his walking stick up under the man's chin. He knew, though, that the frustrated beggar meant him no real harm, and he was not surprised when the man released him, shoving him back a step.

"I could cure you," Cadderly growled.

"Could you?" the man mocked. "And could you cure them?" he cried, waggling a finger toward the distant town. "Could you cure them all? Are all the world's ills to fall before this young priest of Deneir? Call to the wretched, I say!" the beggar cried, whirling and shouting to the four winds. "Line them up before this . . . this . . ." He searched for the word, his dirty lips moving silently. "This *godsend!*" he cried at last.

A nearby squirrel broke into a dead run along the branches across the path.

"I don't deserve this," Cadderly said again, calm.

His tone seemed infectious, for the large man dropped his hands to his sides and his shoulders slumped.

"No," the leper agreed, "but accept it, I pray you, as but a small penance in a world filled with undeserved penance."

Cadderly blinked away the moisture that came into his gray eyes. "What are their names?" he asked.

The beggar looked at him curiously for a moment then his lips curled up in his first sincere smile. "Jhanine, my wife," he answered. "Toby, my son, and Millinea, my young daughter. None have shown signs of my infection as yet," he explained, guessing Cadderly's unspoken question. "I see them rarely— to deliver the pittance I have gained from the guilty arrogants of Carradoon."

The beggar chuckled, seeing Cadderly's blush. "My pardon," he said, dipping into a low bow. "I, too, am sometimes blind, seeing the well and fortunate in a similar light."

Cadderly nodded his acceptance of that inevitable— and excusable—fault. "What is your name?"

"Nameless," the beggar answered without hesitation. "Yes, that is a good name for one such as me. Nameless, akin to all the other Namelesses huddled in the squalor between the towers of the wealthy."

"You hold such self-pity?" Cadderly asked.

"Self-truth," Nameless answered without pause.

Cadderly conceded the point. "I could cure you," the young priest said again.

Nameless shrugged his shoulders. "Others have tried," he explained. "Priests from your own order, and those of Oghma as well . . . I went to the Edificant

Library—of course I went to the library—when the signs first appeared."

The mention of the Edificant Library brought an unconscious frown to Cadderly's face. "I'm not like the others," he asserted more forcefully than he had intended.

The beggar smiled. "No, you're not," he agreed.

"Then you will accept my aid?"

Nameless did not relinquish his smile. "I will . . . consider it," he replied. Cadderly caught an unmistakable glimmer of hope in the man's dark brown eyes, and saw a shadow appear atop the man's shoulder, a shadow of the beggar himself, gaily tossing a small form—Millinea, he somehow knew—into the air and catching her. The shadow fell apart quickly, dissipating in the wind.

Cadderly nodded somewhat grimly, suspecting the dangers of false hope for one in that man's position— suspecting but not truly understanding, Cadderly knew, for he was not, for all his sympathy, standing in the beggar's holey shoes.

The young priest tore the pouch from his belt. "Then accept this," he said, tossing it to the large man.

Nameless caught it and eyed Cadderly, but made no move to return the coin-filled purse. It was an offering holding no false hope, an offering of face value and nothing more.

"I am one of those arrogants," Cadderly explained. "Guilty, as you have accused."

"And this will alleviate that guilt?" the beggar asked, his eyes narrowing.

Cadderly couldn't hold back his chuckle. "Hardly," he replied, and he knew that if Nameless believed the purse would alleviate his guilt then Nameless would have thrown it back at him. "Hardly a proper penance. I give it to you because you, and Jhanine, Toby, and Millinea, are more deserving of it than I, not for any lessening of my own guilt. That guilt I must carry until I have learned better." Cadderly cocked his head to the side as a thought came to him.

"Call the gold a tutor's fee if that helps you to lessen your own guilt for waylaying one as innocent as me!" he said.

The beggar laughed and bowed low. "Indeed, young priest, you are not like those of your order who greeted me at the library's great door, those who were more concerned with their own failings to cure me than with the consequences of my ailment."

That is why they failed, Cadderly knew, but he did not interrupt.

"It is a fine day!" Nameless went on. "And I pray you enjoy it." He held up the purse and shook it. His whole body shaking in a joyful dance, he smiled at the loud jingle of coins. "Perhaps I will as well. To the Nine Hells with Carrion's stinking alleys!"

Nameless stopped his dance and stood stock-still, eyeing Cadderly with a grave expression. Slowly, he extended his right hand, seemingly conscious, for the first time, of his dirty, fingerless glove.

Cadderly understood the action as a test, a test he was glad he could so easily pass. Without a thought for superstitious consequences, the young priest accepted the handshake.

"I pass by here often," Cadderly said quietly. "Consider my offer of healing."

The beggar, too touched to reply aloud, only nodded.

Then he turned and walked briskly away, his limp more pronounced, as though he no longer cared to hide it. Cadderly watched him for few moments then turned and continued away from Carradoon. He smiled as more squirrels scrabbled overhead, but he hardly looked up to see them.

It seemed to the young priest that the day had grown finer and less fine at the same time.

Q

Nameless smiled as a squirrel nearly lost its balance on a small branch, catching hold and righting itself at the last moment. The beggar tried to use that simple, natural movement as a symbol of what had just transpired between him and the curious young priest, viewing himself as the branch and Cadderly as the creature righting its course. The thought made the leper feel good, valuable, for the first time in a long, long while.

He couldn't brood on it, though, and could hardly hope to meet enough people like the curious Cadderly, who would care to see their arrogance laid out before them. No, Nameless would have to continue as he had for more than a year, struggling daily to gain enough trinkets to keep his wife and children from starving.

He had at least a temporary reprieve. He tossed the purse into the air, caught it gingerly, and smiled again. It was indeed a fine day!

Nameless turned around, prepared to pay Jhanine and the children a long overdue visit, but his smile fast became a frown.

"So sorry to startle you, good friend," said a puny

man, his drooping, thick eyelids open only enough for
Nameless to make out his small, dark eyes.

Nameless instinctively moved the coin-filled pouch
out of sight and kept his arms in front of him.

"I am a leper," he growled, using his disease as a threat.

The smaller man chuckled and gave a wheezing
laugh that sounded more like a cough. "You think me a
thief?" he asked, holding his hands out wide. Nameless
blinked at the man's curious gloves, one white, the other
black. "As you can see, I carry no weapons," the little
man assured.

"None openly," Nameless admitted.

"I see we both wear a mixed set of gloves," Ghost
remarked. "Kindred spirits, eh?"

Nameless slipped his hands under the folds of his
badly fitting clothes, embarrassed for some reason he
didn't understand. Kindred spirits? he thought. Hardly.
The fine gloves the little man wore, matched or not,
must have cost more than Nameless had seen in many
months, the young priest's pouch included.

"But we are," Ghost asserted, noticing the frown.

"You're a beggar, then?" Nameless dared to ask.
"Carradoon is but a mile down the road. I was going
there myself. The take is always good."

"But the young priest changed your mind?" the
stranger asked. "Do tell me about that one."

Nameless shrugged and shook his head slightly,
hardly conscious of the movement.

"Ah," the little stranger said, his arms still wide, "you
don't know young Cadderly."

"You do?"

"Of course," the man replied, motioning to the
pouch Nameless tried to hide. "Shouldn't all those of

our ilk know one as generous as Cadderly?"

"Then you are a beggar," Nameless reasoned, relaxing a bit. There was an unspoken code among the people of squalor, an implied brotherhood.

"Perhaps," the stranger answered. "I have been many things, but now I am a beggar." He wheezed another chuckle. "Or soon I will be," he corrected.

Nameless watched as the man unbuttoned the top of his surcoat and pulled the woolen folds aside.

"A mirror?" Nameless muttered then he said no more, transfixed by his own image in a silver mirror.

Nameless felt an intrusion. He tried to pull away, but couldn't, held firmly by strange magic. He saw nothing except for his own image, lined in black as though he had been transported to some other place, some dark, otherworldly place. Nameless tried desperately to look around at his surroundings, tried to make sense of them, find some familiarity.

He saw only his own face.

He heard a clap then he was moving, or he felt as though he was moving, even though he knew that his physical body had not stirred in the least. There came a brief, sharp pain as his spirit left his body and floated helplessly toward the effeminate vessel that awaited it.

The pain came again.

Nameless blinked, fighting against the heavy droop of his eyelids. He saw his own image again, wearing gloves, black and white. His confusion lasted only until he realized that it was no longer a reflected image he saw, but his own body.

"What have you done to me?" the beggar cried, reaching for the stranger in his body. Every movement seemed to drag. His arms had little strength to convey his fury.

He saw himself snap his fingers and the black and white gloves disappeared, replaced by the fingerless gloves. Nameless was pushed back by the man that inhabited his body, and he realized how useful that frail body had proven to the stranger—how benign and unthreatening, the body of a man even a young boy could defeat. Nameless watched his own body offer him a resigned shrug then advance on him. He could only whimper in confusion as his own wretched, diseased hands wrapped around the skinny neck he found himself in possession of.

Nameless fought desperately, as desperately as the stranger's puny form had surely ever battled, but there was no strength in his arms, no power to loosen the larger attacker's hold. Soon he stopped struggling, his resignation founded in grief for those he would leave behind.

Q

Ghost contemplated the change with amusement, thinking it curious, even humorous, that one as obviously wretched as the leprous beggar would lament the end of his life.

There was no mercy in the wicked man, though. He had killed that frail body a hundred times, perhaps, and had killed his previous body a like number, and the body he had used before that as well.

The corpse slumped to the ground, and Ghost brought back his magical device and called upon its powers to watch the beggar's spirit step out of the slain form. Ghost quickly pulled off the fine black glove and placed it on his unoccupied body. He closed his eyes and stiffened his resolve against the ensuing pain, for the simple act had transferred a part of his own spirit back into the corpse.

It was a necessary step for two reasons. The body would heal—Ghost had a powerful magical item concealed in one boot to see to that—and if the receptacle remained open, the beggar's spirit would find its way back in. Also, if Ghost allowed the body to die, if he allowed the item in his boot to call back a spirit, the item's regenerative powers would partially consume the form. Considering how many times Ghost had made the switch, the item would have burned up the puny form long ago.

But that wouldn't happen. Ghost knew how to use the items in conjunction with each other. The *Ghearufu*, the glove-and-mirror device, had long ago shown him the way, and he had spent three lifetimes perfecting the act.

Ghost looked both ways along the empty road then pulled the slender body far from the trail, into some covering brush. He felt the disease in the new form he had taken. It was an unpleasant sensation, but Ghost took heart that he would not wear the disguise for long—just long enough to meet young Cadderly for himself.

He hopped back out to the road and wandered along, wondering how much of the day he would have to watch pass him by before young Cadderly returned down the road.

Q

After the thief in the beggar's body had departed, Nameless's spirit stood beside the puny corpse, confused and helpless. If Cadderly, with his new insight, had gazed upon the spirit then he would have seen the shadows of Jhanine, Toby, and Millinea scattering to the four winds, fading like the images of hope that Nameless had never dared to sustain.

SEVEN

THE MAZE

Q

Cadderly approached the steep-sided, round hillock and the tower of Belisarius with tentative steps, fully expecting that the wizard, as knowledgeable as he was, would offer him little insight into the strange things that had been happening to him. Actually, Cadderly had no idea if the wizard would grant him an audience. He had done some valuable scribing for Belisarius on several occasions, but he couldn't really call the man a friend. Furthermore, Cadderly wasn't even sure Belisarius would be home.

The young scholar relaxed a bit when a wide line up the nearly seventy-degree incline magically transformed from unremarkable grass to a stone stairway with flat, even steps. The wizard was home and had apparently seen Cadderly coming.

Seventy-five steps brought Cadderly to the hillock's flat top and the cobblestone walkway that encircled the tower. Cadderly had to walk nearly halfway around the base, for Belisarius had placed his steps far to the side of the entrance. The steps never appeared on the same spot on the hillock, and Cadderly hadn't yet figured out if the wizard created new steps each time, had some way of rotating the grassy knoll under the stationary tower, or simply deceived visitors of the steps' actual location. Cadderly thought the last possibility, deception, the most likely, since Belisarius used his magic primarily for elaborate illusions.

The tower's iron-bound door swung open as Cadderly approached—or had it been open all along, only appearing to be closed? Cadderly paused as he started over the threshold when there came the sound of grating stone. An entire section of the stone wall in the foyer shifted and swung out, blocking the inner entry door and revealing a cobwebbed stairway winding down into the blackness.

Cadderly scratched the stubble on his chin, his gray eyes flashing inquisitively at the unexpected invitation. He remembered the days when he had come to the tower with Headmaster Avery. Every time, the skilled wizard presented the duo with a new test of cunning. Cadderly was glad for the diversion, glad that Belisarius had apparently come up with something new, something that might take the young man's mind from the disturbing questions the beggar had raised.

"This is a new path, and a new trick," Cadderly said aloud, congratulating the wizard, who no doubt listened in.

Always curious, the young scholar pulled a torch from its sconce on the foyer wall and started down. Twenty spiraling steps later, he came to a low corridor ending at a thick wooden door. Cadderly carefully studied the portal for a long moment then slowly placed his hand against it, feeling the solidity of its grain. Satisfied that it was real, he pushed it open and continued on, finding another descending stairway behind it.

The next level proved a bit more confusing. The stairway ended in a three-way intersection of similar, unremarkable stone passageways. Cadderly took a step straight ahead then changed his mind and went to the left, passing through another door after repeating his pause-and-study test, then another after that. Again he had entered an intersection, but one much more confusing than the last, since each way revealed many side passages.

Cadderly nearly laughed aloud, and silently congratulated the clever wizard. With a helpless shrug, he let his walking stick fall to the floor then followed the path determined by the unseeing gaze of the carved ram's head. Any way seemed as good as another as the young priest moved along, left, right, right again, then straight ahead. Three more doors were left open behind him, and one passage sloped down at a noticeable angle.

"Excellent!" Cadderly exclaimed when he passed a sharp corner and found himself back where he'd started, at the bottom of the second stairway. His torch was beginning to burn low, but the curious young priest pressed ahead once more, consciously selecting different avenues than on his first time through.

The torch burned away, leaving Cadderly in utter blackness. He closed his eyes and recalled a page in *The Tome of Universal Harmony*. He heard a few notes of Deneir's endless song and muttered the appropriate chant, pointing to the tip of his burned-out torch. He blinked many times and squinted against the glare as the magical light came on, much brighter than the flickering torch flame had been. When his eyes at last adjusted, he went on, turning corner after corner.

A scuffling, scraping sound made him pause. It was no rat, Cadderly knew. The animal, if it was an animal, that had made the sound was much larger.

An image of a bull came into Cadderly's thoughts. He recalled a day as a youngster, out with Headmaster Avery, when he had passed a pasture full of cows. At least, Avery had thought they were cows. Cadderly couldn't help but smile when he remembered the image of portly Avery huffing and puffing in full flight from an angry bull.

The scuffling came again.

Cadderly considered extinguishing his magical light, but reconsidered immediately, realizing the predicament that act would leave him in. He crept up to the next corner, took off his wide-brimmed hat, and slowly peeked around.

The thing was humanoid, but certainly not human. It towered seven feet tall, shoulders and chest wide and impossibly strong, and its head—no mask, Cadderly knew—resembled the bull in that long-ago field. Wearing only a wolf-pelt loincloth, the creature carried no weapon, though that hardly brought a sense of relief to the minimally armed young scholar.

A minotaur! Cadderly's heart nearly failed him He was no longer so sure that his trek through the tower's catacombs was arranged by Belisarius. It occurred to Cadderly that something pernicious might have happened to the congenial mage, that some dark force might have overcome the tower's formidable defenses.

His thoughts were blown away, along with his breath, a moment later, as the bull-headed giant scraped one foot on the stone again and charged, slamming into Cadderly and launching him across the corridor. He cracked his shoulder blade as he smashed into the stone, and his torch flew away, though of course the magical light did not diminish.

The minotaur snorted and stormed in. Cadderly took up his walking stick defensively, wondering what in the Nine Hells the minuscule weapon could do against that awesome beast. The minotaur seemed none too concerned with it, striding right in to meet its foe.

Cadderly swung with all his might, but the skinny club broke apart as he connected on the brute's thick-skinned chest.

The minotaur slapped him once then leaned its horned head in, smashing Cadderly against the stone. The young man freed one arm and punched the beast, to no avail. The beast pressed more forcefully and Cadderly could neither squirm nor breathe.

His estimate of how long he had to live shortened considerably when the minotaur opened its huge mouth, putting its formidable teeth in line with Cadderly's exposed neck.

In that brief moment, the young priest recognized the fields of energy floating around him. He looked down at the floor, at his unbroken walking stick.

Cadderly jammed his free arm into the minotaur's gaping jaws, and plunged his hand down its throat. A moment later, he retracted the hand, holding the bull-headed monster's beating heart. The creature fell back a step, not daring to do anything at all.

"I have traveled down two stairways, which actually

went up," Cadderly announced firmly. "And through six doors, two of which were illusionary. That would put me in the west wing of your library, would it not, good Belisarius?"

The illusionary minotaur disappeared, but strangely, Cadderly still held the pumping heart. The scene reverted to its true form, the west wing, as Cadderly had guessed, and Belisarius, a confused, almost frightened look on his bushy-browed, bearded face, stood across the room, leaning on a bookcase.

Cadderly winked at him then opened his mouth and moved as though to take a bite of the thing in his hand.

"Oh, you!" the wizard cried. He turned away and put a hand to his mouth, trying to keep his stomach's contents down. "Oh, do not! I beg, do not!"

Cadderly dismissed the gruesome image, willed it away, though he was not certain how he had brought it into being in the first place.

"How?" the wizard gasped, finally composed.

"My magic has . . . shifted recently," Cadderly tried to explain, "grown."

"That is no clerical magic I have ever heard of," Belisarius insisted. "To create such perfect illusions . . ." Just the words made the wizard picture the heart, and he gagged yet again.

Cadderly understood something that Belisarius apparently did not. "I didn't create the image," the young scholar explained, as much to himself as to the wizard, "nor did I collect the magical forces necessary to create it."

The wizard dismissed any remaining revulsion, too intrigued by what Cadderly hinted at. He moved quietly across the room toward the young priest.

"I saw the energies gathered," Cadderly went on. "I discovered the trick for what it was and . . . perverted . . . your grand imagery."

"Couldn't you have dispelled it all together, as most priests would have?" Belisarius asked.

Cadderly shrugged. "I thought I had," he replied with a wry smile, "in the grand fashion befitting your illusions."

Belisarius tipped his floppy woolen cap to the young priest.

"But I'm not sure," Cadderly admitted. "Actually, I'm not sure of much where my magic is concerned, and that's why I've returned."

Belisarius led the young man to the adjoining sitting room where they both nestled into comfortable chairs. The wizard produced four items—three rings and a slender wand—that Cadderly had given him two tendays before, and laid them aside, anxious to hear Cadderly's revelations.

It took Cadderly a while to begin his many tales—so much had happened to him! Once he began, though, he went on and on, covering every minute detail. He told Belisarius about summoning Shilmista's trees, about healing Tintagel, and about watching the gallant horse Temmerisa's spirit depart. Then he spoke of the more specific and recent incidents, of creating light and darkness in his room and in Belisarius's maze. Most disturbing of all to the young priest were the shadowy images he had seen dancing atop shoulders. Cadderly said nothing immediately about his dreams, though, not quite certain of how they fit into anything, and also a bit afraid of what they might reveal.

"The spells you speak of are not so unusual to one blessed with priestly magic," the wizard said when the obviously exasperated young man had finished his worrisome tale. "Many can be duplicated by a wizard as well, such as the manipulation of light. As for the shadows, well, clerics have been able to determine the general weal of individuals for centuries."

"Aura," Cadderly replied, speaking the one word he had been able to decipher from that particular chant. "I don't understand how 'the dawn' would affect such a spell."

Belisarius scratched his graying beard. "That is unusual," he said at length. "But is 'the dawn' the only meaning of the word? When was this wondrous tome penned?"

Cadderly thought for a moment then had his answer. "Aura," he said firmly, "aura." He looked up to the wizard and smiled.

"Aura means aura," Belisarius agreed, "or at least it used to, referring to the emanation of light, of good, surrounding an individual. There you have it, then, a clerical spell to be sure. Perhaps that is what has happened to you, only you have not yet learned to interpret what you see."

Cadderly nodded, though he didn't really agree. He certainly knew how to—or *felt* how to—interpret the dancing and fleeting shadows. That was not the problem.

"I have witnessed extreme examples of clerical magic," Cadderly replied, "but these powers, I fear, are different. I don't study the prayers before I call on them, as do the priests at the library. I make no preparations at all—as with the illusion that I defeated before your eyes. I didn't expect you to challenge me so. I wasn't even expecting you to know I had come to visit."

Cadderly had to pause for a long moment to compose himself, and during the silence, Belisarius mumbled almost constantly under his breath and scratched at his bushy beard.

"You know something," Cadderly declared, his words sounding like an accusation.

"I suspect something," Belisarius replied. "Since the Time of Troubles, there have been increasing reports of individuals with internal magical powers."

"Psionics," Cadderly said.

"You have heard of them, then," the wizard said. He threw his wiry arms out wide in heightened resignation. "Of course you have," he muttered. "You have heard of everything. That is what is so very frustrating about dealing with you."

The dramatics pulled a smile out of Cadderly and allowed him to relax back in the comfortable leather seat.

Belisarius seemed truly intrigued, as though he desperately hoped his guess was correct. "Might you be a mind mage? A psionicist?" he asked.

"I know little about them," the young priest admitted. "If that is what's happening to me, then it's happening without my assistance or approval."

"The powers of he mind mage aren't so different from those of a wizard," Belisarius explained, "except that they come from the individual's mind and not Mystra's Weave. I am well acquainted with your mental abilities." He snickered, obviously referring to his spellbook, which Cadderly had replaced from memory alone. "That type of prowess is the prime element of a mind mage's power."

Cadderly considered the words and gradually began to shake his head. "The power I manipulated in this tower was born of the Weave," he reasoned. "Could psionics interact so with a wizard's spell?"

Belisarius patted a knobby finger against his lower lip, his frown revealing the snag in the logic. "I do not know," he admitted.

The two sat quietly, digesting the details of their conversation.

"It doesn't fit," Cadderly announced a moment later. "I am the receptacle of the power and the transmuter of the power to the desired effect, of that much I am sure."

"I will not argue that," Belisarius replied, "but such power must have a conduit—a spell, if you will. One cannot simply tap into the Weave on a whim!"

Cadderly understood the growing excitement in the wizard's voice. If Belisarius was wrong, the wizard's entire life, his hermitic devotion to his magical studies, might be revealed as an exercise in futility.

"The song," Cadderly muttered, finally realizing the truth of it all.

"Song?"

The Tome of Universal Harmony," the young priest explained. "A holy book of Deneir. Whenever I have used the powers, even unconsciously, as with the dancing shadows, I have heard the song of that book in the recesses of my mind. My answers are in that song."

"Song of the book?" Belisarius could not begin to understand.

"The rhythm of the words," Cadderly tried to explain, though he knew he couldn't, not really.

Belisarius shrugged and seemed to accept that

insufficient explanation. "Then you have found your conduit," he said, "but I fear there is little I can tell you concerning it. This book would seem to be more a matter to take up with your headmasters at the Edificant Library."

"Or with my deity," Cadderly mumbled.

Belisarius shrugged noncommittally. "As you will," he said. "I can tell you this much, though, and I know I am right simply by looking at your haggard features."

"I have not been sleeping well," Cadderly put in, fearing what the wizard would say.

"The Art, the transference of Weave energies," Belisarius went on, undefeated by Cadderly's announcement, "exacts a toll on the practitioner. We wizards are very careful not to exceed our limitations. Normally we couldn't if we tried, since its in the memorization of a spell where those limits are revealed.

"Likewise, a cleric's granted powers stem from his or her faith and are tempered by agents of the gods, or even by the gods themselves where the high priests are sometimes concerned," Belisarius reasoned. "I warn you, young Cadderly, I have seen foolish mages consumed when trying to cast the spells of those more powerful than they, spells beyond their abilities. If you have found a way to avoid the normal boundaries and limitations of magic use, whatever type of magic might be involved, then I pray you will find the wisdom to moderate your activities, else it consume you."

A thousand possibilities began their progression through Cadderly's thoughts. Perhaps he should go back to the library with his dilemma. He could speak to Pertelope. . . .

"Now for some items that I know more about,"

Belisarius said. The wizard reached for the rings and the wand. He first held up a signet ring inscribed with the trident-and-bottle design of Castle Trinity. It once had belonged to the mage Dorigen.

"There is no detectable magic in this, as you believed," the wizard said, tossing it to Cadderly.

"I know," Cadderly said, as he caught it and put it into his pouch.

The declaration made Belisarius pause and consider the young man. "This ring," he said slowly, holding up the gold band set with a large onyx stone, "is indeed magical, and powerful."

"It evokes a line of flame," Cadderly said, "when the possessor utters '*Fete*,' the Elvish word for fire. I have seen it in use," the young priest added quickly, noticing Belisarius's deepening frown.

"Indeed," muttered the wizard. "And have you ever heard of a wizard named Agannazzar?"

Belisarius smiled as Cadderly shook his head. "He is a mage of no large fame born two centuries ago," the wizard explained.

"Now dead," Cadderly reasoned.

"Perhaps," Belisarius said wryly, flashing a wink. "One can never be certain where wizards are concerned."

"And was this his ring?" Cadderly asked.

"I cannot be sure," Belisarius replied. "Either he or one of his associates created it with this specific power imbued. It is not too powerful, but you may find it useful." He tossed it to Cadderly and took up the wand. The young priest suspected that Belisarius had purposely saved the remaining ring for last.

"This is a common device," the wizard began, but Cadderly stopped him with an upraised hand. At first the wand seemed an unremarkable, slender shaft of black wood just over a foot long, but as he looked at it, Cadderly heard the notes of a distant song playing in his mind.

Cadderly studied deeper, sensed, and saw clearly, the magic of the item.

"Light," he said to the wizard. "The wand's power has to do with the manipulation of illumination."

Belisarius frowned again and looked at the wand, as if ensuring that there were no runes visibly etched on its smooth side. "You have seen it in use?" the wizard asked hopefully, already tired of being upstaged.

"No," Cadderly said, not releasing his attention from the revelations. In his mind, he saw lights forming different images and dancing about.

"*Domin illu,*" he muttered. The light he pictured became constant and of the same intensity as the light he had conjured in his room and in the maze.

"*Illu,*" an arcane word for light, escaped his trembling lips. The light intensified, brightened to where Cadderly squinted against the glare in his mind.

"*Mas illu,*" he said, the literal translation being "great light." The image burst forth in all its splendor, a fiery green explosion of light spewing golden rays and blazing in Cadderly's mind. Cadderly cried out and looked away, nearly shouting, "*Illumas belle!*" as he fell out of his chair.

Cadderly sat up and looked at the wizard, who still sat, holding the unremarkable wand in his extended hand.

"What just happened?" Belisarius asked.

"I saw the powers—four, distinctly," Cadderly replied, "in my mind."

"And you repeated the triggering phrases," the perturbed wizard added, "exactly."

"But how?" Cadderly asked him, honestly perplexed.

"Go see a priest," Belisarius said with a snarl. "Why did you waste my time and effort on things you already knew?"

"I didn't," Cadderly insisted.

"Go see a priest," Belisarius repeated, tossing the wand to Cadderly.

The young man accepted the item and looked at the floor beside the wizard's chair. "We have one more ring to explore," he remarked, backing away into his chair as he spoke.

Belisarius scooped up the remaining ring, a gold band lined with diamond chips, and held it out for Cadderly to see. "You tell me," the wizard insisted.

Again Cadderly heard the distant song playing, but for the sake of his valued friend's pride, he consciously pushed it away.

"It's not magical," he lied, extending his hand to accept it.

"Hah!" the wizard snapped and pulled back his hand. "This is the most potent item of all!" He held it close to his sparkling, admiring eyes. "A ring for wizards," he explained, "to heighten their powers. It would be quite useless to you."

An alarm went off in Cadderly's head. What was sneaky Belisarius up to? The young priest concentrated not on the ring, but on the wizard himself, and saw a shadow image of Belisarius perched on the wizard's shoulder, waggling its eager fingers and rubbing its hands as it peered at the ring. But Cadderly realized that the wizard's greed was indeed for a wizard's item. The bent of the shadow told him beyond any doubt that Belisarius had not lied to him, and he privately berated himself for thinking differently.

"Keep it," he offered.

The wizard nearly toppled from his chair. His smile seemed as though it would engulf his ears. "I will," he said, his voice an unintentional shriek. "What might I pay you in return?"

Cadderly waved the thought away.

"I must insist," Belisarius continued, undaunted. "This is too valuable a gift—"

"Not to me," Cadderly reminded him.

Belisarius conceded the point with a nod, but still searched for some way to give something back to the young priest.

"Your walking stick!" he proclaimed at last.

Cadderly took up the item, not understanding.

"You use it as a weapon?"

"If I must use anything at all," Cadderly answered. "It is harder than my hand." The mere mention of open-handed combat inevitably brought an image of Danica to Cadderly's mind.

"But not as sturdy as you would like?" Belisarius went on, not noticing the cloud of despair that briefly crossed Cadderly's face.

"Do not deny it," the wizard insisted. "You revealed your fears for the feebleness of the weapon in your fight with the minotaur, when you readily accepted the image of it breaking."

Cadderly didn't argue.

"Leave it with me, my boy!" Belisarius cried. "Give me a few days, and I promise you that you will never consider it a feeble weapon again."

"So you are an enchanter as well?" Cadderly remarked.

"There are many wizardly talents that a cleric would not understand," the wizard replied with an exaggerated air of superiority.

"Especially a cleric who does not understand his own talents," Cadderly replied, his simple admission stealing the wizard's bluster.

Belisarius nodded and managed a weak smile then left Cadderly with a final thought: "Moderation."

Q

Cadderly was a bit surprised to find Nameless still wandering the road between the wizard's tower and Carradoon, expecting that the beggar would either have gone to Carradoon to further his day's take, or to his wife and children to enjoy a reprieve from the unenviable lifestyle that had been forced upon him.

Cadderly grew even more surprised when the beggar looked at him and gave him an exaggerated wink, holding up and jingling the purse of gold with a lascivious smile on his dirty face.

Something about that gesture struck Cadderly as badly out of character for Nameless, an act of either greed or thanks, neither of which suited the proud, but unfortunate man Cadderly had met on the road.

Then Cadderly saw the shadows.

He couldn't make them out distinctly, as he had the images of Jhanine and her children. They were hunched and growling things, their forms shifting continually, but always emanating a clear and unrepentant wickedness to the young priest. One imaginary claw reached out from the beggar's shoulder and raked the air in Cadderly's direction.

Cadderly was afraid. His neck hair stood on end, and his heart began to drum in his chest. A sickly sweet smell came to him then, and he thought he heard the buzz of flies. Cadderly shook his head, worried that he was going insane. It seemed as if his senses had heightened, become animal-like, and the sudden intrusion of so much stimulation nearly overwhelmed the young priest.

Then he was calm again and looking at the innocent beggar. He wished that he had his walking stick, and glanced back to the distant tower.

"Fine day!" the beggar said, seeming cheery, though Cadderly instinctively knew better.

Fete. The word came into Cadderly's head and he almost uttered it. He looked down at his hand, the onyx ring upon one finger, and saw that he had subconsciously angled it the beggar's way.

"Must you be gone so soon?" Nameless asked, sounding innocent, almost wounded.

Cadderly looked again at the black shadows crouched upon the man's shoulder, saw the claws and venom-dripping fangs. He nodded briskly, pulled his cloak tightly around his shoulders, and hurried on his way.

He caught a whiff of that sickly sweet scent again and heard the flies. If he'd been alone and not so unnerved, he would have stopped and sought out the source. He glanced to the side only briefly as he passed, at the bushes lining the road.

If he'd looked closer, Cadderly would have discovered the body, already bloated after just a few hours in the late summer sun. And if he had found the strength to work his magical perceptions, Cadderly would have seen, too, the spirit of Nameless, helpless, hopeless, and pitifully wandering until the gods came to claim it.

EIGHT

The young priest had noticed the change!

Ghost cursed himself, considering the implications of the unexpected occurrence. He had never really believed that he would be able to kill Cadderly so easily—according to every piece of information he'd been given, the young priest was a deadly opponent—but when he'd seen Cadderly coming down the road, alone and with no witnesses, Ghost had briefly wondered if the purse might be earned quickly, if his artistry had so easily paid off.

The beggar had gained Cadderly's confidence, that much Ghost knew from eavesdropping on their conversation. Posing as that man, the assassin thought he could get close, catch Cadderly with his guard down. Ghost replayed the brief encounter, trying to discern where he'd failed. Nothing obvious came to him—certainly nothing so blatant as to justify sending a defensively huddled Cadderly running on his way.

A singular fear came to the assassin then: if Cadderly

proved as formidable as the reports had indicated—and as Ghost was beginning to suspect—then he might be strong enough to fend off the magic of the *Ghearufu*. It had been done only twice before, both times by wizards, when Ghost's attempts at possession had been mentally blocked.

"There are other options," Ghost said aloud, reminding himself of his many allies and of the fact that both of those resisting wizards had wound up as worm food.

One of those times, Ghost had possessed a victim that the unsuspecting mage could not suspect—his wife. What a sweet kill that had been! On the other occasion, Ghost had served the attending Night Mask band as an infiltrator, providing them with such an enormous amount of information that the targeted wizard, as powerful as he was, had been among the guild's easiest kills.

"Either way, young Cadderly," the merciless assassin whispered to the wind, "I shall paint my picture, and you shall be dead before the first of winter's snows."

With a malignant snicker, the assassin in a beggar's body went to the bushes and retrieved his own form. The magical ring had nearly completed its healing work on the limp-muscled figure by then. The stench was fast fading and the flies had gone away.

"Do you wear a ring such as mine?" the assassin teased the formless spirit he knew would still be wandering nearby. Ghost willed the *Ghearufu*, white glove, and mirror, back into sight and took the black glove from the hand of the corpse. He fell back into his mind, connecting with the powers of the magical device.

The eyes of the assassin's more familiar form blinked open just in time to watch the beggar's body fall stiffly to the side. Ghost spent a moment reorienting himself to his customary form then propped himself up on his elbows.

"No magic ring?" he laughed at the beggar's corpse. "Then you will stay dead, pitiful fool, though whoever finds your body will have no idea how you died!"

The thought widened Ghost's smile. In his earliest days with the *Ghearufu,* more than a hundred years before, he had hacked up his unmarked victims. His confidence had quickly grown, though, and Ghost soon changed tactics, thinking in his budding arrogance that the mysteries surrounding the demise of an apparently healthy body would serve as an appropriate calling card.

Ghost willed the *Ghearufu* away and brushed the dirt from his clothes. He started down the road for the distant gates of Carradoon, and his room at the Dragon's Codpiece.

Q

The firbolg noted with distaste the apparently normal situation at the farmhouse on the outskirts of Carradoon. A few hens clucked and strutted, pecking at discarded seed here and there, the three horses in the stable beside the barn showed no signs that they had been spooked in the least, and the house itself showed neither a shattered window nor a broken door.

Vander knew better. It was always that way, always done in absolute secrecy. And it all seemed so cowardly to the warrior giant.

"We could have stayed in the forest," Vander

muttered, flipping his white-furred cloak back over his muscular shoulders.

The black-and-silver-outfitted assassins at the firbolg's sides looked at each other with curiosity. "It was by your orders . . ." one of them began to reply, but Vander's upraised hand silenced him.

Not by my orders, the firbolg thought, remembering when Ghost, in Vander's magnificent body, had set the troupe into motion, while Vander could only sit and watch helplessly from inside Ghost's weak form.

"We must get inside," offered the assassin after a few moments of uncomfortable silence. "This yard can be seen from the road."

"The light of day offends you," the firbolg remarked.

"It reveals us," the Night Mask replied.

Vander cast him a threatening scowl but followed the two men to the door anyway. The portal was large enough so that Vander didn't have to alter his size, and he was glad, for he didn't enjoy wearing a human frame, especially not around his murderous compatriots. He liked the imposing strength of his giant body, the long, muscled limbs that could reach an enemy from across a room and easily throttle him.

Vander hesitated at the threshold.

"The house is secure," one of the assassins inside assured the firbolg, misunderstanding his dismay. "Only the elder daughter remains alive, and she is held—" the lewd way the man spoke that word irritated Vander profoundly—"in the bedroom."

Vander strode in. "Where?" he demanded, purposely redirecting his gaze from the bloodied male and female bodies in the corner of the small kitchen. The human assassin, obviously unbothered by the gruesome sight, sat at the table, casually eating breakfast. He motioned to a door at the back of the room.

Propelled by his mounting rage, Vander was across the kitchen and through the door in an instant. He nearly tripped over a smaller bloodied form just inside the second room, and that moved him along only faster.

The second room connected to a side bedroom, its door open a crack. A whimpering sound came from within, revealing to Vander what was going on even before the firbolg shoved the door wide.

The girl lay on the bed, half-dressed and securely tied to the posts by her wrists and ankles, with the sides of her mouth pulled tightly back by a cloth gag. An assassin lay on each side of her, teasing her and taking delight at her terrified movements.

Vander had to stoop low to avoid the ceiling beams, but that didn't slow him. He swept aside the three Night Masks standing in his way with a single movement then stepped to the foot of the bed.

One of the prone assassins looked up and grinned wickedly, misconstruing the firbolg's urgency. The fool motioned for Vander to join in the fun.

Vander's great hands caught both the men by their collars and sent them flying across the room to collide heavily with the wall on each side of the door. The firbolg quickly threw a blanket over the exposed young woman and turned to face his hated associates.

The three on the side of the room looked at each other nervously. One of the men who had hit the wall lay crumpled in a heap at its base. The other, though, was up and outraged, a short sword in one hand.

Vander couldn't help but grin as he considered

the situation. Might this be the long-awaited show-down? A nagging thought stole his mirth. He could kill the men, all five, and probably the other dozen or so that were in and about the house, but what about Ghost?

"You three," he commanded to the men on the side of the room. "Your associate has drawn a weapon on your master."

The three understood the implications immediately, as did the man holding the short sword, if his suddenly fearful expression correctly revealed his thoughts. The Night Masks were a vicious and unforgiving band, but within the organization existed strict codes of conduct and horrible forms of discipline that even the heartiest assassin feared. The three by the wall drew their own weapons and faced the traitor.

The man with the short sword fumbled to put his weapon away. He jerked once then again, a confused expression on his face.

His accomplice, crumpled at the base of the wall, was not as dazed as he'd appeared, and he was eager to regain the taskmaster's favor. In his hand he held the last of three daggers, and that one, too, he whipped across to find a place in the traitor's side.

Anxious to show their respect and loyalty to their powerful leader, the other three promptly rushed the dying man. A club slapped the short sword from trembling hands, and all four loyal soldiers set upon the doomed man, hacking and crushing until he lay in a bloody heap on the floor.

"Put him with the other dead," Vander said to them. He looked back to the bed. "And find a proper prison for this girl."

"She is a witness, and must be killed," an assassin replied. "That is our way."

"On my word alone," Vander growled back, his voice carrying tremendous influence, considering the grim fate of the one who had dared to oppose him. "Now take her!"

The same man who had questioned the decision started immediately for the bed, sheathing his weapon but not relenting his steely-eyed glare.

Vander caught him in one hand by the throat and easily lifted him from the floor.

"You are not to touch her." The firbolg snarled in his face. He noticed the man's hand inching toward his belt. "Yes," Vander purred, "do draw your little knife!"

The three remaining men seemed at a loss.

"She must be killed," one of them dared to offer in support of his threatened colleague.

The man in Vander's grasp twisted free enough to growl defiantly at the firbolg.

Vander heaved him through the nearest wall, back into the kitchen. Several assassins who had gathered in the other room stared through the hole in disbelief at the angry firbolg.

"On your word alone," the three men by the door said obediently.

"I will make my place in the barn," Vander said to them all. "It is more fitting to my size and there I will not have to deal with your impertinence. I warn you just one more time," he growled. "If the girl is harmed in any way. . . ."

Vander left it at that, preferring to end the threat by leading the others' gazes to the squirming, groaning Night Mask caught fast by broken, stabbing planks halfway between the bedroom and the kitchen.

Q

Fredegar Harriman, proprietor of the Dragon's Codpiece, shook his thick-jowled face in disbelief at the request for yet another private room. The inn had only eight such rooms, and while the much less expensive common room was nearly empty, all of the private rooms were occupied. That alone seemed amazing enough, but what struck Fredegar as even more odd was the makeup of his guests. Five of the rooms belonged to visiting merchants, as was common. A sixth had been paid for until the end of the year by Cadderly, and a seventh had been reserved by the Edificant Library for use by a soon-to-arrive headmaster. Even more unexpectedly, the last room had been rented that very day, to a stranger nearly as curious-looking as the brown-haired lad who stood before him.

"Common room won't do?" the flustered innkeeper asked. "At least for a few nights? It's on the back side of the building. Not much of a view, but quiet enough."

The young man shook his head, his stringy brown hair flopping to one side, revealing that half of his head had been shaved. "I can pay you well," the man offered, giving his purse a quick shake to accentuate the point.

Fredegar continued to wipe the bar and tried to find a way around the dilemma. He didn't want to put the young man out, more to protect his own reputation than for the lost coins, but he didn't see a way around it. The hearth room was teeming—as it had been every night since rumors of impending war had spread through Carradoon—mostly with locals. Fredegar peered through the throng, trying to see if any of his private guests were in attendance.

"I have just one room empty," he explained, "but it won't be for long—might even be filled this very night."

"I am here now to fill it," the stranger argued. "Is my gold not as good as any other's?"

"Your gold is fine," Fredegar assured him, hoping to keep the tension low. "The one open room has been reserved for more than a tenday by priests from the Edificant Library. I have assured them that it will be available, and well, if you are from the area, you know that it is not wise for an honest merchant such as myself to displease the Edificant Library."

The traveler perked his ears up at mention of the place.

"Headmaster Avery and Kierkan Rufo will be in soon," the talkative innkeeper went on. "I haven't seen the good, fat headmaster for almost a year now. I expect he and Rufo have come to town to meet with young Cadderly, another of my guests and another of their priests, and to prepare for this potential war that everyone seems to be talking about."

Q

Bogo scrutinized every word, all the while trying to appear unconcerned. The news about Rufo seemed almost too good to be true. Having the two-time stooge so close at hand could aid his plans to kill Cadderly.

The innkeeper rambled on in many unimportant tangents, speaking mostly of the outrageous rumors that had been circulating. Bogo put in an occasional smile or grunt to make it appear that he was listening, but his mind raced with his own plans.

"I have it!" the innkeeper announced suddenly, so

loudly that several patrons at the nearest tables of the hearth room stopped their conversations and turned to regard the innkeeper. "Malcolm," he called across the room.

An older gentleman, a merchant by his rich and fanciful dress, looked up from his table.

"Half price if you will share a room with my Brennan," the innkeeper offered.

The old gentleman smiled and turned to talk with his companions at the table then stood and came over to the bar.

"Fredegar, you know I have only one more night in town," Malcolm answered. "I leave for Riatavin in the morning." He winked conspiratorially, both at Fredegar and the unfamiliar young man standing at the bar. "One can make fine trades with such grim news filling the air, eh?"

"A night with my Brennan?" Fredegar asked once more.

The merchant gazed across the room to a younger woman, fine in stature, who looked back at him with obvious interest. "I had hoped to be, uh . . . accompanied on my last night in town," he explained. Again came a wink, even more lecherous. "After all, back in Riatavin, tomorrow night, I will be forced to spend some time with my wife."

Fredegar, blushing, joined him in his laughter.

"I could spend a single night in the common room," Bogo interjected, not at all amused by the worthless bantering, "if you will guarantee me this man's room by midday tomorrow." Bogo turned his thin lips up in a wry smile, thinking it best to play the conniving buddy game. "Free of charge this night?" he asked coyly.

Fredegar, never one to bicker—especially not when the inn was so full—readily agreed. "And an ale with my compliments, young stranger," the innkeeper offered as he filled a tankard. "And one for your intended?" Fredegar asked Malcolm.

"I will meet it at the table," the lecherous merchant replied, going back to his seat.

Bogo accepted the drink with a smile and turned, leaning with his elbow propped on the bar. The crowd buzzed and laughed. It was a jovial and warm inn, its atmosphere not at all hindered—perhaps even enhanced—by the still-distant rumors of war. The perfect cover, Bogo thought as he watched the bustle, and he nearly laughed aloud as he considered how the events of the next few days might steal a bit of the place's mirth.

"So good that you have returned!" he heard Fredegar say a short while later. Bogo's eyes widened and he purposely shifted farther down the bar as a young man of above average height and solid build moved to join the innkeeper.

He wore a blue, wide-brimmed hat lined with a red sash. Set in its middle was a porcelain brooch bearing the holy symbol of Deneir. There could be little doubt as to his identity—Dorigen's description of Cadderly had not included the beard, but Bogo could see that it was newly grown, and the unkempt, sand-brown hair and gray eyes certainly fit.

"Headmaster Avery and Kierkan Rufo are coming in," Fredegar explained, "perhaps this very night."

Bogo noticed the young man flinch at that remark, though the priest had tried to cover his reaction. "Do they know I'm staying here?" he asked.

Fredegar seemed at a loss by his guest's obvious discomfort.

"Why, Cadderly," he replied slyly, "have you done something wrong?"

The young priest smiled noncommittally and started for the staircase beside the bar. Distracted, Cadderly didn't even notice the odd-looking young man as he passed by.

But Bogo certainly noticed Cadderly. He watched the priest go, thinking how easy this all might be.

NINE

EVIL VISIONS, EVIL DEEDS

Q

He stood in a lighted room, the sitting room of Belisarius's tower perhaps, holding a beating heart in his hand. The slain minotaur lay at his feet and all his closest friends, Danica and the dwarf brothers, stood by it, laughing wildly, uncontrollably.

Cadderly, too, joined in the laughter but as soon as he did, he realized that his friends were not laughing at all. Rather, they were crying, sobbing great tears that streaked their cheeks and fell in impossibly large puddles at their feet.

He didn't understand.

Something was wrong—something about the entire scene was out of place. He felt the warm blood running down his arm, soaking his tunic, but in his perversion of the wizard's minotaur-and-maze illusion there had been no blood. Slowly, fearfully the young scholar looked down.

The minotaur was not a minotaur any longer, nor had it vanished like some insubstantial illusion, as

Cadderly had expected. It was Avery—Cadderly knew it was Avery, though he could not see the face of the man who lay on his back across a table, arms and legs splayed wide and his chest savagely torn open.

Cadderly held Avery's still-beating heart.

He tried to scream but couldn't. There came a rapping noise, sharp but distant.

He could not scream.

Q

Cadderly sat up. The rapping came again, more insistently, followed by a voice that Cadderly could not ignore. At last he dared open his eyes, and sighed deeply when he learned that he was in his own room, that it had all been another terrible dream.

"Cadderly?"

The call was not a dream, and of course he recognized the commanding, fatherly voice. He closed his eyes again, tried to pretend he was not there, or that Avery was not there.

"Cadderly?" The knocking did not diminish.

What day is it? Cadderly wondered. The moon was up, though beyond its zenith, for no direct silvery light played through the young priest's east window.

Resigned, Cadderly pulled himself out of bed, straightened his nightshirt, and went to the closed door.

"Cadderly!"

He cracked open the portal and winced at the sight of Headmaster Avery. Kierkan Rufo, leaning as always in his customary position, leered over the headmaster's broad shoulder.

"It's late," Cadderly mumbled through the cottony

sensation and the lump of revulsion in his mouth. He couldn't look at Avery without the gruesome dream image coming clearly to his thoughts, could not regard the man without the warm sensation of blood running along his arm. Unconsciously, he rubbed one hand against his nightshirt.

"So it is," Avery replied, somewhat embarrassed, "but I thought you would be pleased to learn that Rufo here, and I, have arrived in town. We shall be staying at the inn, just four doors down from you, across from the stairway." The portly headmaster glanced that way, his expression clearly revealing an invitation for the young priest.

Cadderly nodded then winced again as another drop of imaginary blood ran the length of his forearm.

Avery didn't miss the sour expression. "Is something wrong, lad?" the headmaster asked with compassion.

"Nothing," Cadderly replied curtly. He mellowed immediately, guessing that his demeanor would inspire further curiosity. "I'm just tired. I was sleeping."

"My pardon," Avery said, straining to be light-hearted, "but you are not sleeping now." He took a step forward, as though to push his way into the room.

Cadderly shifted to block the door. "I will soon be sleeping again," he said.

Avery stepped back and for the first time since he'd arrived, regarded Cadderly with a less than appreciative glint in his puffy eyes.

"Still stubborn?" Avery asked him. "You tread on dangerous ground, young priest. Your absence from the library might be overlooked. Dean Thobicus has promised that he will allow you to make up your missed duties and studies."

"I do not care for his promises."

"If you continue on your wayward path," Avery went on, his voice a growl against Cadderly's biting remark, "then you may move beyond the order all together. I am not certain even kind Thobicus could forgive your transgressions against Deneir."

"What do you know of Deneir?" Cadderly asked.

In his mind he saw Avery again, lying dead across the table, but he shook the dark thought away, realizing how much he loved the man who had been a surrogate father to him. "And why would you care for me? Did you not once call me a Gondsman?" Cadderly asked, referring to the order of inventive priests who created without conscience, without regard to the implications of their creations.

His tirade exhausted, Cadderly looked at the headmaster, the father he had just terribly wounded with his impertinence. Avery couldn't respond to his last statement and seemed more on the verge of tears than an explosion of anger. Behind him, Kierkan Rufo wore an almost amused expression of disbelief.

"I-I'm sor—" Cadderly stammered, but Avery put a large hand up to halt him.

"I'm tired, that's all," Cadderly tried to explain. "I've had some terrible dreams of late."

Avery's expression shifted to one of concern, and Cadderly knew his apology had been accepted, or soon would be.

"We are but four doors down," the portly headmaster reiterated. "If you feel the need to talk, do come and join us."

Cadderly nodded, though he knew he wouldn't go to them, and shut the door the moment Avery had turned away. He fell back against the door, thinking how flimsy a barrier it was against the doubts and confusion of the outside world. He looked at his table by the window, to the open tome. When was the last time that book had been closed?

Cadderly couldn't even muster the strength to go to it. He slipped over to his bed and collapsed, hoping that he had put the night's bloody dreams behind him.

ℚ

Bogo Rath released his spell of clairaudience and cracked open the common room's door. The room was on the southwestern wing of the inn's second level. Almost directly across from him, over the hearth room, loomed Cadderly's door, closed once more. Avery and Rufo rounded the corner diagonally to Bogo's right, moving toward the door directly opposite the wide staircase. The hearth room had grown quiet and Bogo could clearly hear their conversation.

"His surliness has not relented one bit since he passed through the library," Rufo said in an accusatory tone.

"He appeared weary," Avery answered with a resigned sigh. "Poor lad—perhaps Danica's arrival will brighten his mood."

They entered their room then, and Bogo considered using his eavesdropping magic to hear the rest of their discussion.

"Who is Danica?" came a quiet, monotone question from behind Bogo. The young wizard froze then slowly managed to turn around.

There stood Ghost, in the otherwise empty common room. The puny man held no weapon and made no move toward Bogo, but the wizard felt vulnerable nonetheless. How had Ghost come in so easily behind him? There was but one door to the room, and it had no outside balcony, as did the more expensive private rooms.

"How did you get in here?" Bogo asked, managing to steady his voice.

"I have been 'in here' all along," Ghost replied. He turned and pointed to a pile of blankets. "There, awaiting your return from the hearth room."

"You should have told me."

Ghost's wheezing laughter mocked him and showed him how ridiculous he had sounded.

"Who is Danica?" the dark little man asked again.

"Lady Danica Maupoissant," Bogo replied, "from Westgate. Do you know of her?"

Ghost shook his head.

"She is Cadderly's dearest friend," Bogo went on, "a beautiful wisp of a woman, by all descriptions, but formidable." Bogo's expression and tone grew grave. "This is not good news. Lady Maupoissant has been a terrible foe to Castle Trinity in the fight thus far. If she arrives soon, then you would be well advised to finish your business with Cadderly promptly and be gone from here."

Ghost nodded, considering the warning. "From where will she come?" he asked. "The library?"

"That would seem likely," Bogo replied. He flipped his brown hair to one side and smiled slyly. "What are you thinking?"

Ghost's glare stole the wizard's mirth. "That is none of your concern," he rasped with sudden anger, pushing past Bogo to the door. "If you're thinking of making any move against Cadderly on your own. . . ." He let the implication hang in the air.

"Well, let us just say that the consequences of failure can be terrible indeed," Ghost finished, and he started away. He turned back immediately, though, his gaze directing Bogo to the pile of blankets that had hidden Ghost. "Do watch your back, young wizard," Ghost said then he coughed a wheezing laugh and went to his room, in the corner of the north wing, halfway between Cadderly's room and the room occupied by Avery and Rufo.

Q

"From the library, from the mountains," Ghost mused, closing the door behind him. "Well, we shall see if Lady Maupoissant follows her path all the way to Carradoon." Ghost sat on his bed and summoned the *Ghearufu*. Using its powers, he sent his thoughts out to Vander, in the distant farmhouse.

Ghost felt the firbolg's typical revulsion and knew from its depth that Vander was angry both with the situation at the farm and with Ghost's intrusion.

Let me in, Vander, the wicked man teased, confident that the firbolg could not deny access even if he tried. Vander was Ghost's chosen victim, his special target, and with Vander alone, Ghost could make the body transfer from almost any range. He felt the sharp, burning pain as his spirit stepped out of his body, and he was floating, flying on the winds, propelled straight for the firbolg's shell. As he entered the giant body, he knew that Vander had entered his, back in the room at the Dragon's Codpiece.

Do not leave the room, Ghost instructed telepathically through the continuing mental link. *Admit no visitors, particularly not that foolish wizard, Bogo Rath!*

Ghost willed away the *Ghearufu* and considered his surroundings. Curiously enough, he was in a barn, surrounded by stabled horses and cows. The man in the firbolg's body shook his head at Vander's continuing surprises and made his way to the large door.

The farmyard was quiet under the light of the westering moon, and the house was dark. Not a single candle burned in any window. Ghost made his way across to the porch and heard a shuffle from up above.

"It's only the master," he said to the unseen guards. "Gather the others and come into the barn, all of you. The time has come to tighten our noose."

Just a few moments later, the entire band of nineteen remaining Night Masks assembled around their leader. Ghost noted that one of his henchmen was missing, but he said nothing about it, realizing that Vander probably knew what had happened to the man and that he might confuse them all by questioning the absence while wearing Vander's form.

He drew a quick map on the ground in front of him. "I have word that a woman is on her way to Carradoon from the Edificant Library," he said, indicating the location of the mountain structure. "There are only a few trails down the mountains, and they all exit in this general area. She should not be hard to find."

"How many should we send?" one of the assassins asked.

Ghost paused as much to consider the angry edge to the man's tone as to consider the question itself. Perhaps the missing Night Mask had met an unfortunate demise at Vander's impulsive hands.

"Five," Ghost said at last. "The woman is to be killed, as are any who travel beside her."

"It could be a large and formidable band," the same assassin argued.

"If so, then kill only the woman and be gone from there," Ghost snapped back, his firbolg-strength voice resounding off the barn's walls.

"Which five?" asked one of the group.

"Choose among yourselves," Ghost replied, "but do not take this woman lightly. She is, by all reports, formidable indeed.

"Another group of five is to strike within the town," Ghost went on. "Our information was correct. Cadderly stays at the Dragon's Codpiece. Here," he said, extending his map to show the lakeside section of Carradoon and indicating the lane running along the shore, "on Lakeview Street. Secure positions near the inn, where you will be at my—at *Ghost's* call. But take care to be far enough out of reach so as not to arouse suspicion."

"With five stringers to open a line of contact to the group within the city?" the same questioning assassin put in.

"That is our usual method," Ghost answered.

"That will leave only four here at the farmhouse, excluding yourself," the angry assassin reasoned. Ghost didn't understand the problem. "If we're forced to maintain a continual guard over the girl—"

"The girl?" Ghost didn't mean to sound so startled.

The assassin and several others cocked a curious eye. "The girl that Mishalak died for," he said with open contempt.

Ghost saw a problem building, and he scowled to force the upstart back on the defensive.

"I don't question your decision to let her live," the assassin quickly explained. "Nor do I deny that

Mishalak deserved death for drawing a weapon against you, the taskmaster. But if only four of us remain to guard the farmhouse, the girl becomes a threat."

It all made perfect sense to the cunning impersonator. Vander's soft heart had caused problems before. Oftentimes the firbolg was too intent on honor, placing that foolish notion above his duties. Ghost spent a moment considering how he might punish the giant then smiled as a typically fiendish idea came into his head.

"You are correct," he said to the assassin. "It's time for you to end that threat."

The man nodded eagerly, and Ghost's smile widened. The wicked little wizard thought how furious Vander would become, and how helpless, impotent, the firbolg would be. The proud giant would hate that most of all.

"And end it tonight," Ghost purred. "But first, you and your friends may have your way with her." All around the ring, the assassins smiled. "After all, we cannot survive on duty alone!"

That brought a cheer from the group.

"Go for the mountains tonight, as well," Ghost continued. "I don't know how many days away this Lady Maupoissant is from Carradoon, but she cannot be allowed to enter the town."

"Maupoissant?" one of the assassins, an older killer with salt-and-pepper hair, piped in.

"You know the name?"

"Nearly a decade ago we killed a wainwright by that name," the man admitted, "along with his wife. And we were paid handsomely for the task, I must say."

"The name is unusual and she is, by my informant's

words, from Westgate," Ghost reasoned. "There could be a connection."

"Good," said the man, drawing a dagger and running the flat of the blade slowly along his bony cheek. "I always like to keep it in the family."

The nineteen Night Masks were pleased to see their unpredictable firbolg taskmaster joining in the laughter, the giant's heartfelt roars smothering their own. They were nervous. The time to kill was drawing near, and adding this "Lady Maupoissant" to the victim list was akin to smearing icing on an already delicious cake.

TEN

PROFESSIONALS

Q

"What time is it?" Ivan asked, rolling out of his blankets and giving a profound stretch.

"Hours past dawn," Danica answered, privately berating herself for being foolish enough to take the last watch.

"Ye should've woked me up," Ivan complained. He started to sit then changed his mind and fell back into the bedroll in a heap.

"I have," Danica muttered, though the dwarf was no longer listening. "Six times!

"But not again," the fiery woman whispered.

She was prepared. Danica took up two small buckets filled with the icy cold water of a nearby mountain stream. Stealthily, she slipped up to the dwarves, their bedrolls having merged from their typically wild slumber during the night into a single large tangle. Danica sorted out the mess and moved the blankets aside enough to reveal the backs of hairy necks.

Pikel's presented the most problem, since the dwarf

wore his beard pulled back over his ears and braided with his long hair, which he had recently re-dyed forest green, halfway down his back. Gently Danica moved the tousle aside, drawing a semiconscious "Hee hee," from the snoozing dwarf, and lifted one of the buckets.

The next thunderous roars resounding from the camp sent animals for nearly a mile around scurrying for cover. Even a fat black bear, out to catch some morning sunshine, raced through a tangle and up the side of a thick oak, sniffing the air nervously, fearfully.

The dwarves ran around in circles, crashed into each other several times, and threw their blankets into the air.

"Me weapon!" Ivan cried in distress.

"Oo oi!" Pikel wholeheartedly agreed, unable to locate his tree-trunk club.

Ivan calmed first, noticing Danica standing next to a tree, her arms folded across her chest and her grin spreading from ear to ear. The dwarf stopped running all together and regarded her with dart-throwing eyes.

He should have looked out for his brother instead.

Pikel hit him broadside, and the two flew away into some brambles. By the time they extricated themselves and had stomped back into the camp, their beards were thrown wildly about and their nightshirts seemed almost furry with burrs.

"Yerself did that to us!" Ivan shouted accusingly at Danica.

"I wish to be in Carradoon no later than tomorrow," the woman replied just as angrily. "I welcomed your company, but didn't know it would mean holding camp until after noon each day. I thought dwarves were industrious."

"Oooo," Pikel moaned, ashamed of his perceived laziness.

"Not our fault," Ivan muttered, also on the defensive. "It's the ground," he blurted. "Yeah, the ground. Too hard and comfortable for a dwarf to want to get himself up in the morning!"

"You have forfeited breakfast," Danica scolded.

"When halflings shave their feet!" Ivan roared, and Danica suspected—-correctly—that she was overstepping her bounds. Throwing ice-cold water down the backs of sleeping dwarves was one thing, but denying them food was something all together different, something downright dangerous.

"A quick meal then," she conceded. "Then we're off."

Sixteen trout, four tankards of ale—each—half a sack of biscuits and three bowls of berries—each—later, the dwarf brothers gathered their belongings and skipped off down the mountain trails behind Danica. Impresk Lake was clearly visible whenever they came to an open ridge, and Carradoon soon came into sight as well, far below.

Despite Danica's desire for haste, the trio took all caution in their trek. The Snowflake Mountains were a dangerous place, even in their southern reaches, where the charges of the Edificant Library dominated the region. With war brewing in the north and battles continuing back to the west, in Shilmista, the companions had to assume that the trails would be more dangerous than ever.

Danica led the way, bending low to inspect every track, every bent blade of grass. Ivan and Pikel bobbed along behind her, Ivan in his deer-antlered helmet and Pikel wearing a many-dented cooking pot for lack of any formal headgear. Even though Danica continually searched the ground as she traveled, the speedy monk had little trouble outpacing the dwarves and forced them to scurry along just to keep up.

Danica slowed considerably, and Ivan and Pikel nearly ran her down.

"Uh-oh," Pikel muttered, seeing Danica's curious expression.

"What'd ye find?" Ivan asked, pulling his brother along behind him.

Danica shook her head, unsure. "Someone has passed this way," she declared.

"Avery and Rufo," Ivan replied.

"More recently," Danica said, standing straight again and taking a long, hard look at the nearby brush.

"Coming, or going?" Ivan pressed.

Danica shook her head, unable to decide. She was confident that her guess had been correct, but what bothered her was the nature of the tracks, the scratching marks made over the apparent boot prints. If someone had crossed their trail earlier that morning then they had gone to great lengths to conceal their tracks.

Ivan looked down at the unremarkable ground, and scratching at his yellow beard, produced yet another stubborn burr. "I don't see any tracks," he huffed.

Danica pointed out a slight depression in the ground, barely visible, then indicated the pattern that made her believe that brush had been scraped over the ground.

Ivan snorted in disbelief. "That all ye got to go on?" he asked loudly, no longer afraid of the volume of his voice.

Danica didn't even try to hush him. She remained confident of her guess, and could hope only that some ranger, or one of Elbereth's kin, perhaps, was in the area. If not a ranger or an elf then Danica felt certain the tracks had been made by someone intent on concealing himself.

In the wilds of the mountains, that rarely boded well for travelers.

A few hundred yards down the trail, Danica found further signs of passage. Even Ivan couldn't discount the obvious boot print in the soft trail, though half of it had been just as obviously brushed away.

The dwarf put his hands on his hips and looked around, focusing on the crook of a low branch hanging over the trail.

"I seen some rocks aside the trail a dozen yards back . . ." the dwarf began.

"Uh-oh," muttered Pikel, suspecting what his brother was getting at.

"Got some big enough trees hanging over the trail," Ivan continued, not hearing Pikel's flustered sigh. He looked at Danica, who seemed not to understand.

"Could set us a *trap,*" Ivan spouted. "Could haul a rock up one of them trees and—"

Pikel slapped him across the back of the head.

"You've tried that before," Danica reasoned from the sour look on Pikel's face.

Pikel groaned and Ivan glared at him, but the yellow-bearded dwarf took no retribution against his brother. They had indeed tried that trap before. Though Ivan, stubbornly, if with little real conviction, insisted that it had been a success—they had clobbered an orc after all—Pikel just as stubbornly insisted that the meager kill had hardly been worth the terrific effort of putting the rock in the tree in the first place.

Knowing that this time there would be another witness, Ivan would have conceded the point and gone along without further mention of the trap and Pikel's assault—it was only a slap, after all—but then, without explanation, Pikel whipped his club up in front of Ivan's face. To Danica, standing to the side, it seemed clear that Pikel tried to halt the weapon's momentum short of Ivan, but the club still connected with Ivan's great nose. It knocked him back several steps and sent a stream of warm blood flowing over the dwarf's hairy lip.

"What'd ye . . ." Ivan stammered, hardly believing the attack. He took up his double-bladed axe, snarled, and stepped toward his frantically squeaking brother.

Pikel couldn't explain the action to either Ivan or Danica, but he did manage to turn his fat club around in time, revealing a heavy dart buried halfway into the hard wood.

Now came Ivan's turn to do his brother a good deed. Looking to the thick bushes past Pikel, to where his warrior instincts told him the dart had come from, he saw a crossbow leveled Pikel's way.

A tall form fell from a branch to land softly behind Danica.

Ivan's pointing finger made Pikel turn about.

"Uh-oh," the green-bearded dwarf squeaked, knowing he had no time to get out of harm's way.

Ivan hit him just before the quarrel, though, taking him down in a perfect tackle as the bolt flew harmlessly past.

Ivan didn't relent. As he rolled, he heaved Pikel right over him, and Pikel understood the tactic, likewise heaving Ivan back over him. Like a rolling boulder, the brothers barreled into the brush forcefully enough to tangle the two men concealed there.

The intruder behind Danica, his sword bared and held high, had no reason to believe that the woman, intent on the spectacle of the dwarves, even knew that she was about to die. His surprise was complete when Danica snapped into a bend at her waist, her leg shooting out behind her, high enough to connect with the man's chest.

He flew back several feet, slamming into a tree trunk, but managed to regain his dropped sword. More wary, he began backing away, step for step with the dangerous woman's approach.

Danica broke into a run and came in hard and fast, but skidded to her knees and dipped her head as another form appeared from behind the trunk and launched a shoulder-high swipe at her with a short, slender staff. The weapon banged hard against the tree, spitting flakes of bark.

Danica slipped one foot back under her and kicked out with the other, thinking to break the second enemy's knee. He got his staff down in time to deflect the attack, though, then countered with several sharp thrusts.

The young monk knew she was in trouble. They were no ordinary highwaymen, though their dress seemed mundane enough. She managed to fall out of the way as the other's sword flashed at her skull, but took a hit on the hip from the fast-flying staff.

Then she was up in a crouch a few feet away from the two men, taking careful measure of their tempered approach, looking for an opening where there seemed to be none.

Q

Ivan bit down hard, and continued to bite, until he realized from the steady stream of "Ooooo's" that it was Pikel's calf, not an enemy's, in his mouth.

The dwarf scrambled to gain his footing in the tight quarters, branches and brambles grabbing at him with every move, and the nearest man landing no less than three punches on his already wounded nose.

Then Ivan was up, as was Pikel, with weapons ready. Ivan launched a vicious swipe with his axe, but his arm slipped through another thin but tough branch, shortening his reach so that he never got close to hitting the man.

Pikel yelped in terror and dived aside as his brother followed through, the wild flying axe nearly connecting. Again, albeit unintentionally, Ivan had saved his brother's life, for as Pikel leaped aside another crossbow bolt soared in, cutting the air between the dwarves with a sizzling sound and thudding heavily into the shoulder of the man facing Ivan.

Both brothers paused long enough to look behind them to the crossbowman, who was frantically re-cocking the weapon. Pikel went back at his attacker, who had finally extricated himself from the brush tangle, and Ivan turned to where his closest enemy had been standing.

The man was not to be seen, and Ivan suspected from the still-shaking bushes that he had been laid out flat. Not one to argue with good fortune, the dwarf howled and bolted back the other way, crunching out of the brambles to find a clear path leading to the crossbowman.

Q

The swordsman was wounded; that was something at least. Danica's kick apparently had done some damage, for he winced with every circling step he took. Danica had already come to the conclusion that the staff-wielder was the more formidable of the two, though. His salt-and-pepper hair showed experience, and the perfect balance of his measured strides made her realize that he'd spent his lifetime training in the martial arts. His staff seemed puny compared to the other's sword, but in his hands it was a deadly weapon indeed.

A sword cut sent the woman low, and the staff clipped her shoulder. She had to dive over backward, rolling back to her feet just in time to prevent a killing follow-up attack.

Danica had used the roll to her advantage. Crouched in a ball on the way over, the monk had slipped one of her crystal-bladed daggers from her boot sheath.

The swordsman came on again, seeming more confident.

Danica planted her right foot out in front of her and pivoted on it, launching her left foot high and wide behind her as she twirled. She knew that her circle-kick attack would have no more effect than to force the swordsman's blade out wide, and knew, too, that she had left herself vulnerable to the other attacker. She threw her supporting leg out from under her and completed her circuit as she crashed down to the ground, hearing the whiz of the staff as it flew inches above her head.

Danica broke her fall with one arm and kept her torso high enough from the ground for her to snap her other arm underneath her, releasing the dagger. Its short flight ended in the swordsman's belly, and he fell back, eyes wide in disbelief and mouth wide in a silent scream.

The staff-wielder laughed, congratulated Danica for the cunning move, then came on relentlessly.

Q

Pikel's attacker, too, wielded a club, but he faced two serious disadvantages. First, Pikel's club was much larger than his, and second, he couldn't possibly hit the thick-skinned and thicker-headed dwarf hard enough with a blunt weapon to do any serious damage. Lightning fast, he smacked Pikel twice on the shoulder and once on the pot helmet, which rang loudly.

Pikel hardly cared, accepting the three hits for the one he returned. His tree-trunk club caught the man's exposed side and sent him flying from the brush to roll hard against the base of a tree.

The man's face could not have reflected greater terror if he had been tied to a stake in the path of a horse stampede when Pikel came rushing out in pursuit, his pot all the way down over his face but his club leveled perfectly to squash the man between the tree and its thick end.

The man rolled aside and Pikel slammed in, snapping the young tree down and going headlong over its broken trunk.

"Oo," the dwarf grunted as he skidded to a stop along the felled tree's rough bark. Then came that loud ring again as his stubborn attacker rushed back in and planted a two-hander on the top of his helmet.

Q

Ivan realized he would not get to the crossbowman before the man had the weapon readied, so he hoisted his axe above his head in both hands and roared, "Time to die, ye thieving dog!" as he let the weapon fly.

The man dived over backward, thrusting his crossbow up in front of him as a makeshift shield. The axe took it solidly, tearing it from the man's hands and carrying it along on its flight until the whole connected with a tree, the crossbow falling in two pieces and the axe burying several inches into the trunk.

Ivan slowed his charge as the man came back up to his feet, drawing a long, thin sword, and not at all unnerved by the fine throw. In fact, the killer smiled widely at the unarmed dwarf's approach.

"I could be wrong," Ivan admitted quietly, his ferocious charge withering to a halt.

Q

Danica punched and punched again, both attacks deflected harmlessly wide by the small staff. Her attacker countered with a straight thrust and Danica threw her forearm up at the last moment to push it out of line with her face. She countered with a snapping kick, but her attacker had his staff back in place quickly enough to slow the strike so that it did no real damage.

A groan drew Danica's attention to the side. There stood the swordsman, his trembling hand at last closed around Danica's bloodied dagger. The man's face contorted in agony, but also in rage, and Danica suspected that he would soon be back in the fray. No matter how ineffective he might prove, she feared she wouldn't be able to handle both men at once.

Her temporary distraction cost her. The staff connected on her side. Danica rolled sidelong with the blow, diminishing its painful sting, and grabbed at her other boot as she went over and came back up into a crouch.

The staff-wielder leaped and spun in a flurry of defensive movements, anticipating another dagger throw. Danica pumped her arm several times, delicately shifting her angle with each forward movement. Each time, her intended victim placed himself in a position to block the throw or dodge aside.

The man was good.

Danica carefully aligned herself, pumped her arm once more, and threw. The staff-wielder easily slipped to the side, his expression revealing confusion that the skilled woman would have missed him so cleanly. He understood a moment later, when his companion groaned again, loudly.

The swordsman's trembling hand slipped free of the golden tiger hilt of the dagger in his belly and inched upward to the silver dragon protruding from his chest. Helplessly, he fell back against a tree and slid down to the ground.

"You and I," said the staff-wielder, and he accentuated his point with a furious rush and a blinding, dizzying series of thrusts and swipes.

Ç

Pikel looked mournfully at the tree he had felled, his pause for sorrowful contemplations costing him yet another ringing slam on his pot helmet.

The druidic-minded dwarf felt nothing but a most profound rage welling inside of him. Pikel had always been regarded by those who knew him as among the most even-minded of people, the slowest of the slow to anger. But he had killed a tree.

He had killed a tree!

"Ooooooo!"

The groan issued out of his trembling lips, between gnashing, gritted teeth.

"Ooooooo!"

He turned around to face his attacker, who backed off a step at the sheer strength of the dwarf's bared fury.

"Ooooooo!"

Pikel tripped over the tree stump as he charged, diving headlong. His attacker turned to flee, but the sprawling dwarf caught him by the ankle. The man's club came down repeatedly on Pikel's grasping fingers, but the enraged dwarf felt no pain.

Pikel dragged the man in, grabbed him in both hands, and hoisted him into the air. Gaining his feet, the powerful dwarf held the man above his head and looked around as though wondering what to do next.

The club rang again on Pikel's cooking pot helmet.

Pikel decided he had had enough. He impaled the man on the jagged edge of the broken tree stump.

C

Ivan whipped off his backpack, fumbling with the straps as his enemy rushed in. The dwarf blocked a sword thrust with the pack, tangling the sword in its straps long enough for Ivan to get out a package, six inches square and carefully wrapped.

The swordsman yanked away and tore the pack from his blade then looked back at the dwarf.

Ivan had ripped open the box and removed its contents: a toy he had been making for Cadderly ever since the young priest's heroics against the Talonite Barjin.

The black adamantine border of the spindle-disks contrasted with the semiprecious crystal center. The swordsman paused, wondering what purpose the twin disks, joined in their center by a small rod, might possibly serve.

Ivan fumbled to get his fat finger through the loop in the string wrapping that small rod. He had seen Cadderly use the toy a thousand times, had marveled at how the young priest so easily let the disks roll down to the end of their cord then, with a flip of his wrist, sent them spinning back to his waiting hand.

"Ye ever seen one of these?" Ivan asked the curious swordsman.

The man charged, and Ivan flung the disks out at him. The man got his sword in the way to block, then eyed his weapon in disbelief, regarding the ample nick the harder adamantine had caused.

Ivan had no time to gloat over the integrity of the craftsmanship, though. His throw had been strong, but unlike Cadderly, he had no idea how to recall the spinning disks. They hung near the end of the string, spinning sidelong.

"Ooooooo!"

Pikel's rush from the side turned the swordsman around. He sidestepped the raging dwarf and regained his balance as Pikel swung around, scraping one foot on the ground for leverage to begin yet another furious charge.

The green-bearded dwarf stopped short of passing the man, instead launching a series of furious blows with his heavy club. The swordsman worked hard, but managed to keep out of harm's way.

Ivan shoulder-blocked Pikel aside.

"This one's mine!" the gruff dwarf explained.

The swordsman smiled at the dwarf's apparent

stupidity—together the brothers could have easily finished him.

His smile went away—literally—when Ivan hurled the spindle-disks again. But surprisingly, the small weapon was not attached to the dwarf's finger, and had no encumbrance at all as it zipped past the swordsman's futile attempt to block.

The man's head snapped backward and his face seemed to melt away when the adamantine disks connected, removing every visible tooth, smashing apart his nose and both cheekbones, and neatly tucking his chin up under his upper jaw.

"Didn't think a dwarf could throw like that, did ye?" Ivan bellowed.

The man stood staring in disbelief. His sword fell to the ground.

"Oo," Pikel muttered as the man's head lolled freely to one side, for only then did either of the brothers realize that Ivan's powerful throw had snapped the man's neck.

Ivan reiterated Pikel's grim thought. "Oo."

Q

Kick and swipe, punch and spearing thrust.

Danica and the staff-wielder moved in vicious harmony, attacking and parrying with incredible speed. For heartbeats that stretched into moments, neither scored a hit at all.

But in the heightened competition, the adrenaline pumping fiercely, neither seemed to tire in the least.

"You are good, Lady . . ." the staff-wielder remarked, his voice trailing off as though he meant to say more. "As I expected you would be."

Danica could hardly reply. Had the man just teased her, almost uttering her name? How could he know? A hundred thoughts raced through Danica's mind with the sudden suspicion that it had not been just some random ambush. Was Cadderly safe? she wondered. And what of Avery and Rufo, who had come down that same path just a couple of days before?

Thinking her distracted, her assailant came in viciously.

Danica dropped straight to the ground and kicked out, connecting with the man's knee hard enough to halt his rush.

Danica stepped ahead, coming up right in the man's face. She took a painful hit on the shoulder for her efforts, but got in one of her own, a snapping chop to the man's throat. In the single instant the man was forced to pause and gulp for breath, Danica got one hand planted on his chin and the other around the back of his head to grab a clump of hair.

The man dropped his staff and clamped his hands onto Danica's wrists, preventing her from twisting his head around. They held the pose for several moments, with Danica simply not strong enough to continue the intended maneuver.

The man, sensing his superiority, smiled wickedly.

Never releasing her grip, Danica leaped and rolled right over his shoulder, letting her weight do what her strength could not. They twisted and squirmed, Danica bending her knees to keep her full weight on the hold. The man wisely dropped to the ground, but Danica rolled again, under and to the side, with her forearm locked tightly under the man's chin.

He gasped futilely for breath, scratched and clawed at

Danica's arms, and shoved his own hand into Danica's face, probing for her eyes.

Danica felt the hardness of a stone under her hip and she quickly shifted again, putting the man's head in line. Frantically, brutally, the young monk realigned her grip on the man's hair, leaving the back of his head exposed, and began slamming him down to the stone.

"He's dead!" Ivan cried, and Danica realized only then that the dwarf had been uttering the words over and over.

Horrified and sorely bruised, the young woman released her grip and rolled away from the man, fighting back her nausea.

"That one'll be gone soon, too," Ivan said, indicating the man slumped against the tree, two daggers protruding from his bloody torso. "Unless we tend his wounds."

The man seemed to hear and looked pleadingly at the three companions.

"We must," Danica, composed again, explained to the dwarves. "I think this one knew my name. There may be a conspiracy here and he—" she pointed to the man against the tree—"can tell us what it is."

Ivan shrugged his agreement and took a step toward the man, who seemed to take some comfort in the fact that his life would be spared. But there came a click from the side, and the man jerked violently a moment later, a crossbow quarrel next to the silver-hilted dagger.

C

The lone surviving Night Mask, wounded, with a crossbow quarrel protruding from his shoulder, crashed through the brush on the edge of delirium from the

143

searing pain and loss of blood. One thought dominated his thoughts: he had failed in his mission. But at least he'd stopped his cowardly comrade from revealing the greater strategy—rule number one for the merciless band of assassins.

The man didn't know where to run. Vander would kill him when the firbolg learned that Lady Maupoissant had survived—the man regretted that he had chosen his one remaining shot to finish the potential informant instead of trying again for Danica. Then he took heart as he reminded himself that even if he had been able to hit Danica, even if he had killed her, the dwarves would have had their informant and the more important plan to eliminate Cadderly would have been in jeopardy.

Still, the man regretted the decision, all the more when he heard the pursuit. Even wounded and weakened, he was confident that he could outrun the short-legged dwarves. When he looked back over his shoulder, though, he saw the young monk, running effortlessly through the brush, gaining on him with every sure-footed stride.

The trees and brush opened up to more barren, rocky ground, and the desperate man smiled as he recalled the surrounding terrain. He was a Night Mask to the bitter end, loyal and proud. His duty, wicked though it often was, had been his all, a dedication bordering on obsession.

The cruel monk was only a few strides behind him, he knew.

Loyal and proud, he never slowed as he came upon the edge of the hundred-foot cliff, and his scream as he leaped into the air was one of victory, not terror.

ELEVEN
WHAT THE SHADOWS SAY

Long shadows of the day's last light streaked across the barn's floor and walls. Gray webs glistened across gaps in the rafters then went dark as the sun slipped farther away. Vander leaned against the wooden wall, glad to be back in his body again, but not so glad to learn what had transpired in the few short hours that Ghost had taken his form.

The farmer's girl was dead, and her end had been most unpleasant.

Memories of the time he had fled to his homeland, the Spine of the World, when Ghost had caught up to him and taken his body, coursed through Vander's thoughts, forcing the firbolg lower against the wall. For the proud firbolg, his failure was complete. He could accept defeat in battle, could kneel to a rightful king, but Ghost had dared to take that one step farther. Ghost had taken Vander's valor, his honor, his very identity.

"Have they returned?" the firbolg snapped at the

black-and-silver robed man as soon as he appeared at the barn door.

"The trip to the mountains would have taken them all of last night," the Night Mask replied, as if he sensed Vander's frustration. "Likely, they have not yet even encountered Lady Maupoissant."

Vander looked away.

"The line has been set up to Carradoon, and the group has taken position near the Dragon's Codpiece," the assassin went on.

Vander eyed the man for a long moment. He knew what the human was thinking, knew that the man had only blurted that information in the hopes that the news would be well received and would spare him from the firbolg's unpredictable wrath.

Unpredictable! Vander nearly laughed at the vicious irony of that thought. He waved the man away, and the Night Mask seemed more than happy to comply.

Vander sat alone once more in the deepening shadows. He took some measure of solace in the fact that the noose was apparently tightening around their latest target and that their business might soon be concluded.

Vander hardly began to smile before a frown again captured his visage. The business would be finished and another would soon begin. It would not end, Vander knew, until Ghost decided that the firbolg had outlived his usefulness.

The sun was gone, leaving Vander in the darkness.

Q

"You've indicated that you want to be of help," Ghost said to the surprised wizard. "Now I offer you that chance."

Bogo Rath's beady green eyes seemed to grow even smaller as he studied the sleepy-eyed man. He had just moved his small pack of belongings to the private room that Fredegar had provided, only to find the mysterious assassin sitting on his bed, waiting for him.

Ghost understood both the wizard's suspicion and his hesitation. Bogo didn't trust Ghost, and rightly so. Bogo's agenda was his own. Surely the wizard wanted Cadderly dead, but Ghost knew that the opportunistic and ambitious young wizard wasn't really working with the Night Masks. Rather, he was working independently, hopeful that he might use the assassins to meet his own ends. Ghost, above all others, could understand a healthy dose of self-aggrandizement, but the wicked man was also aware of the dangers that tended to follow.

"I'm to serve as a sentry?" Bogo replied, incredulous.

Ghost thought it over then nodded—that was as good a description as he could think of. "For this minor exploration only," he answered. "The time has come for us to learn a bit more about Cadderly's room and personal defenses. I can do that, do not doubt, but I wouldn't be pleased to have the other two priests of the library return to the inn while I'm otherwise engaged."

Bogo spent a long moment staring at the man. "You are so filled with riddles," he said at length. "You can get near Cadderly, hint that you can get even closer, and yet, the young priest lives. Is it caution or macabre pleasure that makes you play games with your prey?"

Ghost smiled, congratulating Bogo for his perceptiveness. "Both," he answered honestly, more than willing to tout his own prowess. "I'm an artist, young wizard, not a common killer. The game, for that is what it is, must be played on my terms and by my rules." Ghost carefully chose his emphasis for that last sentence, letting it sound just enough like a threat to keep Bogo on edge.

"It's early for the hearth room," Bogo reasoned. "The sun is just down. Most of the patrons are still at home, finishing their dinners, and I'm not yet settled into my new quarters," he added, a hint of dissatisfaction in his tone.

"Do you consider that so very important?" Ghost asked.

Bogo had no immediate reply.

"Take your dinner down in the hearth room," Ghost replied. "It's not so unusual a practice for guests of the inn."

"The priests went to the Temple of Ilmater," Bogo argued. "It's unlikely they'll return within the time you'll need."

"But they might," Ghost said, his voice hinting of mounting anger. "Artist," he reiterated, voicing each syllable slowly and clearly. "Perfectionist."

Bogo gave up the argument and nodded in agreement. Ghost had indicated that he wouldn't yet kill Cadderly, and the young wizard had no reason to believe otherwise. Certainly, if the weakling assassin had wanted to strike against the young priest, he could have done so at almost any time over the last few days, and he wouldn't have had to go out of his way and engage Bogo to stand watch in the hearth room.

They left Bogo's room together, Ghost stopping Bogo at the door and whispering to him, "Do inform young Brennan, the innkeeper's son, that Cadderly wishes to take his dinner now." Bogo cocked an eyebrow at him.

"It will get the door open," Ghost explained, a perfectly reasonable lie.

Ghost turned into his own room, with Bogo continuing on to the stairway. The puny assassin silently congratulated himself for so easily handling the potentially troubling wizard. He willed the *Ghearufu* into sight as he slipped behind the protection of his partly opened door.

The industrious Brennan came hopping up the stairs a short while later, carrying a dinner tray balanced easily in one hand and a long, narrow package in the other. Ghost admired the spring in the teenager's step, the vigor and boundless energy of awakening manhood in the handsome, if a bit slender, Brennan.

"Boy," Ghost called out as Brennan turned the corner past Avery's room. Brennan stopped and turned to regard the curious man, following the waving motion of Ghost's white-gloved hand.

"Let me deliver this and I'll get you whatever—" Brennan began, but Ghost cut him short with his upheld hand, the one adorned with a black glove.

"My business will take only a moment," Ghost said, the significance of his wry smile lost on the unsuspecting youth.

A scant heartbeat later, Brennan found himself staring back into his own face, and to the hallway beyond. At first, he probably thought the strange man had put up some sort of mirror, but then the image, his image, moved independently. And he, or at least his image, wore the black and white gloves.

"Wh-what . . . ?" Brennan stammered, on the verge of panic.

Ghost shoved the trapped youth back into the room

and waded in, closing the door behind him, dropping the narrow bundle—some sort of staff or rod—and setting the tray on his own night table.

"It's just a game," Ghost purred, trying to keep the terrified victim from calling out. "How do you like your borrowed body?"

Brennan's eyes darted around in search of some escape. Gradually, his terror shifted to curiosity. The man standing before him, wearing his body, didn't seem so ominous.

"I feel . . . weak," he admitted then cringed, realizing he might have offended the man.

"But you are!" Ghost teased. "Don't you understand? That's the point of the game."

Brennan's face crinkled in further confusion then his eyes popped open wide as Ghost, moving with the speed of youth, clenched his borrowed fist and launched a roundhouse punch. Brennan tried to dodge, tried to block, but the weak body didn't respond quickly enough. The fist slipped through his pitiful defenses, slamming Brennan between the eyes, and he fell, helpless, with no strength to resist the wave of blackness closing over him.

Ghost regarded the body for a long while, trying to decide on his next move. The prudent act, he knew, would be to strangle Brennan then and there, as he had done with the beggar on the road, and put one glove on the body to prevent the regeneration process from recalling the lad's wandering spirit.

But the wretched assassin felt wonderful in the youth's body, full of barely controllable energy, and with his passions fluctuating almost violently, beckoning him urgently toward base actions he had not seriously considered for decades. The impulsive notion came to Ghost to reach over and remove the boot and the magical ring, to kill Brennan in the weakling body and leave him dead. Ghost could then claim the young man's form as his own until he'd burned it out as he'd nearly burned out his previous, effeminate mantle.

He again wore the black and white gloves when his hands went around the weakling's neck.

But then Ghost realized that he mustn't do it—not yet. He berated himself for even beginning to act on such a rash notion. Moving methodically, he tied and gagged his victim, dragged him behind the bed, and wedged him between the bed and the wall.

The ring had already begun its work, and young Brennan's eyelids fluttered with the first signs of consciousness.

Ghost smashed him again, and again after that.

Brennan groaned through the gag and Ghost leaned in close, putting his lips to the trapped boy's ear. "You must be quiet," he purred, "or you will be punished."

Brennan groaned again, more loudly.

"Would you like me to tell you the punishments I have planned for your disobedience?" Ghost asked, putting a finger into Brennan's eye.

The terrified Brennan made no sound.

"Good, wise lad," Ghost cooed. "Now let us see what you have brought."

The assassin moved away and quickly unwrapped the bundle, revealing a ram-headed walking stick, finely crafted and perfectly balanced. Ghost had seen the marvelous item before, in Cadderly's hands when the priest had gone to the wizard's tower outside Carradoon. Only then did Ghost realize that the young priest had not been carrying the stick when he'd returned down the road.

"How convenient!" he said, moving back over to Brennan. "I said I would tell you of the punishments, but here, let me show you instead," he said, patting the formidable club against his open palm.

Ghost's face contorted with sudden rage, and he launched a two-handed overhead chop. He felt the magic of the weapon thrumming when he slammed the ram's head down on Brennan's shoulder, and smiled even more widely when he saw the skinny limb crumble under the weapon's tremendous enchantment. Ghost had never fancied weapons, but he thought of keeping that one.

Ghost considered the wisdom of turning the walking stick over to Cadderly. The assassin was left in a quandary, for if the young priest was expecting the weapon's return, he might seek out Fredegar, or the wizard in the tower, and either would likely pose larger, more dangerous, questions.

The artist-killer left the room a few moments later, bearing the tray and the retied bundle for Cadderly, and leaving the crumpled, unconscious Brennan hidden behind the bed in a pool of blood. Ghost had beaten Brennan severely, and the young man in the pitiful body would soon have died, except for the persistent healing magic of the ring concealed under the boot.

Q

Semiconscious, Brennan almost hoped he would die. A thousand fiery explosions seemed to be going off within him. Every joint ached, and the man with the club had paid particularly painful attention to his groin and collarbone.

He tried to move his head but couldn't. He tried to wriggle his body out of the tight cubby, despite the pain, but found he was securely bound in place. He coughed up another gout of blood, his survival instincts barely managing to force the warm liquid past the gag so that he wouldn't choke on it.

Broken, Brennan prayed to Ilmater that his torment would soon end, even if that end meant death. He didn't know, of course, that he wore a magical ring, that he would soon be healed once more.

Q

Cadderly wasn't thinking of dinner, wasn't think-ing of anything at all beyond the alluring song playing in his mind as he turned the pages of *The Tome of Universal Harmony*. The book had offered him shelter once again, had chased away the images of Avery and Rufo—they had come back to see Cadderly that morn-ing, and had again been abruptly turned away—and all the other troubles weighing heavily on the young priest's shoulders.

Under the protection of the sweet song of Deneir, Cadderly felt none of that weight, but sat straight and tall. He worked his arms out to the sides when they were not engaged in turning the pages, in a manner similar to the meditative techniques Danica had once shown him back at the Edificant Library. Back then, the movements had been simple exercises, but with the song flowing through his every movement, Cadderly felt his inner strength coursing through his limbs.

"I have your supper!" he heard Brennan call from behind him.

He knew from the young man's volume that

Brennan had probably called him several times and knocked loudly on the door before that. Embarrassed, Cadderly closed the great book and turned to meet the young man.

Brennan's eyes opened wide.

"Excuse me," Cadderly apologized, looking around helplessly for something with which to cover up. He was naked from the waist up, his well-muscled chest and shoulders glistening with sweat, and the rippling muscles of his waistline, newly trim from the meditative exercises, quivering from the recent exertion.

Brennan quickly composed himself, even flipped Cadderly a towel from the dinner tray.

"It would seem that you could use the meal," the boy offered. "I didn't know that reading could be so strenuous."

Cadderly chuckled at the witticism, though he was a bit confused that Brennan had made such a remark. The young man had seen him at his reading many times before, and many times involved, as he was just then, in the meditative exercises.

"What have you there?" Cadderly asked, seeing the long, narrow bundle.

Brennan fumbled with the item. "It came in just this afternoon," he explained, "from the wizard, I would assume."

He unwrapped the bundle and handed the fine walking stick to Cadderly.

"Yes . . . Belisarius," Cadderly replied. He waved the walking stick around easily, testing its balance, then tossed it on the bed. "I had nearly forgotten about it," he remarked. Then he added with obvious sarcasm, "I wonder what mighty enchantments my wizard friend bestowed upon it!"

The boy only shrugged, though secretly he gnawed at his lower lip, angry that he had decided to return the unexpected present.

Cadderly gave the young man a wink. "Not that I'll ever find use for it, you understand."

"We never know when a fight might fall our way," Brennan replied, sliding the tray onto Cadderly's small table and arranging the silverware.

Cadderly eyed him curiously, caught off guard by the grim tones and uncharacteristically reflective thought of the passion-driven youth.

The young man held a serrated knife in his hand for just a moment, with his hand only inches from Cadderly's bare chest. For some reason, that dangerous image suddenly mattered to Cadderly. Silent alarms went off inside him. The young priest fought them away as easily as he rubbed the sweat from his neck, rationally telling himself that he was letting his imagination run wild.

The song played in the back of Cadderly's mind. He almost turned to see if he'd left the tome open, but he hadn't—he couldn't. Shadows began to form atop Brennan's slender shoulders.

Aura.

For some reason he couldn't understand, Cadderly sensed again the unfathomable possibility that Brennan was considering stabbing him with the knife.

But Brennan dropped the knife on the tray and fumbled about with the small bowl and plate. Cadderly didn't relax. Brennan's movements were too stiff, too edgy, as if the boy was consciously trying to act as though nothing unusual had occurred.

Cadderly said nothing, but held the small towel around his neck with both hands, his muscles tight and ready. He didn't concentrate on the young man's actions, rather he shifted back to Brennan's shoulders, to the misshapen, growling shadows huddled there, black claws raking empty air.

Aura.

The song played in the distant recesses of his mind, revealing the truth before him. But Cadderly, still a novice, still unsure of his power's source, didn't know if he should trust in it or not.

Cadderly couldn't recognize the shadows any more than to equate them with the same fearsome things he had seen perched upon the shoulders of the beggar on the road. He sensed that they boded ill, sensed that they were images resulting from vile thoughts. Considering that Brennan had just been holding a knife, that a short stroke could have driven the serrated instrument into Cadderly's bare chest, those sensations hardly put the young priest at ease.

"You must go," he said to the youth.

Brennan looked up at him, confused, but again, the expression didn't seem right to Cadderly. "Is something wrong?" the slender youth asked.

"Go," Cadderly said again, his scowl unrelenting, and placed into the word the strength of a minor enchantment.

But the young man held stubbornly to his position. The shadows on Brennan's shoulders dissipated and Cadderly had to wonder if he'd misread the signals, if those shadows represented something else entirely.

Brennan gave him a curt bow—another unexpected movement from the young man that Cadderly thought he knew quite well—and prudently slipped from the room, closing the door behind him.

Cadderly stood staring at the door for a long time, thinking he must be going mad. He looked back at *The Tome of Universal Harmony*, wondering if it was a cursed book, a book inspiring lies, and a discordant song that sounded true to the foolish victim's ear. After all, how many priests had been found dead, lying across its open pages?

Cadderly labored for breath for a few crucial moments, once more at a crossroad in his life, though he didn't realize it.

No, he decided at length. He had to believe in the book, wanted desperately to believe in something.

Still he remained in the same position, looking back at the door, at the tome, and lastly to his own heart. He realized that his meal was getting cold then realized he didn't care.

The emptiness within him could not be sated by food.

Q

Bogo had given Ghost more than the time the assassin had asked for, but the eager wizard decided to stay in the hearth room anyway, to see what he might learn. The talk among the growing number of patrons settled always on the rumors of war, but to Bogo's relief, none of the gathering seemed to have any idea of the depth of the danger that hung over their heads. When Aballister decided to march, most likely in the early spring, the army of Castle Trinity would have little trouble bringing Carradoon to its knees.

The night deepened, the warm fires and the many

conversations blazed, and Bogo, despite his fears that Ghost had already dispatched Cadderly, remained in the room, listening and chatting. Every time the door to the foyer opened, the young wizard looked up, anxious to note the return of the two priests, thinking that perhaps they would provide him with better information than the misinformed townsmen.

Bogo's smile curled up when Kierkan Rufo entered a short while later, for the more formidable headmaster was not beside the man. Rufo headed right for the stairs, but Bogo cut him off.

"You are of the Edificant Library?" he asked, his tone sounding hopeful.

Rufo's sharp features seemed sharper still in the flickering firelight, and his dark eyes didn't blink as he regarded the curious-looking young man.

"Might I buy you an ale, or fine wine perhaps?" Bogo pressed, seeing no answer forthcoming.

Rufo's answer dripped of suspicion. "Why?"

"I'm not from around here," Bogo replied without the slightest hesitation. The ambitious mage had played that scene out a dozen times in his mind, along with several other potential scenarios concerning the priest who would be stooge. "All night I've been assailed with rumors of war," he explained. "And all the rumors say that the Southern Heartlands' one hope lies in the Edificant Library."

Again Rufo failed to respond, but Bogo noticed the vain man straighten his shoulders with some pride.

"I'm not without . . . skills," Bogo went on, confident that Rufo was falling into his trap. "Perhaps I might aid in the cause. Surely I would try.

"Let me buy you some wine, then," Bogo offered

after a short pause, not wanting to break his budding momentum. "We can talk, and perhaps a wise priest can guide me to where my skills would be most helpful."

Rufo looked back at the foyer door, as though he expected, or feared, that Headmaster Avery would come pounding through at any moment. Then he nodded curtly and followed Bogo to one of the few empty tables remaining in the hearth room.

The talk remained casual for some time, with Bogo and Rufo sipping their wine, and Bogo quickly losing any hope that he would be able to get too much of the drink into the man. Rufo, who had been through many torments the last few tendays, remained cautious and guarded, covering his half-filled glass whenever Brennan, waiting on tables, made one of his frequent visits.

Bogo noted several times that the innkeeper's son seemed to be regarding him suspiciously, but he attributed it to the lad's natural curiosity that a stranger would have business with a priest from the library, and thought no more of it.

Bogo wasted little time in shifting the conversation to more specific topics, such as the Edificant Library and the ranking of Rufo's portly friend. Gradually, casually, the wizard led the talk to include the other priest who was a guest at the inn. Rufo, cryptic from the start, backed off even more and seemed to grow more suspicious, but Bogo did not relent.

"Why are you in town?" Bogo asked, rather sharply.

Rufo seemed to note the subtle shift in the increasingly impatient wizard's tone. He rested back in his chair and regarded Bogo silently.

"I must go," the priest announced unexpectedly, bracing himself on the table and beginning to rise.

"Sit down, Kierkan Rufo," Bogo snarled at him.

Rufo looked at him curiously for a moment, and realized he had not, in the course of the conversation, told the man his name. A small whine escaped the man's thin lips as he fell back into his chair, as though he'd expected what was to come.

"How do you know my name?" Rufo demanded with as much courage as he could muster.

"Druzil told it to me," Bogo answered bluntly. Again came that almost imperceptible whine.

Rufo began to ask another question, but Bogo promptly silenced him.

"You will answer and obey," Bogo explained casually.

"Not again," Rufo growled with defiance that seemed to surprise even himself.

"Dorigen thinks differently," Bogo replied, "as does Druzil, who has been in your room for both nights you have been in town," Bogo lied. "The imp has been in your room since before you and Avery occupied it. Did you think to escape so easily, Kierkan Rufo? Did you think the battle was won despite the minor setback we were given in Shilmista Forest?"

Rufo found no words with which to respond.

"There," Bogo said, settling back into his chair and flipping his stringy brown hair over to one side. "Now we understand each other."

"What do you require of me this time?" Rufo asked, his voice sharp and a bit too loud for Bogo's liking, especially since Brennan was nearby again, regarding the two men with open curiosity. Rufo's visage continued to appear defiant, but Bogo was hardly concerned. The man was weak, he knew, else Rufo would have already left, or struck out against his revealed enemy.

"As of now, nothing," Bogo answered, not wanting to set too many things into motion until he better understood what Ghost and the Night Masks were planning. "I will be nearby, and you will remain available to me. I have some specific things planned for my visit to Carradoon, and you, Rufo, will play a role in those, do not doubt." He tipped his glass to the man and drained it then rose from the table and started away, leaving Rufo lost in yet another irresolvable trap.

"Be wary, young mage," Bogo heard from the side as he took his first step up the stairs beside the hearth room's bar. He turned to see young Brennan, casually wiping down the bar and regarding him dangerously.

"Are you addressing me?" Bogo asked, trying to sound superior, though he was indeed becoming a bit unnerved by the innkeeper's son's sudden attention.

"I'm warning you," Brennan growled. "And know that it's the only warning you'll receive. Your business here is as an observer—that position determined by Aballister himself. If you interfere, you might find yourself lying in a hole beside Cadderly."

Bogo's eyes widened in shock, an expression that brought a satisfied smile to the boy's lips.

"Who are you?" the wizard demanded. "How . . . ?"

"We are many," Brennan replied, obviously enjoying the spectacle of the squirming mage. "We are many and we are all around you. You were told that we do things properly, Bogo Rath. You were told that we take no chances." The young man let it drop there and turned back to his work at the bar.

Bogo understood the reason behind the sudden break in the conversation when Kierkan Rufo and Avery, just returned to the inn, walked past him up the stairs, heading for their rooms.

Bogo followed them at a safe distance, no longer certain that he would have further instructions for Kierkan Rufo, no longer certain of anything.

TWELVE

MORTALITY

The dawn found Cadderly at meditation—his exercises—reaching his arms far to the side one at a time, muscle playing powerfully against muscle. He eyed the open book on the table before him as he moved, heard the song in his head, and felt in tune with it. Sweat lathered his bare chest and streaked the sides of his face, and the young priest felt it keenly, his senses heightened by the meditative state.

When at last he finished, Cadderly was thoroughly weary. He considered his bed then changed his mind, thinking he'd been spending too much time in his room the past few days. The day would be bright and warm. Outside his window, Impresk Lake glittered with a thousand sparkles in the morning sun.

Cadderly closed *The Tome of Universal Harmony,* but looking upon the waters of that lake, so serene and inspiring, he still heard the song. It was time to take the knowledge—and the emotional strength, he hoped—that he had gained from the book out into the world. It was time to see how his new insights might fit into the everyday struggles of the people around him.

Cadderly feared those revelations. Could he control the shadows he would inevitably see dancing atop the shoulders of the many people of Carradoon? And could he decipher their meaning—truly? He thought back to the events of the night before, when he had turned young Brennan away, frightened at the implications of the squirming, growling manifestations he'd seen.

The young priest washed and toweled off, strengthening his resolve. The choices seemed clear: go out and learn to assimilate in light of his newfound knowledge, or remain in his room, living a hermetic existence. Cadderly thought of Belisarius, alone in his tower. The wizard would die there, alone, and most likely, his body would not be discovered for tendays.

Cadderly did not wish to share that grim fate.

C

Still wearing the mantle of young Brennan, Ghost, absently replacing the candles on the lowered chandelier at the top of the staircase, watched the young priest leave the Dragon's Codpiece. He'd heard Cadderly tell Fredegar that he wouldn't return until late, and Ghost thought that a good thing. The Night Masks were in town and ready, and Ghost had to meet with them. Perhaps young Cadderly would have a rather unpleasant surprise waiting for him when he returned that evening.

A patient killer, an artist, Ghost would have preferred to wait a few more days before arranging the strike, would have liked to get even closer to the curious young man, to know everything about him so that there could be no mistakes. The assassin considered that especially important in light of the potential problems arising from the arrival of the two other priests. Powerful priests had been known to resurrect the dead, and under normal circumstances, Ghost would prefer to take the time and discern exactly how much magical interference might be expected from the newcomers, particularly the priest bearing the title of headmaster. Might the Night Masks slay young Cadderly, only to have Avery locate his body and bring him back to life?

Bogo Rath presented even more complications. What might the upstart wizard be planning? the assassin wondered. Bogo had spoken with the other, lesser priest on the previous night, and that could not be a good thing.

Ghost didn't like loose ends. He was a consummate professional who prided himself on being a perfect killer with never a lingering problem left behind. But while the operation seemed ragged to him, he had to believe that the problems could be circumvented—or eliminated. A new wrinkle had come into the picture, a new desire for Ghost that, in his mind at least, justified his seeming carelessness. Ghost felt the vitality coursing through his limbs, felt the powerful urges of adolescence, and remembered the pleasure those urges might bring.

He didn't want to give up his new body.

But he knew, too, that he couldn't continue to play that charade much longer. With a single meeting, Cadderly had come to suspect that something was amiss, and Ghost had no doubt that those suspicions would only increase with time. Also, in Brennan's form, Ghost was severely restricted. His other body remained alive, and it would until the assassin fully committed himself to the idea of taking Brennan's body as his own, a dangerous action indeed until his mission was completed. And while that other, puny form drew breath, Ghost couldn't use the *Ghearufu* on any new victims. Even to get to Vander, his chosen victim, Ghost would have to go through his own body, and doing that would release young Brennan.

Things would become so much simpler when Cadderly lay dead, he knew. Ghost had considered trying the strike the night before, when he'd held a cutting knife in his hand just inches from Cadderly's bare chest. If his aim had been good, the game would have ended then and there, and he could collect his gold, and seriously consider his immediate impulse to retain that young and vital body. In just a few days, his spirit would become acclimated to his new form, and the *Ghearufu* would be his to use again. Vital youth would be his once more.

Hesitance had cost the assassin his chance. Before he had resolved to move, Cadderly was again intent upon him. The loose ends—his ignorance of Cadderly's powers, his ignorance of the other two priests—had held him back.

"Brennan!" Fredegar's cry startled the assassin from his contemplations. "What are you waiting for?" the innkeeper bellowed. "Get that chandelier cranked back to its place, and soon. The hearth room needs cleaning, boy. Now get to it!"

More restrictions accompanied the pleasing young form. Ghost didn't even argue. The Night Masks were not far—he had plenty of time to get to them—and in truth, he was glad for the delay so that he could better sort through the many potential problems and the many interesting questions.

A little while later, the assassin was even more grateful for the delay that had kept him at the inn, when a young woman, strawberry-blond hair bouncing gaily around her shoulders, entered the Dragon's Codpiece, looking for Cadderly and introducing herself as Lady Danica Maupoissant.

Another wrinkle.

Q

"There's the lad!" Ivan called, pointing back toward the front of the Dragon's Codpiece and roughly spinning Pikel around.

"Oo oi!" Pikel piped as soon as he spotted Cadderly, more concerned with getting Ivan's hands off him so that he might stop his spin. Dizzied, the green-bearded dwarf shuffled from foot to foot, struggling to straighten his cooking pot helmet.

Ivan started for Cadderly, who had not yet noticed them, but Danica put a hand on the dwarf's shoulder. As soon as the startled dwarf turned and looked into Danica's pleading eyes, he understood.

"Ye want to go to him yerself," Ivan reasoned.

"Might I?" Danica asked. "I don't know how Cadderly will respond to seeing me. I would prefer . . ."

"Say no more, Lady," Ivan bellowed. "Me and me brother got more than a bit of work afore us, and it's getting late in the day already. I'll get us some rooms there." He pointed to the sign of an inn two doors down from where they stood, and two doors shy of the Dragon's Codpiece. "Ye can come and get us when ye want us.

"And ye can give him this from me and me brother,"

Ivan added, pulling the adamantine spindle-disks from a deep pocket. He started to give them to Danica then pulled them back, embarrassed. As discreetly as he could, the gruff dwarf rubbed off a chunk of the weapon's first victim's face. Danica couldn't miss the movement. With a helpless shrug, Ivan tossed the disks to her.

Danica bent low and kissed the understanding dwarf on the forehead, drawing a deep blush from Ivan.

"Hee hee hee," Pikel chirped.

"Aw, what'd ye go and do that for?" the flustered dwarf asked Danica. He slapped his chuckling brother across the shoulder to set them both into motion, moving away from the inn and away from Cadderly. Ivan knew that if the young scholar saw them all, he would probably invite them in, thus ruining Danica's desires.

Danica stood alone in the crowded street, watching Cadderly's every step as he made his way into the Dragon's Codpiece. Across from her, the waters of Impresk Lake sparkled in the late afternoon sunlight, and she almost followed their spellbinding allure and ran away from her fears. Truly, Danica didn't know how Cadderly would react, didn't know how final their parting in Shilmista Forest had been.

If Cadderly rebuked her, Danica didn't know where she would turn.

For the young monk, who had faced many challenges, many enemies, no moment had ever been so trying. It took every measure of courage that Danica could muster, but finally, she skipped off toward the waiting inn.

Cadderly was on the stairs, heading up, when Danica entered. He held his familiar walking stick in the crook of one elbow and was looking at some wrinkled parchment, apparently oblivious to the world around him.

Quiet as a cat, the agile monk crossed the room and made the stairs. A boy of perhaps fifteen years eyed her curiously as she passed, she noted, and she half expected the lad to stop her, for she was not a paying guest. He didn't, though, and soon Cadderly, still too busy with the parchment to notice her, loomed just two steps ahead of her.

Danica studied him a moment longer. He looked leaner than he had just a few tendays ago, but she knew it was not for lack of eating. Cadderly's boyish form had taken on the hardness of manhood. Even his step seemed more sure and solid, less inclined to skip aside from his chosen path.

"You look good," Danica blurted, hardly thinking before she made the comment.

Cadderly stopped abruptly, stumbling over the next step. Slowly, he lifted his gaze from the parchment. Danica heard him gulp for breath.

It seemed like many moments had passed before the young priest finally mustered the courage to turn and face her, and when he did, Danica stared into a confused face indeed. She waited for Cadderly to reply, but apparently, he either couldn't find his voice, or had nothing to say.

"You look good," Danica said again, and she thought herself incredibly inane. "I . . . we, had to come to Carradoon to . . ."

She stopped, her words halted by the look in Cadderly's gray eyes. Danica had many times before stared intently into those eyes, but she saw something new there, a sadness of bitter experiences.

Again, it seemed like time slipped by.

Cadderly's walking stick fell to the stairs with an impossibly loud thud. Danica looked at it curiously, and when she looked up again, Cadderly was with her, his arms wrapped around her, nearly crushing her.

Danica was independent and strong, arguably one of the very finest fighters in all the land, but never in her life had she felt so secure and warm. Gentle tears made their way down her smooth cheeks, but there was no sadness in her heart.

Q

Still wearing Brennan's body as his own, Ghost watched the pair from the bottom of the stairs as he absently pushed a broom back and forth. His devious mind continued its typical whirling, formulating new plans and making subtle adjustments to old plans. Ghost had to get things moving quickly. The complications were undeniably piling up.

But the skilled killer, the artist, was not afraid. He liked challenges, and compared to the many dead heroes he had left in his wake, Cadderly, didn't seem so much a problem.

Q

Danica.

Cadderly had not seen her in more than three and a half tendays, and while he'd not forgotten her appearance, he was nonetheless surprised by her beauty. She stood inside the closed door of his room, her head cocked patiently to the side, strawberry hair dancing against one shoulder, and her exotic eyes, rich and brown, tender and knowing, gazing at him.

He had initiated their breakup. He had been the one who'd left—had left Danica, the war, and Shilmista. He still wasn't certain of Danica's intentions in coming to see him, but whatever they might be, Cadderly knew it was surely his turn to speak, to explain.

"I didn't expect you to come," he said, moving beside his reading table and gently closing *The Tome of Universal Harmony*. A nervous chuckle escaped his dry lips. "I feared I would receive an invitation to Shilmista Forest to witness the wedding of Danica and Elbereth."

"I don't deserve that," Danica replied, keeping her melodic voice even-toned and steady.

Cadderly threw up his hands, helpless. "I would have deserved it," he admitted.

Danica produced Ivan's gift and tossed it to him. "From the dwarves," she explained as Cadderly caught the heavy disks. "They began it long ago, a present for the man who saved the Edificant Library."

Cadderly could feel the strength of the weapon, and that horrified him as much as it thrilled him. "Always weapons. . . ." he muttered in resignation, tossing the spindle-disks to the floor at the foot of his bed where they bounced against a small clothes chest, dented the hardwood, and rolled to a stop inches from Cadderly's newly enchanted walking stick.

Cadderly regarded the fitting image and nearly laughed aloud, but he wouldn't let Danica's obvious distraction keep him from his point.

"You loved the elf prince," he said to her.

"He is now the elf king," Danica reminded him.

Cadderly didn't miss the fact that she failed to respond to his accusation.

"You did . . . *do* love Elbereth," Cadderly said again, quietly.

"As do you," Danica replied. "He's a dear friend, and among the most extraordinary and honorable people I've ever had the privilege of fighting beside. I would give my life for the elf king of Shilmista, as would you."

Her words hardly came as a revelation to Cadderly. All along, beneath the veil of his fears, he'd known the truth of Danica's relationship with Elbereth, had known that her love for the elf—and it was indeed love—was irrelevant to her feelings for himself. Danica and Elbereth had bonded in a common cause, as warriors with shared values. If Cadderly loved Danica, and he did with all his heart, how could he not also love Elbereth?

But there remained a nagging question, a nagging doubt, and not one about Danica.

"You would give your life for him," Cadderly replied with all sincerity. "I wish I could claim equal courage."

Danica's smile wasn't meant to mock him, but he felt it keenly anyway.

"I ran from there," Cadderly pointedly reminded her.

"Not when you were needed," Danica replied. "Neither I nor the elves have forgotten what you did at Syldritch Trea, or in the heat of battle. Tintagel is alive and Shilmista is back in the hands of Elbereth's People because of you."

"But I ran away," Cadderly argued.

Danica's next question, tinged with innocence and honest trepidation, caught the young priest off guard. "Why did you run?"

She dropped her traveling cloak on the small night table and moved over to sit on Cadderly's bed, and he turned to look out his window, over the still-glittering lake in the dying light of day. Cadderly had never asked himself that question so bluntly, had never considered the cause of his distress.

"Because," he said after a moment then he paused again, the words still not clear in his mind. He heard the bed creak and feared for a moment that Danica was coming to him. He didn't want her to see the pain on his face at that moment. The bed creaked again and he realized she'd only shifted and hadn't risen.

"Too much was spinning around me," he said. "The fighting, the magic, my dilemma over Dorigen's unconscious form, and the fear that I did wrong in not killing her, the cries of the dying that wouldn't leave my ears . . ." Cadderly managed a soft chuckle, "and the way you looked at Elbereth."

"All of that would seem cause to remain beside those who love you, not to run away," Danica observed.

"This madness has been mounting for some time," Cadderly explained, "perhaps even before the Talonite priest began his assault on the library. Perhaps I've been troubled my whole life. That wouldn't surprise me, but still, I must face these troubles and get beyond them." He stole a look at Danica over his shoulder. "I know that now."

"But again . . ." Danica began, but Cadderly, facing the lake again, cut her off with an outstretched palm.

"I couldn't face them with you, don't you understand?" he asked, his voice pleading, hoping she would forgive him. "Back in the library, whenever the many questions threatened to overwhelm me, all I had to do was seek out my Danica, my love. Beside you, watching you, there were no troubles, no unanswerable questions."

He turned to face her squarely, and saw the joy emanating from her beautiful face.

"You're not my answer," Cadderly admitted, and he winced as Danica's light went out, a great pain washing through her almond eyes. "You're not my cure," Cadderly quickly tried to explain, lamenting his choice of words. "You're a salve, a temporary relief."

"A plaything?"

"Never!" The word was torn from Cadderly's heart, bursting forth with the sureness that Danica surely needed to hear.

"When I'm with you, all the world and all of my life is beautiful," Cadderly went on. "In truth, it isn't, of course. Shilmista proved that beyond doubt. When I'm with you, I can hide behind my love. You, my Danica, have been my mask. Wearing it, I could even hide from the horrors of that continuing battle, I'm sure."

"But you couldn't hide from yourself," Danica put in, beginning to catch on.

Cadderly nodded. "There are troubles in here," he explained, pointing to his heart and to his head, "that will remain beside me until I can resolve them. Or until they destroy me."

"And you couldn't face them while your mask was there to hide behind," Danica reasoned. There was no malice in her quiet tone. Honestly sympathetic for Cadderly, she asked, "Have you found your answers?"

Cadderly nearly laughed out loud. "I have found more questions," he admitted. "The world has only become more confusing since I delved into myself." He pointed to *The Tome of Universal Harmony.*"You would hardly believe the sights that book has shown to me, though whether they're true sights or clever deceptions, I cannot tell."

By the way Danica's posture seemed to shrink back from him, Cadderly realized that he had said something revealing. He waited long moments for Danica to respond, to share her revelation with him.

"You question your faith?" she asked.

Cadderly spun away, his gaze again searching for the dying light on the lake. She had hit the mark squarely, he only then realized. How could he, as a priest of Deneir, doubt the vision and magic shown to him by the most holy book of his god?

"I do not doubt the principles espoused by the Deneirrath," Cadderly asserted with conviction.

"Then it's the god himself you question?" Danica reasoned. "Or do you question the existence of any such beings?" her voice nearly broke apart with the words. "How can one who was raised among priests, and who has witnessed so much clerical magic, claim to be agnostic?"

"I claim nothing," Cadderly protested. "I'm just not certain of anything!"

"You have seen the magic bestowed by the gods," Danica argued. "You felt the magic in healing Tintagel."

"I believe in magic," Cadderly reasoned. "It's an undeniable fact on the soil of Faerûn. And yes, I have felt the power, but where it comes from I cannot say."

"The curse of intelligence," Danica muttered, and Cadderly regarded her over his shoulder once more. "You can't believe anything you can't prove beyond doubt. But must everything be tangible? Is there no room for faith in a mind that can unravel any of the lesser mysteries?"

A wind had kicked up across the lake. Ripples rolled to the shore, carrying the last daylight on their crests.

"I just don't know," Cadderly said, regarding the rolling water, trying to find some fitting symbolism in its transport of the dying light.

"Why did you run?" Danica asked him again, and he knew by her determined tone that she meant to force him through it, whatever the cost to them both.

"I was afraid," he admitted. "Afraid to kill any more. Afraid that you would be killed. That I could not bear." Cadderly paused and swallowed hard, forced to come to terms with a difficult realization. His silence went on, Danica not daring to interrupt his train of thought.

"I was afraid to die." There it was. Cadderly had just admitted his own cowardice. He tightened his arms against his sides, fearing Danica's stinging rebuttal.

"Of course you were," she replied instead, and there was no sarcasm in her remark. "You question your faith, question that there is anything beyond this existence. If you believe there's nothing more, then of what worth is honor? Bravery rides the crest of a cause, Cadderly. You would die for Elbereth. You have already proven that. And if a spear were aimed for my heart, you would willingly take it in my stead. Of that I have no doubt."

Cadderly continued to stare out the window. He heard Danica shifting on the bed again, but was too lost in contemplations of her wisdom. He watched the last gasps of light riding the waves, riding the crest, and knew that there was truth in Danica's description. He had been afraid to die in Shilmista, but only because the justification for continuing that fight was founded in a cause of principles, and those principles were, in turn, founded in faith. And he had been so angry at Danica and Elbereth, and all the others, because he'd feared for them and could not appreciate their dedication to those higher principles, their willingness to continue on a course that might easily lead to their deaths.

"I would take the spear," Cadderly decided.

"I never doubted you," Danica replied. There was something in the ring of her voice, something softer and mysterious, that made Cadderly turn back to her.

She lay on her side on his bed, her clothes in a pile at the bedside. If Cadderly lived a thousand years, he would never forget the sight of Danica at that moment. She rested her head against her hand, propped at the elbow, her thick strawberry-blond locks cascading down her arm to dance on the single pillow. The minimal light accentuated the curves of Danica's soft skin, the shine of her sculpted legs.

"Through all the tendays, I never doubted you," she said.

Cadderly sensed the slight tremor in her voice, but still couldn't believe how brave she had been. Without blinking, he unbuttoned his shirt and started to her.

A moment later, they were together. The song played again in Cadderly's mind. No, rather, he felt it, thrumming with urgency through every facet of his body, guiding him through every subtle motion, and convincing him that nothing had ever been so right.

Cadderly's mind whirled through a dizzying jumble of thoughts and emotions. He thought of Danica bearing his child, and considered the implications of mortality.

Most of all, Cadderly focused his thoughts on Danica, his soul mate, and he loved her all the more. Perhaps once she had been his shelter, but only because he had made that her role. But Cadderly had revealed his vulnerability, his deepest fears, and Danica had accepted them, and him, with all her heart, and with the sincere desire to help him resolve them.

Later, as Danica slept, Cadderly rose from the bed and lit a single candle on his table, beside *The Tome of Universal Harmony*. Not bothering to dress, he looked back at Danica on the bed, and felt a surge of love course through his veins. Strengthened by that security, Cadderly sat down and opened the book, hopeful that, in light of the night's revelations, he would hear the song a different way.

C

Many hours before Cadderly lit that candle, Ghost had slipped away from the young priest's door, confident from his eavesdropping that the arrival of Danica Maupoissant would do little to defy his solidifying plans. Actually, Ghost had come to the conclusion that he might be able to use Danica—her body, at least—to substantially increase the pleasure offered by the kill.

If he could possess the body of Cadderly's lover, he might catch the young priest with his guard about as far down as it could possibly go.

But for all the eagerness reflected when Ghost rubbed his hands together, every step of the way back to his own room, he was wise enough to realize that things had become dangerously complicated.

Still bound in the cubby between bed and wall, poor beaten Brennan looked up pleadingly.

"I will release you this night," Ghost promised. "I have decided that I cannot afford to keep your body—and a pity that is, for the body is fine!"

Brennan, desperate to hope, almost managed to smile right up until the point when Ghost's hands—Brennan's own hands—closed around his borrowed throat. There was no pain time for the beleaguered innkeeper's son. There was only blackness.

That task completed, Ghost sat down on the bed, untying the weakling form and waiting impatiently for when he could take back his own body. He lamented that he had lost his chance at a fine young form, but reminded himself of the pressing business and equally pressing danger. He assured himself that he would find another suitable body soon enough, when Cadderly lay dead.

THIRTEEN

THE STOOGE'S STOOGE

Kierkan Rufo eyed the stocked shelves with open contempt. Shopping! For more than a dozen years, he had labored in the Edificant Library, had meticulously attended to his duties, and Headmaster Avery had sent him shopping!

The entire trip to Carradoon had been one humiliation after another for poor Rufo. He knew his actions in Shilmista had angered Avery—though Rufo had convinced himself that none of it had really been his fault—but he never would have believed that the headmaster would degrade him so. Through all the many meetings, with the priests of Ilmater, with several of the other religious sects in Carradoon, and with the city officials, Rufo had been ordered to stand behind Avery and remain silent. Those meetings were vital to the defense of the Southern Heartlands, vital to the survival of the Edificant Library, yet Rufo was, for all intents and purposes, left out of them. Not only was his input not sought by Avery, the headmaster had outright forbidden it!

And he had been sent shopping. Rufo stood before the shelves for many moments, fantasizing that the other side had won in Shilmista Forest, thinking that he would have been better off if Dorigen's forces had slaughtered the elves and had taken him into their ranks as the imp had promised. Perhaps the world would be a better place for Kierkan Rufo if Cadderly had fallen in the sylvan shadows.

Cadderly!

The name screamed out in Rufo's mind like the most damning of curses. Cadderly had apparently forsaken the library and the Order of Deneir, had virtually slapped Headmaster Avery and all the other priests in the face with his desertion—there could be no other word for the young priest's actions. Cadderly had never been a good priest—not by Rufo's estimation—had never attended to the many duties given the lesser clerics with any kind of dedication. And yet, in Avery's eyes at least, Cadderly ranked far above Rufo, far above any except the senior priests.

Rufo grabbed a sack of flour and pulled it to him so forcefully that a small white puff burst up at him, covering his face.

"Someone's not seeming a bit too happy," came a gruff, gravelly voice beside him.

"Uh-uh," agreed a voice on the other side.

The priest didn't have to look sidelong or down to know that the Bouldershoulder brothers had flanked him, and that fact did little to improve his sour mood. He had known that the dwarves were coming to Carradoon, but he'd hoped that he and Avery would be well on their way back to the library before the pair arrived.

He turned toward Ivan and started to push past the

dwarf, through the narrow aisle of the cramped store. Ivan did little to aid the man, and with the dwarf's considerable girth, Rufo had nowhere to go.

"Ye're in a hurry," Ivan remarked. "I thinked ye'd be glad to see me and me brother."

"Get out of my way, dwarf," Rufo said.

" 'Dwarf?' " Ivan echoed, feigning a mortal wound. "Ye saying that like it's an insult."

"Take it for what you will," Rufo replied, "but do get out of my way. I am in Carradoon on important business, something you obviously could not understand."

"I always figured flour to be important," Ivan replied sarcastically, giving the bag a rough pat that sent another white burst into Rufo's face.

The man trembled with mounting rage, but that only spurred Ivan to further taunts.

"Ye're acting like ye're not so glad to see me and me brother," the dwarf said.

"Should I be?" Rufo asked. "When have we ever expressed friendship for one another?"

"We fought together in the wood," Ivan reminded him, "or at least, some of us fought. Others figured to hide in a tall tree, if me memory's working proper."

Rufo growled and pushed ahead, dislodging several packages in his attempt to get past Ivan. He'd nearly made his way past when the dwarf threw out one strong arm, stopping Rufo as completely as a stone wall.

"Danica's in town, too," Ivan remarked, his other hand held high and balled into a fist.

"Boom," Pikel added grimly behind the man.

The reference to Danica's humiliating attack made Rufo's face flush red with rage. He growled again and shoved past Ivan, stumbling all the rest of the way down the narrow aisle and knocking many more items from the shelves.

"A fine day to ye," Ivan called behind him.

Rufo dropped the sack of flour and passed by the counter, fleeing for the street.

Q

"Good to see him," Ivan said to Pikel. "Adds a bit of flavor to a dull trip."

"Hee hee hee," Pikel agreed.

Ivan's face went serious once more as he noticed a tall man selecting goods from a shelf behind Pikel. The man's gait and movements were easy and graceful, his eyes sharp and steady, and he hoisted a twenty-pound bag of meal easily with one hand. His tunic moved up from the back of his trousers as he moved, revealing a dagger tucked securely in the back of his belt.

That alone would not have fired off any alarms in Ivan. Many people carried concealed weapons in Carradoon. Ivan himself had a knife in one pocket. But the dwarf was certain he'd seen the man before, in a different guise. He watched the man for a few moments longer, until the man noticed him, snarled, and headed off the other way down the aisle.

"Eh?" Pikel asked, wondering what problem so obviously bothered his brother.

Ivan didn't reply at first. He was too busy searching his memory. Then it came to him: he had seen a man closely resembling the shopper in the alley beside the Dragon's Codpiece. The man had been more disheveled then, wearing tattered clothing and seeming like an ordinary street beggar, of which Carradoon had its share. Even then, though, Ivan had noted the grace of the beggar's movements, a skilled and measured step.

The dwarf hadn't thought much about it, except for the unpleasant incident on his journey into the city. Danica was convinced that the would-be bandits were no ordinary highwaymen and had been waiting to ambush the three companions. Ivan had little proof either way, and while he held many private doubts, he knew Danica better than to openly disagree with her on that sort of thing. An inspection of the bodies had revealed little, though. The men carried no obvious marks, not even the familiar trident-and-bottle insignia of the enemy, which the companions had expected to find.

By all appearances, they had been simple robbers, coincidentally stumbling into the companions' path, and that had seemed even more plausible when Ivan and the others had arrived in Carradoon to find Cadderly, Avery, and Rufo safe and secure at the Dragon's Codpiece.

But prudent, battle-tested Ivan had not let his guard down, not one bit.

"We should go find Cadderly and Danica," he said to Pikel.

"Tut tut," Pikel argued, blushing with embarrassment and waggling a stubby finger Ivan's way. Danica hadn't returned to her room the previous night, and the dwarves didn't have to struggle to figure out where she'd stayed, and why she'd stayed there.

"We won't bother them if we don't need to," Ivan growled back. "Just want to keep an eye on them, that's all." Ivan nodded to the end of the aisle, where the suspicious shopper was gathering more goods. "I'm not so sure we seen the last of the group that hit us on the road."

"Eh?" Pikel balked.

"Sure, that bunch is dead," Ivan said as Pikel finally hopped around to regard the man, "but me thinking's that they got friends, and me fear's that we were more than accidental targets."

"Uh-oh," Pikel whined. He looked back at Ivan, crestfallen and obviously worried.

"We'll just watch 'em, that's all," Ivan said. "We'll just watch 'em close."

Q

Vander paced nervously around the barn on the outskirts of town. Ghost had telepathically contacted him using the power of the *Ghearufu* that morning to set the plans into motion. The strike against Cadderly would come before the next dawn. All of the other assassins were gone from the farm, sent into position with their remaining associates in Carradoon. There had still been no word of the five who had gone into the mountains, but word of the arrival of Danica and the dwarves in the city did not bode well for the missing Night Masks.

Still, fourteen expertly trained assassins should prove an ample number for a single, unsuspecting kill. At least, that had been Ghost's reasoning when he'd told Vander, the most powerful of the group, to remain at the farm, out of the way.

The firbolg didn't mind. Executions had always left a sour taste in the honorable giant's mouth. What bothered Vander was Ghost's motivations in holding him back. The only other times the devious little assassin had done so was when Ghost sincerely respected the powers of his intended victim. On those occasions, Vander became no more than a secret escape route for Ghost. If the assassin got into serious trouble, he could just summon his magical item and flee into the firbolg's body, leaving Vander back in Ghost's body to suffer whatever peril the assassin had gotten himself into.

How long will this continue? the firbolg wondered for about the ten thousandth time. How long will I remain the plaything of that wicked, honorless little weakling?

For all his pacing and all his painstaking thought, Vander could see no end, and no escape. He could find consolation only by telling himself that in the morning Cadderly would be dead, and one more wretched chapter of his own miserable life would be at an end.

Q

"You seem in a hurry," Bogo Rath commented when Rufo, his face chalk white with flour, entered the Dragon's Codpiece and made his way straight for the stairs.

Rufo looked at the young wizard and snorted derisively, but didn't have the courage to ignore the young wizard's hand gesture that Rufo should go over and join him.

"What do you need?" Rufo snapped, angry at all the world and especially impatient in yet another situation in which he was forced to serve. Everywhere the man turned, he found someone more than willing to give him orders.

Bogo laughed heartily and flipped his stringy hair over to the side, out of his green eyes. "How go your negotiations?" the wizard asked.

Again Rufo snorted. "You should ask Avery," he

replied, venom dripping from every word. "Certainly I, the errand boy, would not know!" As evidence to his point, Rufo held up the few small sacks of purchases he had made in the first shops he'd visited that day.

"You deserve better treatment than this," Bogo commented, trying to sound like an honest friend.

"From you as well," Rufo replied.

Bogo nodded and did not argue. In truth, the young wizard, "Boygo" to his older associates, could sympathize with Rufo's dilemma.

"Well, have you a task for me, or are you merely wasting my time?" Rufo asked. "Not that my time is such a precious thing."

"Nothing," Bogo replied, and the man spun away, heading back for the stairs. "As of yet," Bogo remarked after him, stealing some of the ire-filled thunder from Rufo's determined steps.

The priest looked back one final time.

"You will be informed when you are needed," Bogo said, his visage stern and unyielding.

The young wizard might sympathize with Rufo, but that would offer the priest little reprieve from the duties Bogo would eventually require of him.

G

"You met with the priest again," Ghost said to Bogo when the young wizard entered his room later that afternoon. He hardly seemed surprised to find the sneaky assassin waiting for him, or by the fact that Ghost knew of his meeting with Rufo.

"I've warned you once of your meddling," Ghost went on.

Bogo's face twisted curiously, and Ghost realized that

he had made a mistake. He hadn't warned Bogo of any such thing; the innkeeper's son had done that, at least as far as Bogo was concerned.

"You?" Bogo questioned, his lips turning up in a smile. "I have not seen young Brennan today," he remarked cryptically. "Actually, his father is quite worried about him."

Ghost settled back on the bed and nodded silent congratulations to the observant wizard. "Let us just say that the young man outlived his usefulness," he explained. "A very dangerous thing to do."

Neither man spoke for a very long while, but there remained little tension between them. Ghost studied Bogo long and hard, and the young wizard seemed to sense that the assassin was forming some plan—a plan that Bogo could only hope would include him.

"The time is close then," Bogo remarked. "The disappearance of young Brennan is a question that you cannot let hang unanswered for very long."

Again, Ghost nodded his silent appreciation of Bogo's reasoning powers. "The time is nearly upon us," he confirmed, "but it would seem that some things have changed."

"The arrival of the priests and Danica?" Bogo asked.

"Complications," Ghost replied.

"And what else has changed?"

"Your role," Ghost answered.

Bogo took a cautious step back, certainly fearing that he, too, might have outlived his usefulness.

"I had said you were only an observer," the assassin explained, "and, so, by Aballister's measure, you were meant to be. But you never believed that, did you, Rath?

You never planned to sit back and watch while the Night Masks had all the fun killing this young Deneirrath."

Bogo cocked his head curiously at the assassin, obviously unsure of what that plain fact might mean.

"And you have proven to me," Ghost continued, "both by your astute conclusions and your ability to get close to our enemies, that your value extends beyond your assigned role."

"I thought you didn't want me talking with Rufo," Bogo replied, still a safe distance from the dangerous man.

"I just explained to you that things have changed," Ghost retorted. "We have a headmaster from the library to deal with and a formidable young woman, it would seem. I intend to handle the latter problem personally, and for that I will need to borrow your stooge."

Bogo moved over to the bed, more curious than afraid.

"A simple matter," Ghost explained. "A simple, innocuous task for Kierkan Rufo that will allow me to get at the Lady Maupoissant."

"You will kill her?"

"In a manner of speaking," Ghost replied. "First I will use her so that when the Night Masks come for Cadderly, the one he believes is his closest ally will, in truth, be his most dangerous enemy."

Bogo's smile widened, mimicking Ghost's devious expression. The assassin's plan was beautifully simple, with Bogo, and more particularly, Rufo, being the only potential trouble areas that he could foresee. To that end, the assassin then delivered a secure hook.

His smile abruptly disappeared, causing Bogo's visage to assume a similarly grim tone.

"I offer you a part in this execution," Ghost explained, "something you have craved since before we left Castle Trinity. I assure you that your role will be well received by Aballister.

"But," Ghost continued, "my pay will be as originally agreed."

"Of course—" Bogo started, but Ghost didn't pause long enough to let him continue.

"And if Aballister does not deliver to me the full amount," Ghost went on, "then you must make up the difference—to the gold piece."

Bogo nodded eagerly, appearing more than happy to pay such a pittance in exchange for the prestige, and surely also beginning to understand just how very bad it might be to get on the wrong side of that wicked little man.

FOURTEEN

TO CAPTURE A SOUL

Cadderly and Danica had slept very late that day.
Brennan did not appear with Cadderly's breakfast,
and Cadderly, in his modest way, was glad of that. He
suspected that the innkeeper's son had probably come
to the door, but had turned away, blushing, at what
he'd heard from inside. With a private smile, Cadderly
thought no more about it.

The lovers left their room shortly after noon,
taking a meal together in the hearth room. Fredegar
served them himself—an unusual occurrence that
Cadderly realized was out of sorts only when the innkeeper asked him if he had seen anything of Brennan
that morning.

Still, Cadderly was too consumed by the presence
of Danica to appreciate the implications of the missing
youth. He promised to keep an eye out for Brennan
when he and Danica went out walking. Fredegar
nodded his thanks, but he was plainly worried.

"The mistakes of adolescence," Cadderly explained

to Danica, not too concerned for the welfare of the youth. He figured that Brennan had been out late in pursuit of some young lady, and that maybe Brennan had finally made a catch.

For all of Cadderly's inner turmoil, the world seemed calm that morning, with Danica beside him again, and the young priest couldn't even begin to think dark and ominous thoughts.

They left the inn together, crossed the wide way of Lakeview Street, and moved down to Impresk Lake's sandy shore. The breeze was stiff off the water, chill but not cold, and long-winged birds zipped about at impossible angles and cut sharply in daring maneuvers all around them. The normal morning mist had long since dissipated, leaving the two with a grand view of the island that comprised the wealthier section of Carradoon, and the wide, arching stone bridge that led to it. Several multi-story structures peeked up above the trees, and a fleet of boats, both pleasure and fishing, meandered around the land mass.

"I suppose I might come to accept the beard," Danica said after many minutes of quiet watching. She moved over and tugged at an exceptionally long strand. "As long as you keep it trimmed!"

"And I love you," Cadderly replied with a contented smile. "Will you stay beside me?"

"Are you certain you want me to?" Danica said in a teasing tone, but there was a subtle undercurrent of dread in her question.

"Stay with me," Cadderly said again, more forcefully.

C

Danica looked back at the water and didn't answer. The request seemed so simple and obvious, and yet, the woman realized that many obstacles remained. She had gone to the Edificant Library to study the ancient works of Grandmaster Penpahg D'Ahn, the Most Holy One, prophet and founder of her order. Only in the library could Danica continue her work, and that work was very important to her, the culmination of all her personal goals.

As important as Cadderly?

Danica was not honestly sure, but she knew that if she gave up her goals to remain beside her lover, then she would forever look back and wonder what might have been, what level of perfection she might have achieved.

And there remained, too, the war. The last few days had come as a reprieve to the battle-weary woman, despite the attack on the road, but Danica knew that the quiet time was only temporary. More fighting would break out, in the spring if not sooner, and Danica had long ago resolved to be a part of that struggle.

Cadderly, though, had run away from it, and she didn't know if he would change his mind.

So Danica didn't answer the question, and Cadderly, wise enough to understand her hesitancy and her fears, didn't ask it again. Day by day, she decided. They would pass their time together day by day and see what changes the wind across the lake brought.

They walked quietly along the beach for some time, Cadderly leading Danica to one of his favorite places. The shoreline jutted sharply out into the water in a small, tree-covered peninsula with banks only a foot above the water level. A single path, barely a foot wide, led the way into the thick tangle, ending at a small clearing right in the center of the peninsula. Though they were barely half a mile from the bustle of Carradoon, and barely half a mile from the island section as well, it seemed to Cadderly and Danica that the world had disappeared beyond the shelter of those trees.

Danica looked slyly at Cadderly, suddenly suspecting the reason he had brought her out there.

But Cadderly apparently had other ideas. He led Danica down another narrow path, to the very tip of the peninsula, beside a small pool formed by the waves whenever a large boat passed by. Cadderly indicated a mossy stone and bade Danica to sit.

Cadderly walked the perimeter of the pool, muttering something under his breath that Danica couldn't make out. She soon came to understand that the young priest was chanting, a spell, most likely.

Cadderly stopped walking. His body swayed gently, a willow in the wind he seemed, and his arms moved in graceful circles. Danica's eyes settled on Cadderly's holy symbol, the single eye-and-candle design set in the center of his wide-brimmed hat. She felt a pulse of power from that emblem. It seemed to glow with some inner strength.

Cadderly's arms waved again as he reached low in front of him and swung them slowly out wide to either side.

The water reacted to his call. The center of the pool bubbled with sudden energy then rolled outward, great ripples moving to every edge. Danica moved her feet in close to her, thinking that she was going to get splashed, but the water didn't break the edges of the pool. As the waves crested, there came a great hissing sound and the water vaporized, rolling up into the air to form a grayish cloud.

More water rolled out to be consumed, and when it was done, just a few small puddles remained where the pool had been. The cloud hovered for a few moments until the pull of the wind broke it apart to nothingness.

Danica blinked in amazement and looked at Cadderly, who stood very still, staring at the mud-and-puddle pit.

"You have become powerful," she remarked after some time had passed. "For a nonbeliever."

Cadderly glared at her but could not sustain any anger in the face of her disarming smile. Through his smile, though, Danica recognized the young man's torment.

"Perhaps it's just a variation of a wizard's magic, as you fear," she offered, "but perhaps the strength does come from Deneir. You seem too quick to deny what others of your order—"

"*My* order?" Cadderly was quick to interrupt, his tone both sarcastic and incredulous.

"Your holy symbol vibrated with power," Danica replied. "I witnessed it myself."

"A conduit for magical energy, much like the tome on my desk," Cadderly said more sharply than Danica deserved. He seemed to understand that, and his tone softened considerably as he continued, "Whenever I call on the magic, I merely recall some of the words in that book."

"And it is a book of Deneir," Danica reasoned.

Cadderly shook his head. "Do you know of Belisarius?" he asked.

"The wizard in the tower to the south?" Danica said.

Cadderly nodded. "Belisarius has a similar book—a spellbook. If he attached a god's name to it, would it then become a holy book?"

"It's not the same," Danica muttered, frustrated.

"I don't know that," Cadderly said.

Danica looked at the lake behind her, at the gently lapping waves against the many small rocks at the peninsula's tip, determined to change the subject. Then she looked at the muddy hole. "How long will it take to refill?" she asked, not happy with the results of Cadderly's display. "Or must it wait for the next rain?"

Cadderly smiled and bent low, scooping a few drops of the remaining water into his cupped palms. He pulled his hand in close to his chest, again muttered some words under his breath.

"As the graceful rain must fall!" he ended, then he threw his hands out before him, threw the water to the air above the muddy pit. A tiny cloud appeared, hovering and churning in the air, and a moment later, a steady stream of water poured forth, splashing into the mud.

Before Danica ended her first burst of laughter, the pool had returned, as full as when she had first seen it.

"You find this humorous?" Cadderly asked, narrowing his gray eyes and thumping his fists against his hips so that he seemed a caricature of wounded pride.

"I find you humorous," Danica retorted, and Cadderly's expression revealed that he was truly hurt.

"You have all the proof right before you," Danica explained, "more proof than the vast majority of ordinary people will ever know, and yet you remain so filled with doubt. My poor Cadderly, so damned by the unending questions of his own intelligence!"

Cadderly looked at the pool he had magically evaporated and refilled, and chuckled at the irony of it all. Danica took his hand and led him back to the clearing at the center of the peninsula. Cadderly thought to keep going, down the other narrow path and back out to the wider beaches, but Danica held tight to his hand and did not continue, forcing him to turn around.

They were alone in the sun and the breeze, and all the world seemed peaceful. Danica smiled mischievously, her almond eyes telling Cadderly without the slightest doubt that it was not yet time to leave.

Q

It was nearly twilight when Cadderly and Danica made their way back to the Dragon's Codpiece. Farther down Lakeview Street, fatherly Ivan watched their progress. The dwarf was much more at ease than he had been, and the safe return of Cadderly and Danica made him feel that his suspicions might be unfounded, that he was acting as silly as a mother hen.

But was it a coincidence, just a moment later, when a beggar came to the end of the alleyway next to the Dragon's Codpiece, and appeared to be watching the young couple as intently as Ivan was?

Ivan sensed that the man meant to go after the two, and the dwarf started to make his way slowly up the street. He didn't have his greataxe with him—it wasn't considered proper to stand around on one of Carradoon's streets so obviously armed—but he was wearing his deer-antlered helmet. If the beggar made a move against Cadderly, Ivan resolved to gore him good.

Cadderly and Danica turned into the inn, and the beggar leaned against the wall. Ivan stopped, perplexed, feeling foolish. He looked around, half-expecting everyone else on the street to be pointing at him and chuckling, but of course no one was.

"Stupid dwarf," he muttered under his breath. "What're ye getting so anxious about? Just a poor man, looking for a bit of coins."

Ivan stopped and scratched his yellow beard curiously when he looked back toward the alleyway.

The man was gone.

Q

Danica giggled, but Cadderly was not amused at the knock on his door—not at that particular moment.

"Oh, go and answer it," Danica whispered to him. "It's probably the innkeeper's son, whom you have been worried over the whole of the day!"

"I don't want to go," Cadderly replied, pouting like a child.

That brought another chuckle from Danica, who pulled the bedclothes up tight around her neck.

Groaning with every move, Cadderly pulled himself out of bed and eased over to the door, wrapping himself in his discarded cloak.

"Rufo?" he asked as he cracked the door open.

The hallway was dark, the candles in the great chandelier atop the stairs having long since died away. Only the glow from the hearth room's fireplace offered any light at all. Still, Cadderly could hardly mistake Rufo's tilting posture.

"My greetings," the man replied. "And my apologies for disturbing you."

Cadderly blushed deeply, a sight the man obviously enjoyed.

"What do you want?" asked the younger priest.

"You are needed in the hearth room," Rufo explained, "as soon as you can."

"No."

The answer seemed simple enough, and Cadderly moved to shut the door, but Rufo stuck his foot in the way and said, "Headmaster Avery will return with a delegation from the chapel of Ilmater."

Cadderly looked back over his shoulder to the balcony doors, and the blackness of the night. "It's late," he said.

"It is very late," Rufo admitted. "The Ilmatari wish this done in private. They seek information about the deaths of their acolytes at the Edificant Library during the time of the chaos curse."

"I have already written my testimony—"

"Avery asks that you come," Rufo pressed. "He has not required much of you, certainly less than he asks of me." Obvious resentment rang clearly in the man's tone. "You can do this much for him, impudent Cadderly, after all the headmaster has done for you."

The argument seemed solid enough. Cadderly groaned again then nodded. "I'll be along," he said.

Danica's giggling renewed as soon as the door was closed.

"I will not be gone long," Cadderly promised as he pulled on his clothes.

"It doesn't matter," Danica replied. "I'm certain I shall fall asleep immediately." She stretched languidly and rolled to her side, and Cadderly, cursing his luck, left the room.

He, too, must have been sleepy, for he didn't even notice the weasel-like man—was it a man?—behind a slightly opened door, watching him go.

Q

"Cadderly?" Danica uttered the question, but she heard it as though someone else had spoken the words. A smell of exotic flowers permeated the room.

Somewhere deep in her mind, she was surprised that she had fallen asleep so soon. Or had she? How long had Cadderly been gone? she wondered. And what was that smell?

"Cadderly?" she asked again.

"Hardly."

The word should have sounded like a warning to the woman—she knew she should open her eyes and find out what in the Nine Hells was going on . . . but she couldn't.

She felt a thumb, a gloved hand, she believed, pressed against her eyelid, and her eye was forced open, just a crack. Danica tried to focus her thoughts—why was she so sleepy?

Through the blur, she saw herself in a small mirror. She knew that the mirror was hanging around someone's neck.

Whose neck?

"Cadderly?"

The laughter that came back at her filled her with dread, and her eyes popped open against the permeating drowsiness, suddenly alert.

She saw Ghost for just an instant, too briefly to strike out, or even to cry out. Then she fell back into her own thoughts, into the blackness that suddenly became her own mind, and she felt a burning pain throughout every inch of her body.

Danica didn't understand what was happening, but she knew that it wasn't good. She felt herself moving away, but knew that her body wasn't actually moving.

Another blackness loomed in the distance, across a gray expanse, and Danica felt herself pulled toward it, compelled to sink into it. The first blackness, her mortal coil, was left behind, far behind.

Few in all of Faerûn would have understood, but few in all of Faerûn were as well versed in meditation as Danica.

Her identity!

Someone was stealing her very identity!

"No!" Danica tried to cry out, but control of her body's voice was almost gone by then and the word came out as an indecipherable whimper.

Danica focused her will, dismissed the continuing smell that she suspected was some sort of sleeping poison. She located that approaching blackness and pushed against it with all her mental strength, understanding that to enter it was to be lost.

A moment later, she felt another presence, similarly wandering out of body.

Her thoughts screamed a thousand protests at it, but it didn't respond, it just kept making its way for the blackness that Danica had left behind.

C

"Where are they?" Cadderly asked when he came down into the hearth room. The fire burned low and the place was empty, except for him and Rufo, who sat at a table in the far corner.

"Well?" Cadderly growled as he moved over and took a seat opposite the man.

"Patience," Rufo replied. "It won't be long."

Cadderly leaned back and threw one arm over the back of the chair. By his estimation, it had already been too long. He looked at Rufo again, noting a subtle undercurrent of nervousness in the man. Cadderly dismissed the feeling and any suspicions it started to encourage, reminding himself that Kierkan Rufo was always at least a little nervous.

The young priest closed his eyes and let the moments slip past, let his thoughts linger back to Danica and the pleasures and implications the day had brought. He would never leave her again, of that much he was sure.

Cadderly's eyes popped wide.

"What is it?" he heard Rufo ask.

Cadderly studied the man, and saw Rufo blink— *heard* Rufo blink!

The fire crackled so powerfully that Cadderly thought the whole wall would be aflame, but when he turned to regard the hearth, the embers barely seemed to glow with their last flickers of life.

A fly buzzed by the bar. Gods! Cadderly thought, the thing must be the size of a small pony.

He saw nothing there.

And he was aware of that song again, playing softly in the back of his mind. Instead of trying to figure all of it out, Cadderly just allowed himself to feel.

Something—some danger?—had put him on his guard, and he had subconsciously replayed a page from the tome, enacted a magical spell to heighten his hearing.

"What is it?" Rufo asked him again, more urgently.

Cadderly didn't look at the man, just held a hand up to silence him.

Breathing.

Cadderly heard the steady inhale and exhale of breath a few tables away. He looked over but saw nothing.

But there was something, someone, there. Shifting his probe, Cadderly felt the magical energy.

"What are you saying?" he heard Rufo ask, and he realized only then that his lips were moving, forming the words from yet another page of *The Tome of Universal Harmony*.

Cadderly saw a silvery outline of a young man, recognized the stringy locks of hair hanging down one side of the invisible intruder's head.

Rufo shoved him roughly, forcing his attention.

"What?" the man demanded.

Cadderly started to rebuke him then stopped and instead locked his intent gaze on Kierkan Rufo.

Q

Danica calmed her thoughts; she had to beat the other presence to the void of her physical mind. She turned her spirit around, willed her mind to connect fully with the tiny part of her that she had left behind, the part that had forced her mouth to utter that pitiful sound. She sensed the other presence pushing at the blackness then, nearly entering her form.

She felt a burning sensation.

Danica saw too many things in the next instant for her to possibly sort through them. She saw, most clearly, murders—dozens of murders. She saw the Night Masks.

Night Masks!

The assassins guild, the scourge of Westgate, had killed her parents.

She saw a clan of giants, through the eyes of a giant.

She saw the other giants die at her own giant hands.

She saw Cadderly, on the road to Carradoon, and huddled at his desk over *The Tome of Universal Harmony*, and crouched behind the protection of his partly opened door.

To her horror, Danica realized that she was recalling someone else's memories, had connected with the small part that other identity had left behind on its journey to take her body. And that person, whoever it might be, had been close to Cadderly on several occasions.

Night Masks!

Let me out! her thoughts protested.

The other identity cried out to her in rage and agony and disbelief. She heard no words, but understood its meaning acutely, understood that her focused rage could push her back to where she belonged.

Let me out!

Danica pushed against the foreign blackness with all her mental strength, called upon her rage in combination with her years of mental training. The burning intensified then abated, and Danica felt a physical presence once more—her own body.

The smell returned and Danica felt a cloth pressed against her face. Giving in to her warrior instincts, she locked her fingers into a gouging position and cocked her arm for a strike.

She fell hard against the floor, but she didn't realize it.

Q

Shadows—dark, misshapen things—grumbled and growled from the man's shoulders, their demeanor toward Cadderly obviously hostile. Rufo reached out across the small table to touch Cadderly again, but the young priest slapped his hand away.

"Cadderly!" Rufo responded, but the young priest sensed clearly that the man's apparent concern was a facade.

Before Rufo could move again, Cadderly pushed against the table, slamming its other edge into the man's belly. Cadderly honestly didn't know what to do, didn't know if he was being warned or misled.

"Tell Avery that he can find me in the morning," the young priest said, rising and spinning around to survey the room. He sensed that the invisible wizard was long gone.

"Avery won't like that," he heard Rufo say, but more acutely, he heard a thump from somewhere upstairs that he knew instinctively was his own room.

Danica!

Cadderly bounded across the floor to the stairs, but then he was moving slowly, as if in a dream, barely able to put one heavy foot in front of the other.

The song played in his head. He instinctively pictured a page from the great book, a page describing focused magical energies, describing how to dispel such malevolent collections of magic.

A moment later he was moving again normally, free of whatever magical bonds had been placed on him. The door to his room was closed, as he'd left it, and all seemed as it should.

Cadderly burst through the door anyway. He found Danica, her breathing rapid, sprawled upon the floor, tangled in a pile of blankets next to the bed. Cadderly knew she was alive and not seriously hurt as he held her in his arms.

The young priest surveyed the room. The notes from the song seemed more distant to him and all seemed calm, but still the young priest wondered if someone had come in during his absence.

"Cadderly," Danica breathed, suddenly coming awake.

She looked around her, confused for a moment, pulled the blankets high ,and brought her arms in close—actions that struck Cadderly as curious gestures.

"A terrible dream," Danica tried to explain.

Cadderly kissed her gently on the forehead and told her that everything was all right. He placed his chin atop Danica's head and rocked her in his arms, his own smile widening with growing security.

Danica was unharmed. It had been only a dream.

FIFTEEN

A GOOD DAY TO DIE

As the night wound on toward morning, the guests in half of the eight private rooms at the Dragon's Codpiece slept soundly.

Bogo Rath was simply too agitated to think of sleeping. Knowing what was to come, and knowing the part he'd played, the young wizard thought through the problems facing him that morning. Would Kierkan Rufo remain loyal? And even if he did, would the priest be able to carry out the mission Bogo had set before him? Things could get very troublesome at the Dragon's Codpiece very quickly if a certain headmaster from the Edificant Library wasn't properly and efficiently dealt with.

Bogo understood the merciless Night Masks well enough to realize that Ghost would hold him responsible if Kierkan Rufo failed. The wizard paced his small room, taking care to keep his footsteps as quiet as possible. He wished that Ghost would come to him then, or that one of the band of assassins would at least make contact to let him know how things progressed.

The young wizard resisted the urge to crack open his door, remembering that if he interrupted at an inopportune moment, he might well share Cadderly's grim fate.

Q

In his own room, Ghost sat staring out his window, bitter and full of rage. He hadn't slept at all that night, after Danica's mental discipline had defeated his attempted possession. He had wanted to be close at hand when the assassins roared in. He'd even been forced to go to the band that night and change their orders. Danica must die beside her lover.

For all the unexpected twists, the assassin remained confident that Cadderly would die that day, but even if the young priest fell easily, it had been a messy execution, filled with complications and unexpected losses. Vander had killed one man, and five others were missing in the foothills of the Snowflakes.

And young Cadderly was still very much alive.

Q

And very much awake.

In his room, the young priest sat at his table, dressed for the coming day and flipping through the pages of *The Tome of Universal Harmony*. The hearth room had shown Cadderly many surprises earlier that night, and he searched for an entry that might help explain the sudden heightening of his senses, particularly his hearing.

Danica sat cross-legged on the floor beside the bed in quiet meditation, allowing the priest his needed privacy and taking some for herself. Hers was a life of discipline, of private challenges and trials, and though it was a bit early, she had already begun her daily morning ritual, working her inner being, stretching her limbs, and clearing her mind in preparation for the coming day.

Danica had discovered no answers for her strange experience earlier that night, and truthfully, she hadn't sought any. To her, the encounter with the unknown other mind remained a dream. Since nothing else traumatic or dangerous had occurred, that explanation seemed to satisfy her.

C

"The sun has not even peeked over the horizon!" Headmaster Avery protested, managing with some difficulty to roll his bulky form out of bed.

"That was Cadderly's wish," Kierkan Rufo reminded him. "He desired secrecy, and I believe what he might have to say will be worth the effort."

Avery struggled to clear his throat of its nighttime phlegm and draw in a profound breath, never taking his curious stare off the man.

Rufo struggled even harder to remain calm under that searching gaze. He kept his breathing steady. So many things depended on his maintaining a calm facade, but beneath the calm front, turmoil boiled in Rufo. He honestly wondered how it had all come down to such a dramatic end. He had been used by Barjin when the Talonite priest had invaded the library several months before. He had been the one who'd kicked Cadderly down the secret stairway, nearly leading to the library's downfall.

Rufo had never quite forgiven himself—no, not forgiven himself, but rather, had never quite been able to justify the action to himself. Self-forgiveness would imply that he held guilty thoughts for that treacherous act, and he didn't. With every event that had come after Barjin's invasion, Cadderly had become more Rufo's rival, more his bane. In Shilmista, Cadderly had emerged a hero, while Rufo, through no fault of his own—at least, none that he would admit to, even to himself—had become a scapegoat.

Bleary-eyed, Avery stumbled across the floor and pulled on his clothes. Rufo was glad to be released from the headmaster's gaze.

"Are you coming down with me?" Avery asked.

"Cadderly doesn't want me there," the man lied. "He said he would meet with you alone in the hearth room before Fredegar began his work."

"Before dawn," Avery muttered.

Rufo continued to stare at the portly headmaster's back. He didn't hate Avery—on the contrary, the headmaster had acted on Rufo's behalf many times over the last decade. But that was behind them, Rufo reminded himself. Shilmista had undeniably changed the course of Rufo's life, but looking at vulnerable Avery, he had to pause and consider just how drastically.

"Well, I'm off for the hearth room, then," Avery announced, moving to the door.

He wasn't even carrying his mace in the loop on his belt, Rufo noted. And he hadn't yet prayed and prepared any spells.

"I truly wish Cadderly would be more . . . conventional," Avery remarked, his obvious fondness for the young priest showing through, and that only strengthening the treacherous Rufo's resolve. "But then that is his charm, I suppose." Avery paused and smiled, and Rufo knew the portly man was engaged in some private recollection.

"Meet me in the hearth room for the morning meal," Avery instructed. "Perhaps I'll be able to persuade Cadderly to dine with us."

"Just what I desire," the man muttered.

He moved to the door and watched Avery descend the sweeping stairway to the dimly lighted hearth room then closed the door. Rufo's part was done. He had set events into motion, as the young wizard had instructed him to do. Avery's fate was the headmaster's own to deal with.

The man leaned back against the wall, desperately trying to dismiss his growing guilt. He recalled Avery's recent treatment of him, of the terrible things the headmaster had said to him and the threats to drive Rufo from the order.

For Kierkan Rufo, consumed by resentment, guilt was not a difficult emotion to overcome.

Q

Half asleep in the common room of the inn two doors down from the Dragon's Codpiece, his head resting on the ledge of the alley window, Pikel heard a distinct whistle. The dwarf's grogginess held fast only for the few moments it took Pikel to remember what his brother would do to him if Ivan caught him asleep on his watch.

Pikel stuck his head out the window and took in a deep breath of the chilly predawn air.

Another whistle sounded, from the alley on the other side of the building he was facing.

"Eh?" the dwarf grunted, his instincts telling him that the whistles were surely signals. Pikel hopped up from his seat and ran to the front door, throwing aside the locking bar and hopping out onto the inn's front porch.

He saw shapes pass out of the alley beyond the nearest building, move onto the veranda of the Dragon's Codpiece, and slip through the open door.

Pikel started forward to better investigate when a movement close beside him stole his attention. A large man rushed up to him, sword slicing. The first hit bounced off the dwarf's armored shoulder, not penetrating but leaving a painful bruise.

"Oooo!" Pikel exclaimed in surprise, backstepping the way he'd come. The man kept right with him, flailing away viciously. Pikel had no weapon—he'd left his club back in his room, not really believing Ivan's growing suspicions that dangers were lurking just outside.

The man hacked away at him, driving him backward with every step. Blood rolled down one of Pikel's arms, and he took a glancing hit across the cheek that drew a thin red line.

The relentless beating continued, and Pikel, nearly across the common room, had little distance left to run.

C

The lockpick had been silent. Headmaster Avery, his heavy eyelids drooping, didn't even realize that anyone had entered the Dragon's Codpiece until the assassins were upon him.

Then they were beyond him, slipping up the stairs as quietly as shadows.

Cadderly looked up from *The Tome of Universal Harmony* and glanced over his shoulder at Danica.

"What is it?" the woman asked, her meditation interrupted by the sheer intensity of the young scholar's stare.

Cadderly lifted a finger over pursed lips, beckoning the woman to be silent. Something had called out to him, a distant song, a voice of impending danger. He took up his spindle-disks and his walking stick and started to rise, facing the closed door.

He hadn't even left his chair when the door burst open and dark shapes stormed in.

Danica was still sitting cross-legged when the first assassin, sword in hand, rushed at her. The killer came in low, gaping in disbelief as Danica's coiled legs sprang, her momentum lifting her into the air. She tucked her legs under as she rose, clearing the low strike, and descended on the bending man.

Her legs locked around his neck as she came down, clamping tightly, and she jerked herself to the side, dipping into a full bend and throwing her full weight right under the bending man.

The assassin saw the room spin, but his body had not turned.

Q

Cadderly whipped his walking stick across in front of him and was amazed when he heard something—a crossbow quarrel, he realized—tick off it and fly harmlessly wide. He swung again in a wide, shoulder-level arc as two men bore down on him. Instinctively, Cadderly dropped to one knee and snapped his spindle-disks straight out ahead of him.

The ducking attacker came down right in line with the second weapon, catching the adamantine disks on his forearm.

Cadderly expected the man to immediately retaliate, for the young priest had not yet learned of the power of Ivan's forging. Cadderly stared as the man's arm folded—it seemed as though he had grown a second elbow—under the power of the blow.

But pausing to gape with a second enemy so near was not a wise choice. By the time Cadderly realized his error, realized that a spiked club was on its way down to crunch his head, he knew that his life was at its end.

Q

Pikel managed to keep close enough to his pursuer so that the man hadn't been able to extend his long arms and get in a serious hit. Still, the dwarf said "Oooo!" repeatedly, feeling the sting of a dozen razor-like slashes.

Pikel's first thought was to go for the stairs, but he dismissed the idea, realizing that if he started up, he would rise to his enemy's level and lose his desperately needed advantage of being down below the man's optimum striking area. The dwarf veered to the side, backstepping faster, nearly tumbling over in the effort.

The man stayed with him, every step.

The killer stopped suddenly, and Pikel realized that he could not do likewise, leaving the dwarf wide open for a full-force roundhouse.

"Oooo!" Pikel screamed, desperately hurling himself backward through the air.

He collided with the wall before he'd gotten very far,

and the assassin's sword whipped across just under the breastplate of the dwarf's fine armor.

Pikel didn't even have the time to cry out. He bounced back off the wall and charged forward. The assassin held his sword level in front of him, and Pikel would have impaled himself, except that he grabbed the sharp blade with his bare hand and turned it aside.

Then Pikel was up against the man. He released the sword and wrapped the man's arms in his own, pushing with all his strength, his stubby, muscled legs frantically pumping.

It was the killer's turn to backstep, and Pikel drove forward, gaining speed and momentum. The dwarf could hardly see around the larger man. He aimed for the open door but missed, two feet to the left.

The inn suddenly had a second door.

C

Danica hit the floor harder than she would have liked, but she managed to scramble back under her victim fast enough so that the next closest assassin inadvertently sliced his sword into the back of his still-standing companion.

Out the other side, Danica ran to the foot of the bed, hooked the post in one arm, and spun around, hopping up onto the mattress. An attacker came up on the bed as well, at the other end, bearing down on the apparently unarmed woman.

Danica kept low and kicked straight out. She could hardly brace herself amidst the tangle of blankets, so her kick was not fierce, but neither could the assassin brace himself, so it didn't have to be. The man stumbled in the tangle and lurched over. Danica came up under him, hooking her arm under and behind his shoulder, and heaved him away using his own momentum to launch him over the foot end of the bed.

She was up, grabbing the blankets as she went, knowing the sword-wielder was too close. She lifted the tangle of cloth out in front of her, smiling grimly as she felt it absorb the weight of the coming blow.

Caught in, and concerned with, the impromptu web, the assassin failed to anticipate Danica's next attack, and her foot connected with his belly.

The agile monk let herself drop as the man lurched over, using the spring of the bed to lift her right back up, her forearm slamming against the stooping man's face. Danica's second arm, coiled against her chest, snapped out under the first, thumping into the man's throat, then she reversed the angle of her first arm, flying high over her head in its follow-through, and came down diagonally at her stunned victim, blasting against his collarbone. He flew to the side, and Danica, temporarily free of any immediate threat, was hardly pleased by what she saw beyond him.

Again using the spring of the bed, the young woman leaped out, diving between the posts at the foot of the bed. She heard a heavy thump as a crossbow quarrel hit the wall right behind her.

The man she had thrown that way was back up and turning back to the fight, but hardly prepared as Danica's shoulder-block launched him over the table to crash into the wall.

Q

"Stop!" The word came from somewhere deep inside Cadderly. He wasn't even aware of the magical strength it carried until the killer above him, already beginning his stroke, pulled his spiked club to a halt and stood perfectly still. The weapon hovered just a few inches above Cadderly's head.

The command had no lasting power, and the assassin came out of it quickly, snarling and lifting his club for another strike.

Still acting purely on instinct, Cadderly lashed out in two directions at once, slamming his walking stick against the side of the man's knee, and heaving his spindle-disks straight ahead to collide with the crumbling killer's chest and send him flying backward.

"The balcony!" Danica cried, and Cadderly, seeing the group of killers—some cocking crossbows—still coming in the door, could hardly disagree.

Danica hooked his arm as she passed and threw open the door.

The song had started again in Cadderly's head, somehow passing through the confusion and the many noises.

He grabbed Danica's hair and jerked violently backward just as the woman took her first step out of the room. Fully caught by surprise, Danica fell back.

Cadderly snapped his spindle-disks across her angled torso, to meet head on with a thrusting dagger coming the other way.

Ivan's disks easily won the contest, bending the dagger blade and crushing the hand that held it.

Cadderly recoiled quickly, felt the sting as the disks snapped back into his own hand, and whipped them straight back. They hit the wounded man in the chest, driving him over the railing.

The assassin reached out as he tumbled, grasping

futilely at the rail. His hand hooked the balcony just enough to allow him to continue in his spin, to put his legs straight out under him so that when he fell the twenty feet to the ground, he landed flat on his back.

And he lay very still.

C

Pikel shook the splinters from his beard and hair. "Me brother!"

The call, though emphatic, sounded distant, and was accentuated by the crash of shattering glass and splintering wood as Ivan, hearing his brother's distress, ran full speed down the inn's second story hallway and flung himself headlong through the window above the front door.

He crashed down with a groan, two feet to the right of Pikel and the stunned assassin, showering the two of them with glass and shards of broken wood.

The killer, up first, his back bleeding from many gashes, turned around to discern the newest threat. He saw the lower half of Ivan—the dwarf's upper torso having plummeted right through the raised wooden decking—but he knew by the way the dwarf was flailing and cursing that Ivan would not be held captive long.

He almost got his sword up before Pikel grabbed him by the ankles and yanked his legs out from under him.

Pikel continued to pull, dragging the man away from Ivan. Rage blinded the green-bearded dwarf.

"Ooooooo!" he growled, winding up, beginning his spin, and locking the man's feet under his arms.

The assassin twisted and turned to get at the dwarf, but Pikel's footing was sure and his spin quickly gained enough momentum to force the man out straight.

"Ooooooo!"

The man bounced and flailed, and had all that he could handle in just keeping a hold on his sword.

"Ooooooo!"

Then the only part of the assassin making any contact with the ground was his arms as he struggled to find anything to grab on to.

"Ooooooo!"

Pikel spun furiously. The man, narrowly missing porch posts and the inn's wall, heartily joined in his screaming.

Ivan, back up, watched in disbelief that soon turned to amusement. The dwarf laid his brother's club aside, spat in both his hands, and took up his huge doublebladed axe.

The killer noticed Ivan's preparations and gave a halfhearted swing of his sword, not even coming close to hitting the mark. His arm still extended, he slammed his wrist against the porch support as he came around, his sword flying harmlessly out into the street.

Ivan tightened his grasp on the axe. He started to swing, but the man was past him.

"Gotta lead him," the dwarf reminded himself, taking a bead as the circling target came around again. He saw the assassin's face go ghastly pale, saw the most profound look of horror the tough dwarf had ever witnessed.

Slam!

Distracted by a rare onset of sympathy, Ivan's timing was not so good and he buried his axe deeply into the wooden decking.

Pikel didn't even notice his brother or the axe, didn't notice that the killer's scream had dissipated in a breathless gasp of terror, and had no idea how he would stop the world from spinning in his dizzy head.

"Ooooooo!"

The weight was gone suddenly and Pikel twirled into the wall. He looked down at the empty boots still held tightly under his arms.

The poor assassin took out the closest supporting pole and crashed through the railing, breaking under the top rail and skidding along through the thin, carved balusters. He bounced along for several feet then came to an abrupt halt, his hip driving onto the pointed edge of a broken beam. There he lay, half on the porch and half hanging out over the cobblestone street, groaning softly.

"Nice boots," Ivan remarked, running past Pikel and tossing his brother the tree-trunk club he'd brought along. Ivan started for the fallen man then veered away, hearing a scream as someone went toppling over a balcony of the Dragon's Codpiece, two doors down—Cadderly's balcony.

Both dwarves breathed a sigh of relief when they rushed past the unmoving form of the fallen man, glad that it was neither Cadderly nor Danica who had gone for such a tumble. But the continuing sounds of battle twenty feet above them told them that their friends were not out of trouble just yet.

The door to the inn was closed again, and barred, but such had never stopped the Bouldershoulder brothers. Actually, coming into the hearth room with a dislodged door in front of them proved a good thing for the dwarves, for several crossbow quarrels greeted their entrance, thudding harmlessly into the oaken barrier.

Q

A quarrel ripped past Cadderly's shoulder, drawing a line of blood along his arm. Night Masks bore down on him from behind, and two others waited on the balcony, a sword and a heavy axe gleaming dully in the predawn light.

Still holding Danica by the hair, Cadderly pulled the young woman to her feet. Immediately, she became a blur of motion, snapping a burst of kicks and punches at the already wounded men who were closing from behind. She landed several solid hits, enough to force one of the assassins to back off. But the other caught Danica around the waist and his momentum carried both of them across the narrow balcony to the rail.

Danica got one hand up onto her attacker's face, her fingers seeking out the man's vulnerable eyes. One of the Night Masks on the balcony, though, forewarned of the extraordinary woman's prowess, found a devilish answer. A single swing of his huge axe broke apart the railing that supported both Danica and her attacker.

They pitched over the side together, Danica releasing her grasp on the man's face and swinging both her arms wildly to find a handhold.

Cadderly saw her fall away, his face locked in a stare of helpless denial.

A crossbow quarrel smacked into the back of the young priest's thigh. He turned as he sank to the deck, sheer rage splayed clearly on his usually calm features.

Without even thinking of the movement, Cadderly lifted a clenched fist toward the bowman and uttered, *"Fete!"* the Elvish word for fire, the command word for his magical ring.

A line of flames shot out from Cadderly's hand, seeking his attacker, immolating the man in a burning shroud.

With a mental shriek of revulsion, Cadderly ended the fire. He spun again, his walking stick leading, and got a solid hit on the swordsman. He didn't really care how badly he'd hurt the man, all he wanted was to get the man out of his way, to clear the path to the axe-wielder who had sent Danica away.

Again, inexperience had led Cadderly to an unwise single-mindedness. Before he ever got near to the axe-wielder, strong hands grabbed at his shoulders and drove him to the side railing.

Q

Ivan threw the heavy door aside, meaning to charge right to the stairs. A gruesome sight off to the side slowed him, though, for just a moment, and when he resumed his charge, his fury had heightened tenfold.

Pikel, too, thought to head straight for the stairs. "Uh-oh," he mumbled and he ran to the right, for the cover of the room's bar instead, for several dark shapes knelt in formation on and above that staircase, all holding deadly crossbows.

Pikel dived over the long bar, coming to a crashing halt along the narrow walkway behind, up against kegs of ale. To the dwarf's surprise, he was not alone, and he just managed to convince Fredegar Harriman that he was not an enemy a heartbeat before the terrified innkeeper bonked him over the head with a full bottle of elven brandy.

A quarrel ricocheted off the blade of Ivan's axe, and another struck the dwarf on the head, stunning him, though his fine helmet managed to deflect the thing up between the deer antlers. Perhaps that particular quarrel knocked some sense into the thick-headed dwarf, for Ivan wisely cut to the side, skidding in around the staircase and scrambling for cover underneath it. He slammed hard into one of the structure's supports as he rushed in, getting all tangled up with it. By the time the dwarf figured out that it was just an ordinary wooden pillar and not some lurking enemy, he had battered it to pieces.

Ivan blushed, thinking himself incredibly foolish. Then he looked around, noticing the other four supports—one more on that side, two on the opposite side and one in the middle—and a wide and wicked grin spread over his face.

Q

Danica caught hold of the feeble trim along Cadderly's balcony, and her strong hands would not let go, despite the nagging weight of the assassin still clutching at her waist.

The woman wriggled and squirmed, freed up one foot, and slapped it back and forth across the stubborn man's face.

Only a dozen feet from the ground, the attacker wisely let go, dropping heavily but unharmed to the cobblestones.

Danica's thoughts of climbing back up to join Cadderly on the balcony lasted only a moment, until the trim split away on one end from the main frame, sending Danica on a swinging ride around the corner of the balcony.

She kicked out and leaped before the trim broke away all together, latching on to the sill of a window near the building's corner, opposite from where she'd left Cadderly. Unable to break her momentum, Danica was forced to leap out again, farther from the fight, but landing with a more solid handhold and foothold on a gutter running up the side of the building, just around the corner.

By the time she managed to peek around, the balcony was crowded with black-and-silver-outfitted assassins. She didn't see Cadderly at first amid that throng and couldn't pause long enough to sort him out, for one crossbowman put her immediately in his sights, and two other assassins came over the rail, walking the ledge toward the gutter.

Danica scrambled the ten feet or so to the rooftop. Only as she pulled herself over did she realize that she had somehow badly twisted her knee, probably in the struggle over the railing.

"Cadderly," she mumbled over and over. She was reminded vividly of when she had left the young priest to join the fray in Shilmista, when she had been forced to trust Cadderly to take care of himself.

She started across the roof, thinking to go right above the balcony and leap down upon the enemy. She turned, though, hearing the gutter groan under the weight of a pursuer.

"Do come up," Danica muttered, thinking to clobber the fool as soon as he poked his head over the roof's edge. It never occurred to her that the well-prepared band might already have someone planted on the roof.

She heard the crossbow click behind her.

"A valiant fight, Lady Maupoissant," said a baritone voice at her back, "but a futile effort against the skill of the Night Masks."

Ҫ

Cadderly's walking stick flew away when he collided with the railing. He hardly kept his bearings as he spun over, but did manage to loop one arm around the railing.

It seemed a wasted effort, though, for the assassin clubbed at that arm mercilessly, determined to drop the young priest over the side.

Cadderly's first instinct told him to just drop—the fall probably wouldn't kill him. He realized, though, that another assassin loomed below, and he would be easy prey before he ever recovered from the fall.

None of it seemed to matter when the second Night Mask, the axe-wielder, joined the first at the railing above him.

"Farewell, young priest," the man said, lifting his cruel weapon to split Cadderly's head wide.

Cadderly tried to utter a magical command at that man, but he could do no more than groan as the club connected again against his already wounded shoulder.

The young priest glanced around desperately, only a brief moment left open to him. He saw a tiny ledge along the building a few feet away, behind him, and for some reason he didn't understand a memory of Percival, the white squirrel, skittering happily and easily along ledges at least that thin back at the Edificant Library, came to him.

There was no way any man could make that leap to the ledge, as twisted as Cadderly was. Yet somehow, he was there. Hand over hand, foot over foot, the young priest ran along the ledge.

"Get him!" he heard one of the frustrated and

astonished assassins yell from behind, and the other called for a crossbow.

Cadderly came up fast on the corner, with no intention of turning aside. The alley was only about eight feet wide at that point, but the only apparent handhold on the building across the way was several feet higher than his present perch. By the time Cadderly registered that fact in the still-dim morning light, though, it was too late for him to alter his course.

He leaped, soared, impossibly high and impossibly far. Hardly slowing, he found himself scrambling easily up the side of the other building, disappearing over the top before any crossbowman back on the balcony could get a shot at him.

C

Pikel peeked up over the bar to see one of the assassins bearing down on him, the other two leaning over the far side of the staircase, trying to get a shot at Ivan.

The green-bearded dwarf hopped up, club in hand, ready to meet the challenge.

"Here," came Fredegar's call behind him. Pikel glanced back to see the brandy bottle, stuffed with a burning rag, coming for him.

"Oo oi!" Pikel cried, too startled to catch it, as Fredegar had intended. The dwarf did get a hand off his club fast enough to tap the bottle over him, though, and he spun around and slammed the slow-moving missile with his club, creating a small fireball and showering the approaching assassin with glass shards and flaming liquid.

"Oo oi!" Pikel squealed again, happily, as the man fell

away to the floor and rolled around, desperate to get the stubborn flames off his robes.

When the assassin finally got back up, he ran screaming for the door, having no more heart for the fight.

The dwarf hopped up on the bar then fell back again as the bowmen on the stairs took note of him.

Q

Cunning Ivan's only mistake was that he saved the center support for last. Not until he knocked it out, with a single powerful swipe of his axe, did the grinning dwarf realize that he was standing directly under the heavy structure.

The stairs, and the two surprised assassins standing on them, came tumbling down.

Only one of the men had regained his feet when Ivan finally managed to burst through the pile of broken wood. The dwarf came up with a roar and tried to swing his axe, only to find its head caught fast on a random beam.

The assassin, bruised but not too hurt, grinned at him and pulled out a short sword.

Ivan tugged mightily, and the axe pulled free, coming across so swiftly that neither the dwarf nor the assassin even realized its movement as it struck the assailant, cutting cleanly through the man's belly.

"Bet that hurt," Ivan mumbled with a helpless, almost embarrassed shrug.

Q

Again Pikel hopped up on the bar, and again he reconsidered, seeing a pair of dark shapes rush out of Cadderly's room into the aisle above, right to the lip of the fallen stairway.

The frustrated dwarf groaned loudly—those two also carried the wretched crossbows.

Pikel realized that he wasn't their target, but he knew, too, that Ivan, standing, unsuspecting, right below the ledge, was.

SIXTEEN

SCRAMBLE

Night Masks.

The words stung Danica's heart as surely as could the crossbow bolt aimed her way. Night Masks: the guild that had killed her parents, the wretched assassins of Westgate, the city in which Danica had been raised. The questions that rushed into the young woman's mind—Had they come for her? Were they working for the same enemy that had sent Barjin to the Edificant Library and the invading army into Shilmista?—were no match for the bile, the sheer rage, that climbed up her throat.

Slowly, she turned to face her adversary, locking his gaze with her own. He was a curious sight, bleeding in several places, leaning to one side, and struggling to draw breath. Half his face swelled in a grotesque purple bruise and wooden splinters stuck from his hair, face, and arms. And for some reason, the man was barefoot.

"I will not ask for a reprieve," the assassin slurred, waving the weapon. "Not after the dwarves . . ." He shook away the frightening memory of the fight at the other inn, dropping several splinters to the roof with the effort.

"You shall be offered none," Danica assured, barely able to spit the words through gritted teeth. A growl escaped her lips as she dived to the roof and rolled.

The crossbow fired and Danica felt something thud against her side, though she was too enraged to know the seriousness of the wound or even to realize the pain. She came up near where the man had been, to find that he had taken flight.

Danica was on him in a few strides. He spun to face her, and she leaped into him, grabbing him tightly. Her knee moved repeatedly, each blow connecting with the man's groin.

She hit him a dozen times, grabbed his hair and ears and yanked his head back from her then pulled it forward and drove her forehead in to meet it, splattering the man's nose and knocking out several teeth. Danica kneed him a dozen more times and butted him again. Her fingers raked the beaten man's face, and she drove one finger right through his eye.

Night Masks!

Danica jumped back from the doomed man, spinning a circle kick that snapped his head to the side and forced him into a series of stumbling steps. Somehow he didn't fall down, though he was hardly conscious of his surroundings.

Danica leaped high behind him, lay herself flat out, planted both feet on the man's back, and sent him in a running takeoff over the roof's edge.

She pulled herself back to her feet and saw that two men had gained the roof by the gutter, though neither had summoned the courage to charge the furious woman.

Too many emotions assaulted the wounded and weary monk. The appearance of the assassins, the knowledge that they were Night Masks, sent her mind careening down a hundred corridors of distant memories—and more recent memories, too, like the strange dream of the previous night, when she had, for a moment, entered the consciousness of some mysterious attacker.

And what had happened to Cadderly? Danica's fear multiplied when she learned the identity of the killers. Had the Night Masks again taken the love from Danica's life?

She fled, her eyes filled with tears, her arm and side throbbing. Up the sloping rooftops, across the uneven angles, leaping the small gaps, the young monk ran.

The two killers followed her every step.

Q

Ivan looked down, an inch to the side, to the neat hole the crossbow quarrel had drilled into the lumber pile. Slowly, the dwarf lifted his gaze to the men standing ten feet above him. One leaned over the broken ledge, smiling grimly, with a cocked crossbow pointed Ivan's way.

Sheer desperation shoved new heights of insight into the mind of Pikel Bouldershoulder. Ivan—his brother!—was about to die. Pikel's eyes darted around, taking in a surrealistic view of the grim scene.

Bar . . . pile . . . dead man—guts, yech . . . struggling men . . . Ivan . . . precipice . . . crossbowman . . . chandelier . . .

Chandelier? A chandelier above the leaning man.

They had to bring the thing down to light the candles, Pikel reasoned. The dwarf whipped his head around, his gaze coming to rest on the crank, conveniently located at the back of the bar.

The assassin standing over Ivan paused long enough to wave good-bye to the helpless dwarf.

Pikel could have just pulled the pin out of the crank to set the spindle spinning, but the time for finesse had passed. With a "Whoop!" to try to distract the cross-bowman a moment longer, the green-bearded dwarf hopped from the bar to the shelving along the wall, crashing aside scores of mugs and bottles, the shelves breaking away under his weight.

"Ooooooo!" he wailed as he slammed his club against the crank.

Spindle and all broke out from the wall, hanging stubbornly by a single peg. Pikel, on his knees beside Fredegar, looked at it as though it had tricked him, but then, with a loud popping noise, the last peg gave and the whole assembly rocketed up into the air.

"What?" the confused crossbowman asked.

His companion behind him gasped.

The chandelier took the crossbowman on the shoulder, spinning him over the precipice.

He crashed into the wood pile beside Ivan, the stunned dwarf nodding, stupefied. As though the gods had decided to play some macabre joke, Ivan heard the distinctive *click* a moment later as the crushed man's crossbow, pressed harmlessly between the man and the broken stairs, fired.

"Hee hee hee," chuckled Pikel, standing again to watch the spectacle. He forgot that the spindle above him was fast unwinding, and dropping, and he was back to his knees when it ricocheted off his skull.

"Oooo."

"Set the rope!" he heard Ivan cry, and shaking away his dizziness, Pikel wrapped the rope in his arms.

Ivan grasped his axe handle in his teeth—not an easy thing to do!—and started up. He noticed that the remaining assassin in the pile behind him was getting to his feet, so he jumped back down to the raised end of a plank lying between him and the man. Ivan's end snapped down and the end under the crawling assassin went up, slamming the man under his chin. He groaned and rolled away, grabbing at his shattered jawbone.

That done, Ivan leaped up again, stubby arms pulling him up the rope to the level of the other crossbowman. To the side, he noticed that Pikel was similarly climbing.

Ivan rushed on, finally getting his head high enough so that he could see the other man.

It was not a pleasant sight.

For the second time in the last few moments, Ivan Bouldershoulder stared into the wrong end of a readied crossbow.

Pikel made the ledge and let go of the rope, realizing only then that he had not secured it below him.

Ivan dropped like a stone. The crossbow fired, harmlessly high. And the stubborn assassin on the first level, his jaw grotesquely shattered, realized his folly in going to the rope under the climbing dwarf.

As he sat atop the man, atop the pile of broken stairs, Ivan, for perhaps the first time, thought it was not such a bad thing to have a scatterbrained brother.

C

Still on all fours, the young priest skittered fast and sure-footed along the edge of the adjoining building. His spindle-disks clung tightly to his hand, hanging to the end of their cord and bouncing along the building's side. Cadderly hardly noticed them, and had no time to stop and replace them in any event. Nor did the young priest note that the pain in his wounded thigh was no more.

He spotted Danica, running weakly away from him, limping, and saw the two black-robed killers in pursuit, gaining on the stumbling woman with every stride.

Cadderly came up on the other side of the building, where the alley opened perpendicularly to a wide lane of craft stores called Market Square. Two merchants, up at dawn to prepare for the coming day, spotted the young priest and stared, then pointed up and called out something that Cadderly didn't bother to decipher.

Too enraged to think of his movements, Cadderly slipped headfirst over the side of the building, going down hand over hand. A banner had been strung along thick ropes across the alley as a sign for one of the craftsmen's shops.

Hand over hand, foot over foot, Cadderly ran across the tightrope. He heard a shout of disbelief from the street below, but didn't even realize that it was aimed his way. Back on the many-angled roof of the Dragon's Codpiece, the young priest charged off, nothing but Danica in his thoughts.

He spotted her a moment later—she had leaped across the narrow alley to the next building—stumbling over the crest of a dormer, going headlong. The two men went over right behind her.

"No!" the young priest tried to call out, but his word came out as a strange, squealing sound.

Never slowing, his eyes focused straight ahead, Cadderly flew over the short alley expanse.

One of the black-robed killers emerged from the place Danica had gone, in full flight. Cadderly feared he was too late.

Ç

The remaining man in the corridor darted into Cadderly's room, brushing aside the smoke and stench of charred flesh that blocked the doorway.

Pikel grabbed the rope again, and Ivan began to climb, his efforts aided by his brother's hauling movements toward Cadderly's door.

Pikel drove on, much relieved when he saw Ivan's stubby hand come over the lip of the hallway. But then four shapes emerged from Cadderly's room.

Pikel instinctively let go of the rope. He winced at Ivan's diminishing wail and the dull thump as his brother landed again on the assassin at the bottom of the rope. Pikel couldn't worry about it, though, not with four killers just a few strides away.

But the assassins were no longer interested in battle. Seeing the stairs gone, they sought other avenues of escape. One grabbed the rope and without even testing to see if it was secured, leaped over the precipice. The others ran the other way down the hall, scrambling over the railing wherever they found high spots—tables mostly—where they could get down.

Pikel thought to give chase, but he paused when

he heard a door creak open, and heard chanting. The next thing the green-bearded dwarf knew, he was lying several feet from where he had been standing, a sharp burning pain in one side, and his shocked hair wildly dancing on end.

Me brudder. The words cried out in Pikel's mind over and over, a litany against the swirling dizziness, a reminder that he could not remain up there, lying helplessly on the floor.

Q

Ivan heard the man land beside him, and he felt the other one squirming slowly beneath him. The dwarf opened one heavy eyelid to see the assassin standing over him, sword in hand.

The thrust came before the dwarf could react, and Ivan thought he was dead, but the assassin struck low, beneath Ivan.

Ivan didn't question his luck. He struggled to a sitting position, trying to locate his axe, or anything else he might use against the standing killer.

Too late. The assassin's sword came up again.

"Me brudder!" Pikel cried as he flew over the precipice.

The assassin dived away, rolled to his feet, and followed his companions out the door.

Pikel hit Ivan full force.

Ivan groaned as he waited patiently—he had no choice in the matter—for Pikel to crawl off him.

"If ye're looking for thanks, keep looking," Ivan grumbled.

Q

Cadderly was too late in getting to the scene—for the sake of the other assassin.

The young priest relaxed as soon as he crested the steep roof. Danica was below him, in a valley between several gables. The remaining assassin was there, too, kneeling before Danica, his arms defenselessly by his sides and his head snapping to one side then the other, blood and sweat flying wide, as Danica landed blow after blow to his face.

"He's dead," Cadderly remarked when he got beside the young monk.

Danica, sobbing, slammed the man again, the shattered cartilage of his facial bones crackling under the blow.

"He's dead!" Cadderly said more emphatically, though he kept his tone calm and unassuming.

Danica spun, her face contorted with a mixture of rage and sorrow, and fell into his arms. Cadderly wrapped his arms around her, and Danica jumped back, staring at the young priest in disbelief.

"Wh-what—?" she stammered, stepping back even farther, and Cadderly, noticing the change for the first time, had no answers for her.

His arms and legs, covered in white fur, had become those of a squirrel.

SEVENTEEN

MENTOR

Q

"Turn it back," Danica pleaded, her voice edged in desperation, her hands trembling at her sides.

Cadderly stared, helpless, at his squirrel-like limbs. He hadn't the slightest idea how to begin to reverse the process, and he admitted as much to himself and to Danica.

Danica moved to him, or tried to, until the pain in her side sent her lurching over. She grasped at the bloody wound in her abdomen just above her hip, and slumped to one knee.

Stubbornly, Danica got back to her feet, one hand held out in front of her to keep her concerned lover at bay.

"That must be tended," Cadderly pleaded.

"With squirrel arms?" Danica's retort stung the young priest more than she had intended. "Turn your arms and legs back to human, Cadderly. I beg you."

Cadderly stared long and hard at his limbs, feeling deceived, feeling as though his god—or the Weave— had led him astray. Danica stood before him, needing him, and he, with the limbs of a rodent, could do nothing for her.

The young priest searched his memory, let page after page of *The Tome of Universal Harmony* flip through his thoughts in rapid succession. Nothing explained the transformation he'd somehow brought upon himself.

But while Cadderly found no clear answers, he did begin that distant harmony, that sweet, inspiring song where all the mysteries of existence drifted past him, waiting to be grasped and deciphered. The song rang out a single word to the young priest, the name of the one person who might help him make sense of it all.

"Pertelope?" Cadderly asked no one in particular.

Danica, still grimacing, stared at him.

"Pertelope," he said again, more firmly. He turned his gaze to Danica, his breath coming in short gasps. "She knows."

"She knows what?" the young woman asked, wincing with every word.

"She knows," was all Cadderly could answer, for in truth, he didn't really know what information the headmistress might have for him. He sensed only that the song was not lying to him, nor was it leading him astray.

"I must go to her."

"But she's at the library," Danica argued. "It will take you three—"

Cadderly stopped her with an outstretched palm. He closed his mind to the stimuli around him and focused on the song again, felt it flow across the miles, calling him to step into it. Cadderly fell in with the tune, let it carry him along. The world became a dreamscape, surreal, unreal. He saw the gates of Carradoon and the western road leading into higher ground. Mountain passes zipped along beneath his consciousness then he saw the library fast approaching, came upon the ivy-strewn walls, and passed right through them . . . to Pertelope's room.

Cadderly recognized the tapestry on the back wall, to the side of the bed, the same one he had stolen so that Ivan could use it in making a replica of the drow crossbow.

"I have been waiting for you to come to me," he heard Pertelope say. The image of the room shifted and there sat the headmistress on the edge of her bed, dressed as always in her long-sleeved, high-necked black gown. Her eyes widened as she regarded the presence, and Cadderly understood that she saw him, with his rodent limbs, though he had left his corporeal form far behind.

"Help me," he pleaded.

Pertelope's comforting smile fell over him warmly.

"You have found *Affinity,*" the headmistress explained, "a powerful practice, and not without its dangers."

Cadderly had no idea what Pertelope was talking about.

Affinity? He had never heard the word used in such a way.

"The song is playing for you," Pertelope remarked, "often without your bidding." Cadderly's face revealed how startled he was.

"I knew it would," Pertelope continued. "When I gave you *The Tome of Universal Harmony*, I knew the song would begin to play in your mind, and I knew that you would soon find the means to decipher the mysteries hidden within its notes."

"I have not," Cadderly protested. "I mean, things are happening around me, and to me—" he looked helplessly at his own limbs, translucent replicas of his corporeal form—"but they are not of my doing, not of my control."

"Of course they are," Pertelope replied, drawing his attention away from his polymorphed limbs. "The book is the conduit to the magical energy bestowed through the power of Deneir. You summon and guide that energy. It comes to your call and bends to your will."

Cadderly looked down, helpless and doubting, at his deformed body. He knew Pertelope could see his problem, and wondered if Danica could as well, back on the rooftop in Carradoon. Those squirrel limbs flew in the face of what the headmistress was saying, for if Cadderly could control the magic, as Pertelope insisted, then why had he remained half a rodent?

"You have not learned to control your power," the headmistress said to him, as though she'd read his mind, "but you're still a novice, after all, untrained but with magnificent powers at your fingertips."

"Powers . . . from Deneir?" Cadderly asked.

"Of course," answered Pertelope coyly, as though Cadderly's next remark would come as no shock whatsoever to her.

"Why would Deneir grant me such powers?" the young priest asked. "What have I done to warrant such a gift?"

Pertelope laughed at him. "You are his disciple."

"I am not!" Cadderly said, and he gave a horrified expression, realizing that he had offered that admission to a headmistress of his order.

Again, Pertelope only laughed. "You are, Cadderly," she said. "You are a true disciple of our god, and of Oghma, as well. Do not measure fealty in terms of rituals and attendance to duties. Measure it by what lies in your heart, by your morals and your love. You are a scholar, in all your inquisitive mind and in all your heart—a blessed scholar. That is the measure of fealty to Deneir."

"Not according to Avery," Cadderly argued. "How often has he threatened to throw me out of the order for my failings in those rituals you dismiss so quickly?"

"He couldn't throw you out of any order," Pertelope replied. "One cannot be 'thrown out' of a religious calling."

"Religious calling?" Cadderly replied. "If that's what you call it then I fear I was never in the order to begin with. I have no calling."

"That's absurd," replied Pertelope. "You're as attuned with the precepts of Deneir as any person I have ever met. That, my young priest, is what constitutes a religious calling. Do you doubt the powers you've begun to unlock?"

"Not the powers," Cadderly replied with typical stubbornness, "but their source."

"It is Deneir."

"So you say," answered Cadderly, "and so you are free to believe."

"You will too, in time. You are a priest of Deneir, a follower of a god who demands independence, the exercise of free will, and a reliance on intellect," Pertelope continued, again as though she had read Cadderly's mind. He had to wonder if Pertelope hadn't played through the same conversation herself, many years ago.

"You are *supposed* to question—to question everything, even the nature of the gods and the purpose of being alive," Pertelope continued, her hazel eyes taking on a faraway, mystical look. "If you would follow blindly from ritual to ritual, you would be no better than the cattle and sheep that dot the fields around Carradoon.

"Deneir doesn't want that," Pertelope went on, calmly, comfortingly, and looking directly back at the frightened young priest. "He is a god for artists and poets, free-thinkers all, else their work would be no more than replicas of what others have deemed ideal. The question, Cadderly, is stronger than the answer. It's what drives growth—growth toward the wisdom of Deneir."

Somewhere deep inside, Cadderly prayed that Pertelope was speaking truthfully, that the apparent wisdom of her words wasn't just the feeble hope of one as confused and desperate as he.

"You have been chosen," Pertelope went on, bringing the conversation back to more concrete terms. "You hear the song and will come, over time, to decipher more and more of its notes, to better understand your place in this confusing experience we call life."

"I am a wizard."

"No!" It was the first time the headmistress had appeared angry during the conversation, and Cadderly, wisely, didn't immediately reply. "Your magical gifts are priestly in nature," Pertelope asserted. "Have you cast anything but spells you've witnessed other priests cast?"

Cadderly thought long and hard. In truth, everything magical he had done in some way, at least, replicated clerical spells. Even the so-called "affinity" wasn't so different from the shapechanging abilities exhibited by the druids who'd been caught up in the chaos curse. But still, his powers were different, Cadderly knew it somehow.

"I do not pray for these spells," he argued. "I don't get out of bed in the morning with the notion that I should be able to create light this day, or that I will find need to turn my arms into a squirrel's paws. Nor do I pray to Deneir, at any time."

"You read the book," Pertelope replied. "That is your prayer. As far as selecting spells and memorizing their particular chants and inflections, you have no need. You hear the song, Cadderly. You are one of the Chosen, one of the few. I had suspected that fact for many years, and came to understand just a few tendays ago that you would take my place."

"What are you talking about?" Cadderly asked, his near panic only intensified by the fact that Pertelope, as she spoke, had begun to unbutton her long gown. Cadderly gaped in amazement as the headmistress peeled the garment off, revealing a featureless torso covered by skin that resembled the hide of a shark, covered not with skin, but with sharp pentacles.

"I was raised from childhood on the Sword Coast," the headmistress began wearily, "near the sea. My father was a fisherman, and often I would go out with him to tend the nets. You see, I found affinity with the shark, as you have with squirrels—with Percival in particular. I came to marvel at their graceful movements, at the perfection of that oft-maligned creature.

"I already explained to you that affinity is a practice that is not without its dangers," Pertelope went on, giving a small, ironic chuckle. "You see, I too fell prey to the chaos curse. Under its influences, I assumed my affinity with no regard for safety, no practical restraints at all."

Cadderly winced to think that that wonderful woman, always a dear friend to him, had suffered from the curse that he had brought upon the library. But there was no malice, no blame, edging Pertelope's voice as she continued.

"The change I enacted is permanent," she said, rubbing a hand along her arm, the denticles drawing several lines of blood on her human palm. "It is painful, too, for my whole body is part human and part fish. The very air is poison to me, as would be the waters of the wide sea. I have no place left in this world, my friend. I am dying."

"No!"

"Yes," Pertelope replied. "I am not young, you know, and have labored long on this confusing path we call life. The curse killed me, do not doubt, but I have struggled to hang on for the very purpose that is before me this day. You, Cadderly, are my successor."

"I do not accept it."

"You cannot avoid it," answered the headmistress. "Once begun, the song never ends. Never."

The word sounded like the bang of a drum to Cadderly, suddenly terrified of what horrors he may have unlocked in the pages of that awful book.

"You will come to know the limitations of your powers," Pertelope went on. "And there are indeed limitations." She looked at her own destroyed arms as she spoke, making her point all too clear. "You are not invincible. You are not all-powerful. You are not a god."

"I never said—"

"Humility will be your preservation," Pertelope interrupted. "Test the powers, Cadderly, but test them with respect. They will drain you and take a bit of you with them whenever you summon them. Exhaustion is your enemy, and know that enacting magic will inevitably weary the spellcaster. But know, too, that if Deneir has chosen you, he will demand of you."

Pertelope smiled warmly, revealing her confidence that Cadderly would be up to meeting the challenge.

No reciprocal smile found its way to Cadderly's face.

Q

"Do you plan on going somewhere?" Ghost whispered to Bogo Rath, seeing the young wizard in the upstairs hall of the Dragon's Codpiece with a sack in hand. The assassin stepped out of Cadderly's room and motioned for Bogo to follow him to his own room.

"The city guard has been called," the wizard explained. "They will swarm all over this place."

"And find what?" Ghost replied with a snicker, thinking it an ironic statement, given that he had just deposited Brennan's body in Cadderly's room. "Certainly there's nothing here to implicate either one of us."

"I hit the green-bearded dwarf with a lightning bolt," Bogo admitted.

"He didn't see you," Ghost retorted. "If he had, you would be dead. Both he and his brother are up and about, downstairs with Fredegar. They would have come back for you long before this if the stupid dwarf suspected you had launched that magic."

Bogo relaxed a bit. "Did Cadderly and Danica get away?"

Ghost shrugged, unable to answer. He had seen little beyond the carnage left in the wake of the attack. "Temporarily, perhaps," he answered at length, and with as much conviction as he could muster. "But the Night Masks have been set on the trail now. They will not stop until the young priest is dead."

"Then I am free to return to Castle Trinity," Bogo reasoned.

"If you try to leave now, you will invite only suspicion," Ghost replied. "And if Cadderly has managed to elude the assassins, he will likely return here. This is still the best seat at the game, for those who have the courage to play to the end."

The last words sounded clearly like a threat.

"Aid the city guard in their investigation," Ghost continued, a sudden ironic smile crossing his features. He was the artist, he privately reminded himself, already weaving new webs of intrigue. "Tell them you possess some knowledge of magic, and that you believe a bolt of lightning was set off in the upstairs corridor. When the dwarf confirms your story, you will be viewed in a favorable light."

Bogo eyed the assassin doubtfully, even more so when he remembered that Kierkan Rufo was still about, carrying information that could certainly damn him.

"What is it?" Ghost asked, seeing Bogo's mounting concern.

"Rufo."

Ghost chuckled darkly. "He can say nothing without implicating himself. And he, by all of your descriptions, is too much a coward to do that."

"True enough," Bogo admitted, "but I'm still not convinced of the wisdom of remaining at the inn. We've underestimated Cadderly and his friends, it would seem."

"Perhaps," Ghost said in reluctant agreement, "but don't complicate the error by overestimating them now. For all we know, Cadderly might lie dead in an alley even now."

Bogo hesitated then nodded.

"Be gone," Ghost commanded. "Go back to your room, or to aid in the investigation, but say nothing to Rufo. Better that the cowardly priest be left alone to stew in his guilt and terror."

Again Bogo nodded and was gone.

Ghost's confidence disappeared as soon as he was alone. It had been a complicated visit to Carradoon, and had not been a clean kill. Even if Cadderly was dead, the toll had been horrendous, with more than half of the Night Masks killed.

Ghost was no longer sure that remaining at the Dragon's Codpiece would bode well for either himself or Bogo, but he feared the consequences of trying to slip away with the city guard, and two rambunctious dwarves, snooping around. He moved to his door and cracked it open an inch, curious to see what might be transpiring outside.

He watched carefully for Rufo, thinking that if the treacherous priest made any dangerous moves, he might have to kill him.

No, it hadn't been without complications, but that

was part of the fun of it all, wasn't it? It was a new challenge for the artist, an intricate landscape for the filling canvas.

Ghost smiled wickedly, taking comfort in the fact that he wasn't in any personal danger—not while he had the *Ghearufu,* and had Vander as a waiting and helpless host on the outskirts of town.

Q

Cadderly was relieved to see Danica still up and conscious when he rejoined his corporeal form on the rooftop beside the Dragon's Codpiece. The young woman's face remained contorted in pain. A crossbow quarrel protruded from her right side, hanging from skin and tunic and surrounded by a widening crimson stain.

Cadderly didn't immediately go to her. He closed his eyes and forced the song back into his thoughts. The notes drifted past until Cadderly recalled that part of the song, that page in the tome, he had been hearing back on the balcony when he'd enacted the change to squirrel form.

Danica whispered to him softly, sounding more concerned for his own safety than for her own. With some effort, Cadderly pushed her words away and concentrated on the music. His mouth moved in silent prayer, and when he at last opened his eyes, Danica was straining to smile and his arms and legs were back to normal.

"You found your answers," the young woman remarked.

"Along with more questions," Cadderly replied.

He pulled his spindle-disks from their tight hold on

his finger and tucked them away then moved beside his love.

"You were speaking," Danica said to him, "but not to me. It sounded like half of a conversation, the other half . . ."

"Was with Pertelope," Cadderly explained. "I, or at least my consciousness, was back in the library." He hardly noticed Danica's stare, more interested in her sorely wounded side.

When he recalled the song once more, it sounded more distant to him, required more effort to get near it. Pertelope's warnings of exhaustion welled up in him, but he pushed his mounting fears away. Danica's health was more important.

Cadderly focused on the dangling quarrel as much as on the wound it had caused. His thoughts were as much on destruction as on healing, and his chant was uttered through gritted teeth.

Danica grunted and winced. Black smoke wafted from her wound. Soon a small cloud of the stuff covered her side.

The quarrel was his enemy, was Danica's enemy, Cadderly determined. Poor Danica, dear Danica.

When the smoke dissipated, gone too were the crossbow quarrel and the wound.

Danica straightened and shrugged, not knowing how she could possibly thank Cadderly for what he had done.

"Are you injured?" she asked, concerned.

Cadderly shook his head and took her arm. "We must be gone," he said, his tone absent, as though he was talking more to himself than to Danica. "We must go and sit together in private, and try to sort through the turns fate has shown us."

He cocked his head, turned his attention to the growing tumult in the awakening lanes around the Dragon's Codpiece, particularly to the clip-clap of many hooves echoing from every direction.

"The city guard is about," Danica replied. "They will require information."

Cadderly continued to pull her along.

"We have nowhere to go," Danica argued as they neared the building's back edge, many soldiers coming into sight along Market Square.

Cadderly wasn't listening. His eyes were closed again and he was deep in song.

Danica's eyes widened one more time as she felt herself become something less than substantial. Somehow Cadderly kept his grip on her arm and together they simply blew away, off the rooftop, riding the currents of the wind.

Q

Bogo Rath slipped out of the Dragon's Codpiece a short while later, rushing briskly past the dwarves and the bereaved innkeeper in the hearth room. After brief consideration, the frightened young wizard decided that Ghost's presumptions were not worth risking his life over, and he decided, too, that departing the inn after such tragedy wouldn't necessarily raise suspicions.

The only thing the city guardsman asked of him as he passed through the hole where the front door had been was that he remain in town.

Bogo nodded and pointed to an inn a few doors farther up Lakeview Street, though the wizard had no intention of staying around for very long. He would go to the inn and get a room, but would remain in

Carradoon only until he had studied the spells that would allow him to leave quickly and without the possibility of being stopped.

EIGHTEEN

REFLECTIONS ON THE WATER

The morning light was still new, and the mist had not yet cleared from the waters of Impresk Lake. The great three-arched bridge connecting the mainland to Carradoon's island district loomed a ghostly gray above Cadderly and Danica as they drifted in a small rowboat. The pair was quiet with their thoughts and the lap of the gentle waves against the prow.

The weather fit Cadderly's grim mood. He had killed a man, burned him to a blackened coal, and had knocked another from the balcony, leaving him for dead as well. Cadderly knew he'd had no choice, but he couldn't easily dismiss the guilt. Whatever the reasons, he had killed a human being—again.

He tried hard not to think of the man's family, children perhaps, waiting for a father that would never return.

Cadderly took up the oars and gave a single stroke, reversing the drift and pushing the boat farther out from the imposing bridge. He let the oars hang in the water and turned to face Danica.

"Night Masks," Danica muttered grimly.

Cadderly looked at her. The words meant little to him.

"A guild of assassins from the city of Westgate," Danica explained. "They're among the deadliest killers in all of Faerûn. We were fortunate to escape them, and I now believe I've escaped them twice."

Cadderly's expression showed that he still didn't understand.

"On our journey down from the library," Danica continued, "the dwarves and I were attacked by a band of men we thought were bandits."

"Many bandits have been reported on the roads during these troubled times," Cadderly remarked.

Danica shook her head, obviously certain there was a connection between the attack on the road and the one in Cadderly's room.

"Why would an assassins guild from Westgate come after us?" asked Cadderly.

"Us?" echoed Danica. "No, they are after me, I fear. It was the Night Masks who killed my parents, years ago. Now they have come to finish the job."

Cadderly didn't believe her. He sensed that—if Danica's theory about the identity of the killers was correct—there was more at work than the completion of some decade-old vendetta. Cadderly contemplated his own experiences of the last few days, thought of his meeting with Rufo in the hearth room and the presence of the invisible wizard. And what had happened, he wondered, back in his own room that night?

He said to Danica, "I found you on the floor, terrified. Tell me about your dream."

"I don't remember much," Danica admitted, and by

her tone she didn't see the point of his question. Cadderly was determined, though. He thought for a moment then took out his crystal-centered spindle-disks.

He held them up in front of Danica's eyes and set them spinning. Even in the dim light, the crystals flickered. "Concentrate," Cadderly said. "Let the crystal into your mind. Please, do not use your meditative talents to block me now."

"What will this tell us?" Danica argued. "It was just a dream."

"Was it?"

Danica shrugged—it was a dream that contained references to the Night Masks, after all—and relaxed, focusing her gaze on the spindle-disks. Cadderly watched her intently then closed his eyes and thought of the sacred tome, heard the song playing the words to a simple spell of hypnosis.

Danica sank deeper, her shoulders visibly slumping, as Cadderly quietly chanted. His words became prying questions that Danica heard only subconsciously.

Cadderly, too, allowed the hypnosis to fall over him, used it to achieve complete empathy with Danica.

The questions rolled out of his mouth, though he was barely aware of them. And Danica answered, as much with her posture and her facial expressions as with mere words.

Danica blinked her eyes open, and Cadderly followed her lead. Neither of them knew how much time had passed, but Cadderly understood then, beyond any doubt, that Danica's nighttime experience had indeed been an important clue.

"It was not a dream," he announced.

Cadderly recalled what Danica had imparted to

him under the hypnosis: the sense of departure from a black sphere that the young priest knew represented her identity. The image reminded the young priest vividly of his own telepathic experiences with the imp Druzil and the wizard Dorigen.

Cadderly dropped a hand into his pocket to feel the amulet he had taken from Rufo in Shilmista Forest, an amulet that Druzil had given Rufo to improve telepathic contact between the two. With the amulet, Cadderly had been able to sense the imp's proximity, and he took comfort that it had not signaled Druzil's presence in many tendays, not since the battle in the forest.

But who then? he wondered.

Dorigen remained a distinct possibility.

"Possession?" he muttered, using the word as a catalyst for his thoughts.

Another image struck Cadderly then, an image of Nameless, the beggar on the road, and the horrible, shadowy shapes writhing atop his shoulders. He remembered, too, that night when Brennan had come to his room, projecting the same vile aura. Perhaps the song of Deneir had not lied to him. Perhaps the attempt on Danica was not his enemy's first try at possession.

Cadderly winced, remembering Fredegar's worries that young Brennan had not been seen since that night. He tried to recall clues as he took up the oars for another single stroke against the drift.

"What is it?" Danica asked. Her tone revealed her understanding that Cadderly's mind had unlocked some of the secrets.

"They have not come for you," the young priest answered with certainty, looking over his shoulder.

"They were here before you, around me, close to me." Cadderly exhaled deeply, fearing for Brennan and Nameless, and let his gaze drift across the water to the gray outline of the great bridge. "Too close."

Danica started to reply—something comforting, Cadderly knew—then she stopped and cocked her head.

Cadderly began to turn his whole body around, to fully face Danica, understanding that something was wrong and fearing that the young woman had come under some mental assault.

Danica spun, rocking the boat so suddenly that Cadderly, though he was seated near the center, almost went over the side.

"Stubborn!" Danica cried.

Her hand snapped in front of her just in time to grab the wrist of the man who had tried to drive a dagger into her back. Holding tight, Danica leaped to her feet, stretched her attacker's arm to the limit, and pulled him farther over the bow.

She gave her attacker's arm a quick, violent twist and brought her free hand over the back of his fingers, jerking the man's hand back toward his wrist.

Cadderly tried to get around in the rocking boat to go to Danica's aid, but all he wound up doing was stumbling over the boat's center seat and slamming himself on the side of the head with one of the oar handles.

He realized that the stumble was a good thing, though, as a knife soared up over the side of the boat and whipped across above his head. Reacting instinctively to the threat, Cadderly forearmed the oar, freeing it from its lock to tumble into the water near the unseen attacker.

The young scholar got his spindle-disks looped onto his finger. The boat rocked, and he looked back the other way, across the boat, to see still another assassin coming up over the side.

Danica held her balance easily in the rocking craft. She continued her vicious press on the captured man's hand, finally forcing him to release his dagger.

She wasn't done with him yet.

Danica's foot snapped out wide, coming back around the man's head and forcing his chin over the prow rail. Holding him tightly against the wood, Danica yanked his arm back out over the water. She locked his elbow so that he couldn't bend the limb and pressed straight down.

The man's eyes bulged as the bow pressed his throat up under his jaw.

Cadderly's off-balance throw soared lower than he'd hoped, but while he didn't get the man's head, he did get a few fingers—and the top plank of the boat. Wood splintered, the remaining oar flew off, and so did the assassin, clutching his blasted belly as he fell away into the lake.

Free of the weight, the boat rocked back so far that Cadderly feared its other side would dip under the water where the knife-thrower waited.

The young priest realized how vulnerable he was, and how vulnerable Danica was. They needed a distraction, something to allow them to get their bearings.

Water did come in over the broken side of the boat when it rocked back again, but Cadderly took no note of it, intent on the wounded man fumbling in the water with the floating oar. The shape of the oar caught the young priest's attention.

With one foot planted in the rocking boat, and with the choking man struggling frantically against her, Danica amazingly held her balance.

The struggling killer tried to come up over the side, but Danica jammed his arm down mightily, dislocating his shoulder.

The man couldn't even grimace at the obvious pain. His face went blank, weirdly serene. Danica understood. She brought her foot back around, released its hold on the man's head, and let him slip under the water.

Her sensibilities returned to her then, her sheer rage at the presence of the Night Masks temporarily sated by the reality of the kill. Danica realized for the first time that others were likely about.

She turned, and to her horror saw Cadderly disappear under the water in the grasp of a killer. Another boat, with several men in it, approached from behind. Danica didn't know if they were friend or foe—until a crossbow quarrel cut the air beside her face.

Instinctively, she dived to the floor of the boat. She knew she had to get to Cadderly, but how? If she went under the water, how could she hope to stop the approaching menace?

A scream to the side turned Danica around to peek over the broken plank. There floundered the wounded Night Mask, the one Cadderly had hit with his spindle-disks, fighting desperately to free himself from the clutches of a long, thick snake—a constrictor about the same size as one of the boat's oars.

The man somehow broke free and began swimming with all his might toward the approaching boat. The snake slithered off in pursuit, slipping under the water as it went.

Despite the peril, Danica couldn't help but smile. She knew that the appearance of the snake was no natural coincidence. Cadderly, with his mysterious powers, had struck again.

Danica got up to her knees. The other boat had come closer, and she could see a man in the prow leveling a crossbow her way. She jerked up as though she meant to stand then fell flat and heard the whistle of the high-flying bolt.

That bought her the time to get over the side, into the water after Cadderly. Before she moved out of the boat, though, the water churned and the Night Mask appeared, his face contorted in terror and the second snake, the second oar, wrapped around his shoulder and chest. He reached for the boat, and slapped at the water and the beast.

Then he was gone.

Again the water churned, a short distance to the side. Up came Cadderly, impossibly fast, his body breaking out of the water too high.

He stood on the water, still wearing his hat. The holy symbol set in its front glowed furiously.

Danica nearly laughed, too amazed to react any other way. Cadderly took in a few gulps of air, seeming more surprised than Danica.

He looked back toward the approaching boat—the swimming man had just about met it by then—and saw that the crossbowman was preparing another shot.

"Get in!" Danica cried, thinking Cadderly too vulnerable standing on the water out in the open.

Cadderly seemed not to hear her. He chanted, sang actually, and waved one hand slowly to and fro.

Danica looked back to the other boat, saw the man

leveling the crossbow—and saw Cadderly standing in the open, vulnerable.

She scrambled to the side, grabbed at a piece of broken wood floating in the small pool at the bottom of her boat. She came up throwing, skimming the wood sidelong so that it spun and swerved . . . and splashed harmlessly into the water a dozen feet to the side of the approaching craft.

But the crossbowman had flinched, had looked her way.

A sudden swell erupted in the calm lake, near where Danica's wood had disappeared. The water reared up and rolled, as if aimed at the enemy boat. The crossbowman had set his sights on Cadderly again when the wave collided against the side of his boat. The man lurched over the side and nearly lost his weapon.

Cadderly, still standing calmly, sung his soft song and waved his hand back and forth. Another swell rose and crashed against the enemy boat, turning it around so that it faced the bridge.

Cadderly smiled, and another swell turned the boat so that it faced the shore directly away from him.

"Come," Cadderly said to Danica, extending his hand. "Before they get their bearings."

Danica at first misunderstood, thinking that Cadderly wanted her to help him into the boat. He resisted her pull, though, beckoning her to go to him.

The assassin who had pulled Cadderly under the water bobbed to the surface, face down. The snake that had wrapped itself around him became an oar again at Cadderly's command and floated to the surface, a harmless piece of flotsam.

"Come," Cadderly reiterated, tugging Danica. She jumped onto him and wrapped herself around him.

Cadderly looked around then ran for the island. Danica watched over his shoulder, taking note that his footsteps hardly disturbed the water. The young priest left depressions in the water's surface, which quickly disappeared, as though he was running across soft ground.

Behind them, the enemy boat finally straightened and the crossbowman pulled the swimmer up over the side. The oar that had been chasing him bobbed up over the waves.

Danica kissed Cadderly on the neck and rested her weary head on his shoulder. The world had gone mad.

Cadderly came to the shore mumbling, thinking aloud. He kept chugging along but slowed under the weight of his burden when he hit more solid ground.

"Cadderly . . . ?"

"If those are professional assassins," he was saying, "we must assume they were hired by our enemies, by Dorigen, perhaps."

"Cadderly . . ."

"Someone has made the connection to us," Cadderly continued, undaunted. "Someone has determined that we are, or at least that I am, a threat to be eliminated."

"Cadderly . . ."

"But how long have they been hovering around me?" the young priest muttered. "Oh, Brennan, I pray I'm wrong."

"Cadderly!"

Cadderly looked right at Danica for the first time since he had stepped off the surface of the lake. "What?"

"You can put me down now," Danica replied.

She hit the ground running, grabbing Cadderly's wrist and tugging him along. They heard the enemy boat skid to shore through the brush behind them.

"Stubborn," Danica said, looking over her shoulder gravely.

Cadderly knew she wanted to turn and finish the fight.

"Not now," he begged. "We must get back to the inn."

"We may never get our enemies so out in the open again," Danica reasoned.

"I'm weary," Cadderly replied. And indeed, the young priest was. The song no longer played in his head, but had been replaced by a severe headache, the likes of which young Cadderly had never before experienced.

Danica nodded and sped on. They crashed through a hedgerow into the backyard of one of Carradoon's finer estates. Dogs began to bark from somewhere nearby, but Danica didn't veer from her path through another hedgerow and into another open yard.

Several people, older merchants and their spouses, stared at the fleeing couple as they passed.

"Get to cover and alert the city guard!" Cadderly called to them as he followed Danica past. "Thieves and murderers pursue us! Call out the city guard and send them to the bridge!"

The couple burst through another row of bushes, coming out onto a wide, flat cobblestone lane, running between lines of beautiful manor houses, between lines of staring, curious people.

Not a horse or wagon was seen on the bridge at

that early hour, something Cadderly took comfort in as he and Danica started across. The young priest would have hated to place anyone directly in the path of his deadly pursuers, and he knew by the continued bark of distant, unseen dogs that the Night Masks had not given up the chase, were only a few moments behind.

Cadderly skidded to a stop when they came to the high point in the first of the bridge's three arching supports. Danica started to question him, but was stopped by his conniving smile.

"Watch for the assassins," he said to her as he fell to his knees. He used his soaked cloak to trace a square on the stone of the wide bridge.

"The first page I ever looked at in Headmistress Pertelope's book always amazed me," he explained, not slowing in his work. "I knew it was a spell, similar to one I had seen in the book of Belisarius."

The square completed, two lines of wetness running parallel across the structure, Cadderly rose and led Danica a few dozen steps farther along.

Cadderly called up the song and began to chant, knowing the words intimately. He had to stop, though, and rub his temples to relieve the throbbing the casting caused.

They will drain you and take a bit of you with them whenever you summon them, Pertelope had warned him. *Exhaustion is your enemy . . .*

"They're on the bridge!" he heard Danica say, and he felt her tug at his arm, trying to hurry him along.

It could not be helped. Cadderly fought through the pain and weariness, forced the song into his mind and to his lips.

> *What is the bond that holds the stone?*
> *A bond that wetness breaks.*
> *What are you without the bond?*

Danica knocked him to the ground; he barely heard the crossbow quarrel pass them by.

Still he sang, his concentration complete.

> *Seep, my water, seep*
> *Through the bond, so deep.*

The leading assassin stumbled suddenly, lurched forward as though his feet had been ensnared, fell face down onto the bridge . . . and sank into the mud that the section of bridge had become.

Danica and Cadderly heard splashes below as chunks of mud and stone dropped into the lake. Another assassin hit the area but managed to fall back, knee-deep in the collapsing morass.

The man who had gone in headlong screamed as he dropped out the bottom, plummeting the twenty feet or so to the churning lake.

The entire section Cadderly had marked off slipped down right behind him.

Four stunned assassins stood at the edge of the fifteen-foot gap separating them from their intended quarry, staring in disbelief.

"She said that Deneir would demand of me," Cadderly remarked to Danica, rubbing his throbbing temples. "And he will again, when we get to the inn."

"You have come into some faith?" Danica asked as they fled, leaving behind the frustrated assassins' curses and the *clip-clap* of many horses coming onto the bridge, bearing city guardsmen.

Cadderly looked at Danica as though she'd slapped him, but he calmed quickly and shrugged.

They heard the shouts of guardsmen and killers as the trapped assassins, one by one, dived for the cover of the water.

The way was clear, all the way back to the Dragon's Codpiece, to dead enemies and dead friends.

NINETEEN

SORROW AND DIVINE JOY

Q

Shouts continued to follow Cadderly and Danica after they left the bridge and made their way onto Lakeview Street. The steamy rays of the rising sun were quickly burning away the mist.

Carradoon had awakened to a travesty.

Lakeview Street was jammed with curious citizens and city guardsmen. Many heads turned to regard the young priest and his escort, Cadderly's wide-brimmed hat, soaked, drooped on all sides. Pointing fingers turned the companions' way as well, and soon a horseman, a city guardsman, pushed his way through the throng to stop in Cadderly's path.

"Are you a priest of the Edificant Library?" the guardsman gruffly asked.

"I am Cadderly, of the Order of Deneir," the young priest replied. He turned to Danica and shrugged, embarrassed and almost apologetic, as soon as he had spoken the last few words.

"We're making our way back to the Dragon's

271

Codpiece, the inn of Fredegar Harriman," Danica explained, tossing Cadderly a sidelong glance, "to check on the friends we were forced to leave behind."

"Forced?" Cadderly and Danica knew the question was a test. The guardsman's eyes remained narrow and searching as he continued to scrutinize them.

"You know what occurred," Cadderly replied without hesitation.

The guardsman nodded gravely, apparently satisfied with the explanation. "Come, and quickly," he bade them, and he used his horse to nudge aside any who stood to block the couple's progress.

Neither Cadderly nor Danica enjoyed that stroll down Lakeview Street, fearful that among those many watching eyes loomed some belonging to their assassin enemies. And even more fearful to the companions, considering the guard's grim tone, loomed the possibility that the victory back at the inn had not been without cost.

Their fears did not diminish when they passed the inn two doors down, where Ivan and Pikel had been staying, to find that the front rail, the window above the door, and the wall beside the door all had been smashed apart. The innkeeper, sweeping glass and wood shards from his front porch, regarded the two with suspicion, not looking away and not blinking once as they passed.

Cadderly paused and sighed deeply when the Dragon's Codpiece came into sight. He spotted the balcony of his room, the place he had used as a sanctuary from the harshness of the world for the past several tendays. The front rail lay in the street. One plank, the one that had supported Danica's ride to safety, hung out at a weird diagonal angle. There were no bodies in the street—thank the gods!—but Cadderly saw a crimson stain on the cobblestones beneath his room, and a larger one halfway across the wide street.

Danica, apparently sensing his distress at the sight, hooked her arm around his and lent him support. To her surprise, Cadderly pulled away. She looked at him, to see if she had done something wrong, but his return stare was not accusing.

He stood straight and tall, took another deep breath, and squared his shoulders.

Danica understood the significance of those simple gestures. Cadderly had finally accepted what he'd been forced to do. He would not run away, as he had in Shilmista, he would meet the threat head-on, strike back against those who meant to strike at him. But could he do so, Danica wondered, without ghosts like Barjin's hovering beside him for the rest of his days?

Cadderly walked past her then smiled and waved when "Oo oi!" sounded from the door of the Dragon's Codpiece.

Pikel Bouldershoulder stepped onto the front porch. The dwarf held Cadderly's lost walking stick high above his head and waved excitedly with a heavily bandaged hand.

Danica waited a moment longer and let Cadderly get far ahead of her, considering the perceived shift in the young priest's demeanor. A continuing stream of violent events was forcing Cadderly to grow up, to thicken his hide, in a hurry. Violence could be a numbing thing, Danica knew. No battle is ever harder to accept and fight than the first, and no killing blow made with more reluctance than the first.

Watching her lover stride confidently to join Pikel, the young monk was afraid.

By the time Danica caught up to Cadderly, he stood silently inside the inn with both dwarves, to her relief, and with a teary-eyed Fredegar Harriman. Danica held in check her elation at Ivan and Pikel's good health, though, for she followed Cadderly's gaze to a table in the hearth room, to Headmaster Avery's sprawling corpse. The chest was torn wide and revealed a gaping hole where the heart should have been.

"My Brennan," broken Fredegar sobbed. "They killed my poor Brennan!"

Cadderly let his gaze drift across the sacked room to the broken stairwell, the shattered chandelier atop its rubble, and to the charred floor beside the long bar. A young, unmarked body had been laid beside the bar along with a row of six corpses, one of them still releasing wisps of smoke from under the cloth that covered it.

"Four of them, at least, got away," Ivan informed them.

"You will find another one on the roof," Danica remarked.

"Oo oi," Pikel chirped, snapping his stubby fingers and motioning for one of the guards to go and check.

"Maybe only three got away," Ivan corrected.

"Seven got away," Cadderly said, remembering the three men who had assaulted him and Danica from the water, and the four others in the pursuing boat.

Ivan shook his yellow-bearded face and grumbled, "Well, there's a pack of trouble for ye."

Cadderly hardly heard the dwarf. The young priest walked slowly across the cluttered floor toward the body of the man who had served him as a father for as long as he could recall. Before he got there, though, a tall man, a city guardsman, intercepted him.

"We have some questions," the man demanded.

Cadderly eyed him dangerously. "They will wait."

"No," the man retorted. "They will be answered when I say. And fully! I'll brook no—"

"Leave." It was a simple word, spoken quietly and in controlled tones, but to the city guardsman, it struck like a thunderbolt. The man stood up very straight, glanced around curiously, and headed for the front door. "Come along," he instructed his fellow soldiers, who, after exchanging surprised glances, obeyed without complaint.

Ivan started to say something to Cadderly, but Danica put a hand on the dwarf's shoulder to stop him.

Cadderly wouldn't have heard Ivan anyway. The young priest moved beside Avery's torn body and wiped a tear from his gray eyes. Avery had gotten in the way of something that really did not concern him, Cadderly suspected, and the notion brought disgust to the young man, brought yet another layer of guilt to his growing burden.

But it wasn't guilt that drove Cadderly but sorrow, a grief more profound than any he had ever known. So many images of Avery's life flowed through the young priest. He saw the portly headmaster on the lane outside the Edificant Library, trying to enjoy a sunny spring day but continually hampered by Percival, the white squirrel, who dropped twigs on him from the branches above. He saw Avery at Brother Chaunticleer's midday canticle, the headmaster's face made content, serene, by the melodious song to Avery's cherished god.

How different that fatherly face seemed in death, its mouth open in a final scream, an unanswered plea for help that did not come.

Most of all, Cadderly remembered the many scolding the headmaster had given him, Avery's blotchy face turning bright red with frustration at Cadderly's apparent indifference and irresponsibility. It took the insidious chaos curse for the headmaster to finally admit his true feelings for Cadderly, to admit that he considered Cadderly a son. In truth, though, Cadderly had known it all along. He never could have upset Avery so completely and so many times if the headmaster didn't care for him.

Only then, standing beside the dead man, did Cadderly realize how much he'd loved Avery.

It occurred to Cadderly that Avery should not have been down in the hearth room at such an early hour, especially not dressed so informally, so vulnerably. Cadderly digested that information almost subconsciously, filing it away with the myriad other facts he had collected and scrutinized since his flight from the Night Masks.

"My Brennan, too," Fredegar blubbered, coming to Cadderly's side, draping an arm over Cadderly's shoulder to lean on the young priest.

Cadderly was more than willing to give his gentle friend the needed support, and he followed the innkeeper's lead across the floor toward the bar.

The contrast between Brennan's body and Avery's was startling. The teenager's face showed neither horror nor any signs of surprise. His body, too, seemed intact, with no obvious wounds.

It appeared that he had simply, peacefully, died.

The only thing Cadderly could think of was poison.

"They couldn't tell me how," Fredegar wailed. "The guardsman said he wasn't choked, and there's no blood anywhere. Not a mark on his young form." Fredegar panted desperately to find his breath. "But he's dead," the innkeeper said, his voice rising to a wail. "My Brennan is dead!"

Cadderly shuffled to the side under the weight as Fredegar fell into him. Despite his sincere grief at the sight of Brennan, the death had raised a riddle that Cadderly couldn't leave unanswered. He remembered the horrible shadows he'd seen dancing atop Brennan's shoulders that night at supper. He recalled Danica's story, her dream, and knew beyond doubt that someone, something, had possessed the young man then discarded him.

Perhaps some lingering trace of what had happened remained to be seen. Perhaps telltale shadows remained on Brennan's shoulders. Cadderly opened his mind and let the song of Deneir into his consciousness again, despite the continuing, painful throb in his head.

Cadderly saw a ghost.

The spirit of Brennan sat atop the bar, looking forlorn and lost, staring with pity at his distraught father and with disbelief at his own pale body. He looked up at Cadderly, and his nearly translucent features twisted with surprise.

All the material world around the spirit became blurry as Cadderly allowed himself to fall more into Brennan's state.

Poison? his mind asked the lost soul, though he knew he had not spoken a word.

The spirit shook its head. *I have nowhere to go.*

The answer seemed so very obvious to Cadderly. *Go back to your father.*

Brennan looked at him with confusion.

The song played louder in Cadderly's throbbing head, its volume becoming ferocious. The young priest would not let it go, though, not yet. He saw Brennan's spirit tentatively approach the corpse, seeming confused, hopeful yet terribly afraid. To Cadderly's eyes, the room around the spirit went dark.

Everything went dark.

"By the gods," Cadderly heard Danica whisper.

"Oooo," Pikel moaned.

A thump on the floor beside him jolted Cadderly awake. He was kneeling on the hard floor, but beside him, Fredegar was out cold.

In front of him, young Brennan sat up, blinking incredulously.

"Cadderly," Danica breathed. Her shivering hands grasped the young priest's trembling shoulders.

"How do you . . . feel?" Cadderly stammered to Brennan.

Brennan's chuckles, as much sobs as laughter, came out on a quivering, breaking voice reflecting astonishment, as though he really didn't know how to answer the question. How did he feel? Alive!

The young man looked to his own hands, marveled that they again moved to his command. Fists clenched, and he punched them up into the air, a primal scream erupting from his lips. The effort cost the lad his new-found physical bearings, though, and he wobbled and swooned.

Ivan and Pikel rushed to catch him.

Cadderly steadied himself suddenly, his gaze snapping back across the room to Headmaster Avery. The determined young priest rose briskly, brushed Danica aside, and stalked to the corpse.

"They took out his heart," Danica said to him meekly.

Cadderly turned on her, not understanding.

"That is their usual method," the young monk, familiar with the dark practices of the wretched Night Masks, replied. "It prevents an easy recalling of the spirit."

Cadderly growled and turned back to Avery, back to the task at which he would not fail. He called up the song, forcefully, for it would not readily come to his weary mind. Perhaps he should rest before continuing, he thought as the notes continued on a discordant path. Perhaps he had pushed the magic too far for one day and should rest before delving back into the spiritual world.

"No!" Cadderly said aloud. He closed his eyes and demanded that the music play. The room blurred.

Avery's ghost was not there.

Cadderly, though his material body did not move, looked all around the room. He saw marks of blackness, supernatural shadows, on the floor beside the bodies of the dead assassins and sensed a brooding evil there.

The spirits were gone, and Cadderly got the impression their journey had been forced, that they had been torn away.

Would they receive punishment in an afterlife?

The thought did not bring compassion to Cadderly. He stared hard at the puddles of residual blackness. He thought of recalling one of those lost spirits, to question it about Avery's spirit, but dismissed the notion as absurd. The fate awaiting those souls had nothing to do with what awaited the goodly headmaster.

With sudden insight, Cadderly reached with his thoughts beyond the parameters of the room and sent out a call to the Fugue Plane for his lost mentor's departed spirit.

The answer he received did not come in the form of words, or even images. A sensation swept over Cadderly, an emotion imparted to him by Headmaster Avery—he knew it came from Avery! It was a divine calmness, a contentment beyond anything Cadderly had ever experienced.

A bright light gave way to nothingness. . . .

Ivan and Danica helped the young priest to his feet. Cadderly, coming fully from his trance, looked at Danica with a most sincere smile.

"He is with Deneir," Cadderly told her, and the joy in his voice prevented any reply.

Cadderly realized that his headache had flown. He, too, had found contentment.

"What do ye know?" Ivan asked him, and Cadderly understood that the dwarf was not speaking of Avery's fate. Danica also looked at the enlightened young priest with curiosity.

Cadderly didn't answer right away. Pieces of the puzzle seemed to be falling from the sky. Cadderly looked over at the dead assassins then looked to Brennan and Fredegar, in the thick of an unabashed hug.

Cadderly knew where he would find more of those tumbling puzzle pieces.

Q

The passing hours came as a reassurance to Ghost, who sat quietly in his room, going about his day as routinely as he could. Massacres were certainly not a common thing in Carradoon, but these were troubled times and Ghost was confident that the news would grow stale soon enough. Then young Cadderly would become vulnerable to him once more.

Thoughts of abandoning the mission had crossed the assassin's mind soon after he'd learned that Cadderly had escaped—and that many of his Night Masks had not. He dismissed those thoughts, though, choosing instead to personalize the kill even more. He would get Cadderly, get him through one of his friends, and the young priest's death would be all the sweeter.

Ghost was a bit dismayed when he saw Bogo depart, more because he wanted Bogo to serve as a scapegoat if Cadderly and his friends closed in on the truth than for any practical services the wizard might provide.

The wicked man looked out his window at the afternoon sun's reflection on quiet Impresk Lake. He saw the bridge to the island clearly. Masons huddled out there, in boats and on the structure itself, studying the wide hole.

Ghost shook his head and chuckled. He had already contacted Vander telepathically, back at the farm, and learned from the surviving Night Masks that Cadderly had created that hole. Four assassins had returned to the farm—four out of fourteen.

Ghost continued to stare at the gaping break in the great bridge. Cadderly had beaten them. Ghost was impressed, but he was not worried.

C

Every detail of the battle scene came together in the overall picture he was beginning to form in his mind: Avery's presence in the hearth room, where he should not have been; the curious, continued absence of Kierkan Rufo, who had come down from his room only long enough to identify Avery's body and answer the city guards' few questions; even the peculiar scorch mark on Pikel's tunic registered clearly in Cadderly's thoughts.

He spoke with Brennan, though the young man's recollections were foggy at best, dreamlike. That fact alone confirmed Cadderly's suspicions of what had happened to Danica. The young priest made a point of telling Brennan to keep out of sight, and bade Fredegar not to tell anyone that his son was alive again.

"We must press on quickly," Cadderly explained to his three companions, gathered around him in an out-of-the-way room. "Our enemies are confused for now, but they are stubborn and will regroup."

Danica leaned back in her seat and placed her feet on the table in front of her. "You are likely the most weary among us," she replied. "If you're ready to continue then so are we."

"Oo oi!" Ivan piped, before Pikel got the chance. The yellow-bearded dwarf offered his surprised brother an exaggerated wink, and Pikel promptly tugged hard at Ivan's beard.

Though it took him and Danica several moments to quiet the boisterous brothers, Cadderly was glad for the distraction, for the break in the exhausting tension.

"You have spoken with the guard?" Cadderly asked Danica when order was finally restored.

"Just as you suspected," the young woman replied.

Cadderly nodded as another piece fell squarely into place. "The wizard won't be there for long."

"But are ye ready to battle the likes of that one?" Ivan had to ask.

Cadderly chuckled and stood, straightening his trousers, still moist from his dip in the lake. "You make it sound as if I'm going alone," he quipped.

Ivan was up in an instant, bouncing his huge axe atop one shoulder. "Can't trust that type," the dwarf explained, wanting to clarify his atypical hesitance. "Dangerous sort."

"Can't trust an angry priest, either," Cadderly retorted, taking up his walking stick and sending his spindle-disks into a few short up-and-down snaps.

"Dangerous sort," Danica finished for him, and after the sights the young woman had experienced that day, the tremendous magical powers Cadderly had revealed, the words were spoken without any hint of sarcasm.

TWENTY

I TELLED YE SO

Bogo Rath paced anxiously in his small room. He kicked a basket aside and watched a cockroach skitter across the floor, seeking the shadows under the bed.

"Flee, little bug," the young wizard muttered.

Bogo flipped his stringy brown hair to one side and ran his fingers through it repeatedly. He was the little bug.

He looked out the window, which was too small to get any real view, but enough to tell him that the afternoon light finally was beginning to wane. Bogo meant to leave the city at twilight, disguised among the host of beggars that departed Carradoon every evening.

Outside the gates, he could conjure a magical mount, and his ride to Castle Trinity would be swift and unhindered. The thought of getting far from Carradoon, from the young priest and his cohorts, appealed to Bogo, but the thought of facing Aballister did not. Even worse, if Ghost succeeded in finishing the task, the assassin's return to Castle Trinity would cast an unfavorable, cowardly light on Bogo.

"Boygo," he muttered. He figured he had better get used to hearing that name. Aballister and Dorigen would not soon let him forget his cowardice. The lone consolation for the young man was the fact that he had arranged the library headmaster's death.

The cockroach skittered back out for an instant and zipped across the floor and under the folds of the over-sized curtain.

"That will silence them!" Bogo said to the roach. Especially Dorigen, who had been so humiliated in Shilmista Forest.

A smile found its way through the tension on Bogo's boyish face. He had killed a headmaster!

A glance at the window told him it was time to start for the western gate. He selected the components for a spell that would alter his appearance and placed them in a convenient pocket then took up his pack.

He put it right back down when he heard chanting in the hall.

Q

"Fire and water," Cadderly said in an intense, monotone voice. "Fire and water, the elements of protection. Fire and water."

Danica and Pikel stood in front of the young priest, between Cadderly and the door. Danica flipped her hair out of her face and looked at the stairway, at the top of the crouching, nervous innkeeper's balding head. Every so often, the man peeked over the top stair, fearful for his property.

Still, Cadderly had easily convinced the man to let

the three up the stairs to the mysterious stranger's room. Danica looked at Cadderly again, who chanted more forcefully with his eyes closed and his hands waving up and down in front of him, creating a magical tapestry. The young priest had shaved his beard before they had left the Dragon's Codpiece, and he appeared much like his old self.

And yet, he didn't. Danica couldn't explain it, but somehow Cadderly appeared more confident with every move. His encounter—whatever had happened—with Avery's spirit had put a sense of calm on top of that growing confidence.

Danica hadn't questioned him about it, but she sensed that Cadderly walked with the knowledge that his god was with him.

"Fire and water," Cadderly chanted, "the elements of protection."

As one of his hands came up, he loosed a few drops of conjured water against the door. As the other came up right behind, Cadderly sent from it a gout of flame. The fire hit the wet door with a hiss, the signal for Pikel.

"Oo oi," the dwarf chirped and slammed his club like a battering ram against the door.

The weapon popped cleanly through the thin wood, creating a fair-sized hole but not forcing the door open. As the dwarf retracted his club, Danica realized Pikel's mistake. She reached over the dwarf, turned the handle, and easily opened the door—out.

"Oh," the deflated Pikel remarked.

A chanting from inside the room joined Cadderly's continuing prayer when the door came open. The wizard held a small metal rod in front of him, a conductive component that Danica had seen before.

Pikel had, too, and both he and the woman dived to the side, expecting a burst of lightning.

Cadderly didn't move, didn't flinch. An almost transparent, slightly shimmering field of energy appeared in the open portal.

The man's blast struck it with fury, the lightning driving hard against the barrier, sizzling and throwing multicolored sparks, sending a spiderweb of green and orange energy across the breadth of Cadderly's field to burn at the door jamb. When it ended, a tiny pool of water lay at the base of the intact defensive field.

Wide-eyed, the frightened wizard began another spell, as did Cadderly.

The man pulled another component and began a fast-paced chant.

"Sneeze," Cadderly commanded.

The wizard complied, and his spell was disrupted.

The stubborn wizard growled and began again.

"Sneeze."

"Damn you!" the young man cried, wiping the wetness from his face.

"You could not be farther from the truth," Cadderly replied calmly. "Shall we continue to play this game?

"Dispel!" Cadderly cried suddenly, his face twisting to an angry glare. The shimmering field in the doorway disappeared, and Danica and Pikel burst into the room.

He must have realized his mistake. He should have continued to "play" as the young priest had called it, continued to force Cadderly into a defensive posture in the hope that his spell repertoire would outlast the priest's.

Danica dived straight ahead, came up in a leap,

and jolted forward with her landing, too fast for the surprised man to react. He threw his arms out, but the monk wrapped them, bringing her arms up through the wizard's then down and around, locking him fast.

He did twist one wrist, though, cutting a line of blood on Danica's sleeve.

An invisible dagger!

Danica's foot shot up between her and the wizard, crunching his nose. Dazed, the man offered no resistance as Danica released his other arm, cupped her free hand over the back of his clenched fingers and yanked his hand back toward his forearm, pulling his arm in the other direction at the same time.

The wizard's face contorted in agony. He tried to hold his only weapon, but Danica's foot came up again and her hand continued to pull.

Pikel joined her a moment later. "Oo," he said glumly, disappointed that the fun was already over. He heard the *clang* as the unseen dagger hit the floor, and he looked down for it, scratching his green-dyed hair.

Cadderly walked to the bed and motioned for Danica to lead her prisoner to it. "You can let him go," the young priest offered.

Danica gave a quick, painful jerk as she released the wizard's arms, and she pushed him, knocking him to a sitting position.

"We must talk, you and I," Cadderly demanded.

The man glared up at him from the bed, an impotent threat, but Danica cuffed him anyway, on the ear.

She scowled and showed Cadderly her cut arm in answer to his surprised expression, and that seemed to satisfy the young priest's nagging conscience.

"Dorigen sent you," Cadderly said to the man.

"No."

"I have ways of telling when you lie," Cadderly warned.

"Then you detect nothing," he replied.

"You were with the Night Masks, but you are not a part of their guild," Cadderly remarked.

"You will die," the wizard promised, drawing another cuff from Danica.

"Why have they come for me?" Cadderly asked. With no answer forthcoming, he added, "I could speak with your corpse, if that would please you."

For the first time, the man seemed afraid. The sincere calmness of Cadderly's tone gave weight to the threat, and because he wanted to grow to be an old wizard, he replied. "You—you got in the way," the young wizard stammered, "at the library and in the forest. You forced Abal—" He stopped abruptly.

"Who?" Danica demanded, putting her face right up to Bogo's.

"Aballister," he admitted, "Dorigen's mentor, and mine."

Cadderly looked at Danica, concerned. Dorigen had been a powerful adversary. How strong might her mentor be?

"I came only to observe," the stranger went on, "as I was told."

"Oh?" Pikel cut him short, stepping past Danica, pushing her aside, and displaying the scorched hole in his leather tunic, the hole the wizard's lightning had made back at the Dragon's Codpiece.

The blood drained from the man's face, and his growing desperation forced him to a desperate act. He shoved his hand into a pocket, grabbed a handful of pebbles, and flung them to the floor.

A burst of minor explosions went off, blowing in rapid succession and shooting variously colored puffs of smoke into the air. The pops did nothing to the companions, other than distract them. With a quick chant, the wizard diminished to the size of a cat and slipped between Cadderly and Pikel.

Cadderly tried to call out but couldn't decide fast enough whether he should shout for his friends to stop the man or cry out a warning to the wizard. Danica finally pushed past him and Pikel, following the wizard's expected path to the door.

They heard the door close—the smoke began to clear and the wizard, outside the room and man-sized again, began a new chant.

Danica stopped, wisely not going through the portal.

From behind the door they heard the man cry out in terror. The friends heard a shuffle of feet, a sickening thud, and something heavy slammed against the door.

Cadderly shook his head and looked away. The tip of Ivan's double-headed axe protruded through the door, dripping crimson. As if that weren't macabre enough, the wizard's fingers, grasping helplessly and twitching, reached through the circular hole Pikel's club had made in the door. Pulled by the unbalancing weight, the door slowly creaked open.

Pikel walked past Danica and opened the door the rest of the way, peeking around it and saying, "Oo" as he regarded the hanging wizard.

"I told ye ye couldn't trust a wizard," Ivan, standing

a dozen feet down the hall with his hands on his hips, asserted. He strode up to the door and motioned for the group to come out of the room.

The young priest couldn't help but look over at the dead young wizard, a man probably not even as old as himself. "We never asked his name," Cadderly remarked.

Ivan kicked the door closed, spat in his hands, and put one boot up beside the corpse for leverage. "Wondering what to put on his stone?" he asked.

Danica watched the young priest closely, looking for any sign of weakness, but Cadderly appeared to control his emotions and accept his guilt.

"Just wondering," he answered Ivan, giving a resigned shrug as though he had pushed the incident from his mind. "Get the body back into the room," Cadderly instructed the dwarves.

He shook his head at the irony of one of his earlier statements, which he had made merely to scare his prisoner.

Cadderly could indeed speak with the strange wizard's corpse.

Q

There was only the lake and the empty street. Carradoon quieted considerably as twilight neared, and the morbid interest in the outrageous events at the Dragon's Codpiece had finally dissipated. Only a few guests had remained at the battered inn, and with Cadderly and his companions out of the building, the place was quiet—too quiet for Kierkan Rufo.

The man stood in front of his room's small window, the tilt of his stance making him appear almost like a diagonal crosspiece to the glass. Many moments passed, but Rufo didn't move.

He'd gone too far, he realized, had crossed the line to the dark side of his nature. He doubted he could ever step back. He stood in reflection, trying to follow the course that had led to his horrible position. It had begun in the library, when he'd met Barjin and on the priest's command sent Cadderly tumbling down the stairs to the hidden catacombs.

Rufo could excuse himself for that indiscretion, and all of the other members of his order, including Cadderly, had excused him as well. In the forest, Rufo had betrayed them once more, but he had redeemed himself, had come through in the end to provide his companions with the information they needed to ultimately win out. As in the library, the efforts of Cadderly and the others had averted disaster, had helped to cover Rufo's weaknesses.

Avery lay dead downstairs. Rufo had put the headmaster in the path of a guild of assassins. Rufo had stepped over, had crossed the line. He tried to justify his actions, told himself repeatedly that he had been given no choice, that the assassins would have killed them all if he hadn't cooperated.

The facts didn't support his excuse. Cadderly, Danica, and the dwarves—where had those two come from, anyway?—had won, had chased off the band. If Rufo had gone to them soon after his initial meeting with the young wizard, their victory would have been more swift.

Avery would be alive.

The man whimpered and turned from the window, suddenly feeling vulnerable.

"He deserved his fate," Rufo muttered, reminding himself of the way Avery had treated him since the trouble in Shilmista.

Avery would have held him back in his ascension through the Order of Deneir. The headmaster had even threatened to have him removed from the library. That was not justice, Rufo's sensibilities argued, not when the headmaster held all the power and Rufo could only stand and let Avery's whims determine his fate.

By the time Rufo crossed the small room and collected his pack, anger had replaced guilt. He had struck back at Avery in the only way he could. No one suspected him. The conspiring wizard had already fled, and Rufo had easily deflected the city guards' questions. Even more comforting, Cadderly had apparently taken the guards' conclusions for truth. The priest hadn't asked Rufo a single question.

Rufo had to hide his smile as he paid Fredegar, from Avery's purse, for the time he'd spent in the inn. He explained to the hospitable innkeeper that he had to return at once to the Edificant Library and report the tragic loss.

It was getting dark outside when he exited the Dragon's Codpiece, dark like the path Kierkan Rufo had stumbled down.

C

The four friends left the other inn a short while later, Cadderly tossing the fearful innkeeper a bag of coins to cover the damages and the cost of disposing of the wizard's body.

"Where do we go?" Ivan asked, impatient to get on with the fighting.

"Back to the Dragon's Codpiece," Cadderly replied.

"What do we do when we get there?" Ivan said, not sounding happy about the choice.

"We wait," Cadderly answered, trying to calm the volatile dwarf. "We have struck hard today. All of us need some rest."

Cadderly's extensive use of magic had drained him, and he wanted nothing more than to spend the next several hours in peace. After what he'd learned from the wizard's spirit, though, the young priest wasn't confident he would get his wish.

The air was chill outside as the night grew dark and the first stars made their appearance.

Cadderly knew it would be a long night.

TWENTY-ONE

PIKEL BAIT

Cadderly paid his friends' banter little heed. He sat at his small table, in front of *The Tome of Universal Harmony,* pushing the pieces of the mental puzzle closer together, seeking information from every memory he could summon. Cadderly lingered on the image and the sensation of Avery's spirit, on the divine joy he knew the dead headmaster had found. The young priest's doubts, which had followed him through all of his spiritually bereft life, could not penetrate the holy barrier of that sensation. Cadderly's logic, founded on information he could see and test with his own senses, seemed ridiculous when compared to the serene smile of Avery's ghost.

The foundation of Cadderly's existence had once again been violently shaken, and yet the young priest felt no remorse or sense of loss. Quite the opposite—the mystery of it all gave Cadderly a sense of hope beyond anything he had ever known. Rather than deny what he had felt, the young priest would simply have to expand his foundation to include wonderful new revelations.

Cadderly's unconscious chuckle turned Danica and Ivan, who sat on the bed, toward him, and their stares, in turn, awakened the young priest from his musing. Cadderly shrugged, not knowing how to begin to explain.

"Peoples," Ivan grumbled, but Danica nodded to the young priest as though she understood what Cadderly was going through.

Dear Danica, Cadderly thought, and he had no doubt she knew, and that she approved.

Q

Pikel crept along the first floor of the Dragon's Codpiece, slipping in and out of the shadows in search of the cupboards. It was late, and the dwarf was hungry, having missed three out of four meals during the course of the exhausting day.

"Hee hee hee," the dwarf tittered when he found biscuits and sweet dough. He dropped the amulet Cadderly had given him into a pocket and rubbed his plump hands together briskly, his cherubic dimples revealing his glee.

The dwarf sported an armload of food as he ascended the makeshift stairway to the second level, each step on the stairs that he and Ivan had put back together helping him to justify his filching.

His smile disappeared before he got back to Cadderly's room, though, and as a puny human approached him a moment later, half a biscuit fell out of his mouth.

Q

Danica and Ivan struggled on the bed, the young woman proving, to Ivan's disbelief, that her concentration could prevent Ivan from taking her hand down in wrist wrestling. The mighty dwarf, his bright red face framed by his yellow beard, pushed and yanked vigorously to the side, but the woman's arm, tiny compared to Ivan's gnarly and corded muscles, did not budge an inch.

"You have met your better," Cadderly remarked to Ivan, which only set the dwarf into a deeper frenzy. He hopped up on his toes and pushed with all his strength, moving the bed several inches, but Danica's position remained unchanged.

The sudden and somewhat loud scrape of the bed set off silent alarms within Cadderly. The young priest had made no secret of the fact that he and his friends were back at the inn, but he didn't want to give his potential enemies too much information.

"Quiet!" he whispered harshly, and remembering Pikel, he closed his eyes and sent his thoughts to the missing dwarf. He expected to find the same sensations—hunger mostly—waiting for him, but when Cadderly made contact, through the power of the telepathy-enhancing amulet, his eyes popped wide open. The sensations were vague, as expected, but instead of distant thoughts of muffins and ale, Cadderly visualized hunched, black shadows.

It was not Pikel on the other end! Images of Brennan and Nameless filtered through Cadderly's rising sense of panic. The young priest broke contact and jumped from his seat.

"I'll get ye yet!" Ivan snarled at Danica, oblivious to Cadderly's alarm. The dwarf tugged her arm to the bed as she came from her meditative state, and he growled victoriously until he noticed that Danica paid him no heed.

Danica scrambled over the bed, past Ivan. The dwarf turned to see her and Cadderly exit the room, and realized then that the trouble likely involved his absent brother. Not pausing, even long enough to locate his axe, Ivan half-crawled, half-ran out the door in pursuit.

Q

Poor Pikel had never felt so weak! He stared, dumbfounded, at himself, or at his body at least, or at whatever the monster was that had stolen him.

Holding the weakling body by the throat in one hand, Pikel's body reacted to a rumble down the hall and seemed to realize that Pikel's friends would soon be upon him. The thought brought an evil chuckle to his dwarf lips. He slapped aside Pikel's new, human, skinny arm and reached into one of his pockets, producing a small packet.

"Oooo," Pikel wailed. He nearly swooned, thinking the item to be some horrible magical thing and suspecting that his life was at its end.

He watched his own body bring the packet up between them. But whatever inhabited his body broke the packet over itself, over the dwarf body, instead.

"Eh?" Pikel queried, for the imposter dwarf's face was covered in blood, blood from the packet.

With one arm Pikel's body lifted the puny form from the ground and hurled Pikel's new body across the room, where he slammed into a wall and slumped to the floor.

The false Pikel, too, fell back, leaning heavily on the wall perpendicular to the door, and groaned.

Q

Enraged Ivan grabbed both Cadderly and Danica by the backs of their tunics and hurled himself past them as soon as he discerned where Cadderly was leading them. The dwarf, without his deer-antlered helmet, hit the door head first, bursting into the room.

Staggering, Pikel lifted a shaking finger and pointed accusingly across the room at the slender human form crawling around the base of the wall.

"Me brother!" Ivan roared, and he charged across, hands leading to throttle the weakling killer.

Danica, too, followed the imposter dwarf's trembling finger, but Cadderly came into the room more slowly, warily, paying full attention to the apparently wounded dwarf.

He had brought the song of Deneir into his thoughts. He saw the shadows crouched on Pikel's—on the imposter's!—shoulders.

"Ivan!" he cried, and trusting in the song, he whipped his adamantine spindle-disks straight into Pikel's face.

The dwarf flew back against the wall, real blood mingling with false on the green-dyed beard. "Oooo," he moaned.

Across the room, Ivan let go of the weakling and came rushing back to throttle the new target.

Cadderly hadn't released the dwarf from his knowing gaze. He watched the shadows break apart then melt down into Pikel's shoulders.

Ivan caught his brother in both hands and hoisted him off the floor, slamming him against the wall.

"Oooo," Pikel moaned again.

"Hold, Ivan," Cadderly said calmly. "Pikel is back where he belongs."

Cadderly nodded to Danica, and she turned to face the assassin again, ready to spring at him in an instant.

"You have nowhere to run," Cadderly said to the strange little man. He walked up to join Danica. "I know you."

"Shouldn't have made the damn disks so fine," Cadderly heard Ivan say behind him, to Pikel's continuing groans. The young priest glanced back to see Ivan tending Pikel's bloodied face.

When he turned back, the shadows were gone from the puny assassin's shoulders. Cadderly's gaze darted around the room, fearing that the man had stolen one of his friends' identities once again. His three companions appeared the same, though, looking to him for direction—and with confusion, apparently recognizing the young priest's sudden distress.

"Who are you?" Cadderly muttered under his breath when he turned back to the weakling man. He let the song of Deneir sound louder in his mind, and studied the aura of the new identity.

He felt a cold wind, pictured a rocky, forlorn shore backed by towering mountains. Huge ice floes dotted the bay, waves breaking against their invulnerable sides, and a giant ship sat quiet in the calmer waters near the shore, awaiting the mighty arms that could pull its monstrous oars.

Cadderly looked into the weakling's face and saw true fear and unexpected resignation.

Danica sensed that the puny man was about to dart

for the door, and she tensed for a spring to intercept him. A whisper came into her ear, though, a magical message from Cadderly. She looked at her companion curiously.

The little man broke for the door. Danica went for him, as did Cadderly, the two getting conveniently tangled, enough for the man to get by.

Ivan dropped Pikel hard to the floor, wincing at his brother's ensuing groan.

"Halt!" Cadderly cried, looking to the fleeing man. That command was not aimed at the weakling, though, and it carried the weight of considerable magical energy.

Ivan stopped in spite of himself and the man rushed out the open door. Danica halfheartedly took up the chase, as Cadderly had instructed. She came out the front door of the Dragon's Codpiece a few moments later, saw the man turning a corner one way, and purposely went the other, to return empty-handed after an appropriate amount of time had passed.

Back in the room, Ivan stood staring in disbelief at Cadderly, tapping one heavy boot impatiently on the wooden floor.

"More waiting?" the yellow-bearded dwarf asked gruffly.

Cadderly smiled and nodded. "Not too long," he promised.

The puzzle was nearly complete.

TWENTY-TWO

STRIKING BACK

Q

"Well I'll be a smart goblin," Ivan whispered, peering over the back edge of the roof of the building adjacent to the Dragon's Codpiece. Market Square was bustling, as was usual for that time of day, but the dwarf had picked out one figure clearly, a tilting man with angular features making his way through the crowd.

Danica, following the dwarf's pointing finger to spot Rufo, was over the side in an instant, picking her way down into the alley and quickly falling into step some distance behind the man.

"I'd have thought that one'd be long gone from here by now," Ivan remarked to Cadderly, who sat farther from the edge, *The Tome of Universal Harmony* open in front of him, his eyes closed. The young priest shook his head, not at all surprised.

"Rufo would not dare the trails alone," Cadderly explained, the same argument he had used when Fredegar had told the friends Rufo intended to go back to the library. "It's likely he's found refuge within the city, in the temple of Ilmater perhaps."

Ivan and Pikel shrugged at each other, neither willing to dispute Cadderly's logic. Their young friend had been leading them through the continuing mysteries as if he knew all the answers, or knew where to find them. Pikel shrugged again and crossed the roof to watch over Lakeview Street, while Ivan continued his scan of Market Square. They had been on the roof for more than a day, waiting with all the patience that could be expected of dwarves.

Danica returned a little while later, easily scaling the back wall of the building. "He's with the priests of Ilmatari," she reported.

Cadderly nodded silently, not opening his eyes, not breaking the trance he had spent hours attaining.

"He knew that," Ivan remarked dryly, the dwarf starting to feel like a pawn in somebody else's sava game. Under his breath Ivan muttered, "Damned cocky priest knows everything."

"Not yet," Cadderly replied, drawing another disbelieving shake of the head from Ivan. There was no way that Cadderly, twenty feet away, could have heard his remark.

Defeated, Ivan went back to watch for the escaped assassin, for Kierkan Rufo, or for anyone or anything else that might give the friends a clue.

Not that he believed Cadderly needed one.

ℂ

As soon as he regained control of his giant form, Vander began to pace the barn nervously, stretching his huge arms out wide. He'd nearly been caught, and honestly, the firbolg didn't know how he'd moved that weakling body fast enough to get out of the room and out of the inn.

He'd spent a miserable night on the streets of Carradoon, fearful that Ghost would never give back his true form and continually looking over his shoulder, expecting to find Cadderly, the woman, or the two fierce dwarves, bearing down on him.

But he was back, at the farm and in his familiar body. He peeked out the door at the quiet house and empty yard, not sure whether the four remaining assassins were still around.

Four remaining assassins! At least eleven of the killers were dead, with five others missing. Ghost alone walked the streets of Carradoon, except, perhaps, for the wizard, Bogo Rath. And Cadderly, surrounded by powerful allies, remained alive and alert.

In their last spiritual passing, though, Vander had sensed clearly that Ghost remained confident, had sensed that the little man was actually enjoying the challenge of a difficult chase.

Ghost had been in trouble before, had lost entire bands of killers only to turn the tables and bring the intended victim down. He was confident, cocksure, the quality of a true warrior.

Of course, the firbolg's admiration of the little man was tempered by the knowledge that Ghost's confidence was rooted in the fact that the weakling had a quick way out of any situation. With Vander a safe distance from the fight, Ghost always had a quick and easy escape route.

How convenient.

C

"What is it?" Danica posed the question just a moment after Cadderly opened his eyes for the first time in several hours. The young priest had searched the city, reaching out with detection spells to locate the particular magical emanations of the strange item the little assassin carried.

"A shift in the power," Cadderly explained absently, his thoughts still firmly locked on the item.

Ivan, a few feet away but overhearing the conversation, waggled his bearded face in disbelief. "If ye know where the damn thing is . . ." he began.

"I do not," Cadderly interrupted, "not exactly. Our enemy is in the city, somewhere south of here, or I should say, our enemy has just returned to the city."

Danica cocked her head and pushed the stubborn lock of hair from her face.

"He departed the city while we had him cornered back in the room," Cadderly tried to explain, "magically. The man who physically ran away, or at least the spirit of the man occupying the killer's body, was not the same conniving person that captured Pikel."

Ivan waggled his face again, too confused to offer any remarks.

"Now he has returned to Carradoon," Cadderly went on.

"And we're going to find him?" Danica stated as much as asked, and she was surprised when Cadderly shook his head.

"What would we gain?" the young priest asked. "Our enemy would only flee once more."

"What're ye thinking, then?" Ivan huffed, tired of Cadderly's cryptic clues. "Are we to sit here and wait for them killers to find us?"

Again Cadderly shook his head, but accompanied by a wide and wicked smile. "We're going to catch our tricky friend from behind," he explained, thinking of the farmhouse that Bogo Rath's spirit had described to him. "Are you ready for a fight?"

Ivan's dark eyes popped wide at the unexpected invitation, and his response pleased his brother. "Hee hee hee."

Q

"There!" Cadderly whispered, pointing to a window under the spreading limbs of a wide elm tree. "Someone walked by that window, inside the house." Cadderly scanned the farmyard, wondering where Danica's stealthy progress had put her. The young monk was nowhere in sight, had disappeared into the shadows.

"Time for going," Ivan said to Pikel as he hoisted his great axe.

Pikel grabbed his brother's shoulder and cooed, pointing plaintively to the tree.

"I'm not for going up another tree," Ivan growled, but his anger couldn't hold out against Pikel's pitiful expression. "All right," the gruff dwarf conceded. "Yerself can get up the tree."

Pikel hopped at the news, and his wide smile disappeared under his helmet as the cooking pot dropped over his face. Ivan roughly adjusted it, realigned his own deer-antlered helm, and pushed his brother off.

"Ivan," Cadderly said gravely before they had gone two steps. The dwarf turned a sour expression back at the young priest.

"Do not kill anyone if it can be avoided," Cadderly said, "as we agreed."

"As yerself agreed," Ivan corrected.

"Ivan." The weight of Cadderly's tone brought a frown to the dwarf.

"Damn boy's taking all the fun out of it," Ivan remarked to Pikel as the two turned and headed off once more, skittering, hopping, crawling, falling over one another, and somehow, finally getting to the base of the wide elm.

Cadderly shook his head in disbelief that the dwarven racket hadn't alerted the whole countryside of their presence. He continued to shake his head as Pikel clambered up onto Ivan's shoulders, reaching futilely for the lowest branch. The green-bearded dwarf hopped up, dropping his club on Ivan's head, but managed to grasp the branch. Hanging by his fingers, his feet wiggling wildly, Pikel would never have gotten up, except that Ivan promptly returned the club, slamming it against Pikel's rump and nearly launching him over the thick branch.

"Oooo," Pikel moaned softly, rubbing his seat and taking the club from Ivan.

Cadderly sighed. What the dwarf brothers lacked in stealth, they more than made up for in tactical defense.

Q

The one guard for the four remaining Night Masks shook his head in disbelief, too, watching the dwarves' escapades. He crouched in the tight and smelly chicken coop, one leg up on the wall-to-wall-perching bench, and peered through a crack in the old boards, a crack wide enough for him to level his crossbow and take aim. He figured the one with the antlers on his helm for the tougher foe, and thought that if he could take out the dwarf on the ground, the one in the tree would be in serious trouble.

Squawk!

The startled Night Mask spun and fired, seeing a flurry of movement. The air was full of chickens—one less when the crossbow quarrel cut through—but in the dim light and close quarters, the birds seemed like one ominous, feathered foe.

He got hit twice, on the face and neck, and felt blood oozing under his tunic. He grabbed for the wounds, hoping to stop the flow.

The relieved man nearly laughed aloud when he found the blood was really eggs . . . until he realized that someone, behind the barricade of flapping chickens, must have thrown them at him. The man snarled, dropped his crossbow, and drew out a slender dagger.

The chickens quieted quickly. He saw no enemy in the small coop.

The bench, the man thought. His enemy had to be under the bench. His smile disappeared and his mouth dropped open as he started to bend.

Under the bench, and maybe behind him.

A hand slapped across the man's mouth, and another grabbed his weapon hand. His eyes opened wide then closed tight at the searing pain as his own knife pierced his throat, under the chin, and slid unerringly into his brain.

Q

Danica dropped the man aside and turned to regard the dwarf brothers. Ivan was under the farmhouse window by then, with Pikel carefully picking steps in the tree right above him. It was a recipe for disaster, Danica knew, and she figured she had better get back outside and into a new position, just in case.

She paused before stepping over the dead assassin and considered the kill. Cadderly had prompted an agreement that no man would be slain if it could be avoided, and Danica, though she, like Ivan, had thought the agreement absurd, felt some pangs of guilt for not honoring the spirit of her lover's wishes. Perhaps she could have taken this guard out without killing him.

Danica felt no sympathy for the man she'd killed, though. She, above all the others in her party, understood the motives and methods of the Night Masks, and she reserved no mercy for anyone who would don the silver-and-black mask of the amoral guild.

Q

Ivan, directly under the window, looked up in frustration as Pikel sought a secure perch in the tree branch's shaky outer reaches. Finally, when Pikel seemed on solid enough footing, Ivan placed the edge of his axe against the house and ran it slowly down the wall, scraping and bumping over each shingle.

A moment later, a curious face peered out beside the curtain. The man, sword in hand, straightened, seeing nothing there, and gradually peeked over the sill.

"Ha!" he cried, spotting Ivan. Above, a branch cracked.

"Me brother," Ivan explained, pointing up.

"Oh," the confused assassin replied.

"Oooooo!" Pikel roared, swinging down like a pendulum, his club thick end out, like a fat lance, and securely braced. The man tried to get his sword in front of him, but got slammed in the chest and went flying away as if he had been sitting in the basket of a giant-cranked catapult.

"Come on!" Ivan cried, hopping up to the windowsill and pulling himself in beside his upside-down brother.

Pikel shrugged. Things had not gone exactly as planned. The branch had snapped and Pikel's thick ankle was firmly stuck in a fork, leaving him hanging, helpless.

"Come on," Ivan, inside the room, said again. He grabbed Pikel's free hand and tugged, dragging the dwarf halfway into the room.

"Uh-uh," Pikel tried to explain.

Thinking his brother was just being stubborn, Ivan dropped his axe, grabbed with both hands, and yanked with all his strength. Pikel came into the room, the bending, grasping branch being pulled in right behind him.

Q

Vander held the barn door firmly, supporting it tightly against its hinges so it wouldn't creak so loudly as he gingerly cracked it open. He couldn't see the fight at the window from his angle, but he did see the trembling branches of the elm above the corner of the farmhouse roof. That, and the previous squawking of the chickens, told the giant that intruders were about.

Vander stopped, staring incredulously at a ball of fire hovering in the air a few feet above him, just outside the barn door. The firbolg tensed, sensing the danger, sensing that if he moved, the pausing magic would go off.

Why was the spellcaster waiting?

Slowly, Vander leaned back into the barn.

A line of flames roared down from the fireball, scorching the ground at the firbolg's feet. Vander dived to the barn floor, pulling the door closed behind him, fearing that the magic would follow him in.

Black smoke rose from the bottom of the door.

Everything went pitch black.

The stubborn firbolg rose to his feet, knowing that he had to get out the door, out of the trap.

Everything went absolutely silent.

Vander growled and eased one foot in front of the other, toward the door. He had no way of knowing if the flames remained, but he had to find out.

He heard no sound, but it seemed as if the ground rushed up in front of him, twirling dust nipping at his eyes and forcing him to fall back. He tripped over unseen crates and crashed silently to the dirt.

The disoriented firbolg's vision returned in the blink of an eye, the magical darkness dispelled. Vander heard the snap of wood as a plank broke under his hand, and he heard, too, a whirling sound above him that alerted him a moment before he tried to rise.

The firbolg stared helplessly at the air only inches above his head, at the air that had suddenly filled with magical manifestations of whirling blades.

Vander heard the door creak open and looked across his body to see a young man in a wide-brimmed blue hat.

"The blades will cut," the young man said.

The trapped Vander didn't doubt it for a moment.

Q

"Ooooooo!"

Danica, making her way toward the far side of the farmhouse, heard Pikel's cry as the branch holding the dwarf druid flew out of the window.

When the pliable branch reached its end and reversed direction, Pikel's ankle slipped free and the dwarf went sailing, turning a perfect two-and-a-half back somersault to land headfirst into a pile of dust.

"I telled ye not to let go!" a frustrated Ivan, holding Pikel's club, shouted from the window.

Pikel shrugged, adjusted his cooking pot, and rushed back to join his brother.

Together, the dwarves crept across the small room. It had two doors, both fortunately closed, one along the wall to their right, and the other directly across from the window, leading to one of the front rooms.

"Makes a nice rug, that one," Ivan remarked, heading for the front room and stepping over the back of the clobbered Night Mask, who lay spread-eagle and face down on the floor, his arms flung out wide.

Instinctively, Pikel, wearing open sandals, wiggled his gnarly toes as he crossed the man's back behind Ivan, and the green-bearded dwarf nodded, surprised at just how good a rug a clobbered human might make.

"Ye know they know we're here?" Ivan asked when he reached the door.

Pikel quickly shrugged, as though that fact hardly mattered.

Ivan nodded his agreement and looked at the wooden door, his smile widening under his yellow-haired face. "Ye remember the charge at the inn?" he asked.

The door burst from its hinges, crossbows clicked, and Ivan and Pikel, behind the impromptu shield, smiled wickedly to see the two darts protruding through the wood.

"These men is so predictable!" Ivan declared, and he flung the broken door aside. The dwarf brothers had entered a kitchen.

Pikel swerved left, toward a man caught between the charge and the wall who was trying to squeeze through the room's tight window. Ivan bolted right, in chase after the other assassin, heading for the growing daylight beyond the open door.

Pikel considered the struggling man's predicament for just a moment then slammed his heavy club at the window's top frame, collapsing it to further ensnare the man.

"Hee hee hee." Thoroughly enjoying himself, the dwarf pulled the kitchen table over, unlaced the man's boots, and retied them around one of the table legs.

The remaining man stopped abruptly and swung around, thinking to catch his dwarf pursuer off guard by the sudden change in tactics.

Ivan was too crafty for that simple trick. He skidded to a halt, lifting his huge axe to easily deflect the slicing sword blade.

The assassin twirled the weapon up above his head and came in again with it, furiously, angling it left then right to poke holes through the dwarf's defenses. He scored a hit on Ivan's side, but Ivan turned with the thrust, pressing the top of his axe against the thin blade and slamming it against the wall.

The assassin fell back, holding only the hilt and first two inches of his snapped sword.

Ivan looked at the severed strap on the side of his armored suit. A single metal plate hung out an inch, but the assassin's hit had not come close to penetrating the dwarf-forged armor.

"Was it worth it?" Ivan asked in all seriousness.

The assassin snarled and flung his broken sword at the impertinent dwarf then turned and darted out the door.

Ivan batted the missile away and broke into a charge. He dived for the man's ankles but came up short and bumped down off the front of the porch.

The Night Mask never looked back as he rushed for the stable. He leaped atop an unsaddled horse, set the beast into a dead run, and flew over the fence rail.

Ivan groaned, angered that one had escaped, and rolled to his back—and saw Danica kneeling on the farmhouse roof, crossbow loaded and level.

"Ye ever use one of them things?" the surprised dwarf asked.

Danica fired. The fleeing assassin's head snapped forward, the quarrel entering at the base of his skull. He held his seat for a few moments longer then drifted off the horse's side, dropping to the dust as the steed ran on.

"Yup," answered Pikel, coming to the door behind Ivan.

TWENTY-THREE

AN OFFER HE COULDN'T REFUSE

Q

Where's the big one?" Ivan asked when he, Danica, and Pikel found Cadderly standing in the farmyard, leaning against a young tree.

Cadderly pointed to the barn. "He's occupied," the young priest explained, his gray eyes turning up at their corners with his satisfied grin. "Not hurt, but not in any mood to fight back."

Danica nodded. "Then your guess was right," she remarked, her voice unmistakably revealing her distaste. "The band was led by a giant."

Cadderly recalled the images he had seen on the little assassin's shoulder back in the Dragon's Codpiece. The aura change had revealed much to the observant young man, had told him the identity and more importantly, the demeanor of the Night Masks' leader.

"Dead giant." Ivan snickered hopefully.

"No," Cadderly answered him.

"Soon?" Ivan asked.

"I don't think so," Cadderly replied. The young

priest looked around the yard, to the chicken coop, to the window by the tree, and to the corpse lying in the dust by the road. "I didn't want these men killed," he remarked sharply.

Ivan looked to Danica. "Better to let that one get away," the dwarf whispered with obvious sarcasm.

Cadderly heard the comment and locked a deep frown on the yellow-bearded dwarf.

"It was a fight, ye . . ." Ivan began to protest, but he threw his thick hands up in disgust, snorted "Bah," and stomped away.

A few strides off, beyond the nearest corner of the house, he caught sight of the lone living Night Mask, wedged tightly in the kitchen window and no longer struggling against the pressing weight.

"There ye go, lad," the dwarf bellowed. "Me brother held out some mercy for yer foolhardy wishes."

The other three moved over to join Ivan, to see what the dwarf had discovered.

"What'll ye do with him?" Ivan asked Cadderly when the young priest saw the trapped man. "Do ye have some questions ye need to ask this one? Or are ye going to give him to the city guard, ye merciful fool?"

Cadderly regarded the dwarf curiously, not understanding Ivan's anger. His ensuing question sounded clearly as an accusation. "Are you so eager to kill?"

"What do ye think the city guard'll do with him?" Ivan balked. "Ye forgetting yer fat friend, sprawled across a table with his heart cut out? And what of them that lived in this place? Do ye think the farmer and his family'll be coming back anytime soon?"

Cadderly averted his gaze, stung by the honest words.

He preferred mercy, hated killing, but he could not deny Ivan's observations.

"Ye bring us out here and ask us to fight with half our hearts," Ivan blustered, spittle glistening the bottom edges of his thick mustache. "If ye're thinking I'm one to risk me own neck to give a few more days of life to that scum, then ye're thinking wrong!"

Confusion dictated Cadderly's next move. He brought the song up in the recesses of his mind, heard the flow of Deneirrath magic, and found a point where he could join in that sweet river. He had stepped fully into the spirit world several times—in Shilmista Forest to bid farewell to Elbereth's gallant horse, in the Dragon's Codpiece to find Brennan's wandering spirit and learn the truth of Avery's heavenly bliss—and he had come to find the journey short and not so difficult.

As soon as he arrived, as soon as the Prime Material Plane faded into indistinct grayness behind him, he heard the desperate screams of lost souls.

Leaving his corporeal body standing with his unknowing friends, Cadderly willed his spirit toward the corpse lying in the road, the man Danica had shot from the horse. The young priest ended his trek abruptly, though, terrified by the images. Huddled, shadowy things, shapes akin to those growling pools of darkness he had seen on the shoulders of evil men, encircled the doomed assassin's spirit. The dead man noticed Cadderly then and looked at him with desperation.

Help me, came his silent plea.

Cadderly didn't know what to do. The growling, shadowy things tightened their ring, dark claws reaching out for their victim.

Help me!

Cadderly willed his spirit toward the man, but something, his fears, perhaps, or his knowledge that it was not his place to interfere, held the young priest's spirit firmly in place.

Shadows grabbed the doomed assassin. He twisted and jerked, but the dark grip did not relent, did not release him.

Help me! The cry tore at Cadderly's heart, horrified him and filled him with sorrow all at once.

The shadows melted into the ground, taking the man's spirit with them. Only the spirit's legs remained visible, kicking futilely.

Then they, too, were gone, pulled down to the Nine Hells, the Abyss, or some other dark domain.

Cadderly found himself back in his corporeal form, his eyes open wide, sweat beaded on his forehead.

"What're ye thinking?" Ivan demanded.

"Maybe I was wrong," Cadderly admitted, looking at Danica as he spoke the words, looking for judgment in her knowing gaze.

Danica grabbed him by the arm and put her head on his shoulder. She understood the trial Cadderly had just undergone, the realization once again that war precipitated cruel actions, that their survival against their merciless foe demanded a resolve equally vicious.

"But he goes back to the town," Cadderly went on firmly, pointing to the man trapped in the window. "The city guard will decide his fate. He cannot harm us now, and we have no cause to kill him."

Ivan, deadly in battle but certainly no merciless killer, readily agreed. He and Pikel immediately started for the man.

"Not now," Cadderly called to them, turning them around. "Will the window hold him?"

The dwarves turned to study the broken structure.

"For a hunnerd years," Ivan decided.

"Hee hee hee," Pikel chuckled and patted his trusty club, the compliments to his mighty clubbing bringing a blush to his cherubic, fuzzy cheeks.

"Then let it hold him," Cadderly said to them. "We have other business." The young priest turned and nodded to the barn door, realizing that his spell of whirling blades would not last. If they didn't get to the giant soon, they would likely wind up in yet another fight.

On Cadderly's command, Ivan and Pikel each took hold of one of the barn doors and pulled it wide. The dwarves remained behind the doors, out of sight, for Cadderly knew that most giants were not particularly fond of the bearded folk and that the sight of the brothers might send it into a rage that would be quieted only by the monster's death.

The giant wasn't up for any fight, though. It wasn't up at all. It lay on its back, helpless before the magically conjured blades. The creature lifted its head at the sound of the opening doors and looked across his prone form to see Cadderly and Danica regarding him.

Cadderly studied the giant intently, the forms on Vander's shoulders. He saw again the wide mountains, the great boat in the iceberg-dotted bay, and he knew it was the same being—the same spirit at least—that the assassin had switched bodies with when Cadderly and the others had cornered the wily little man.

"I will release you," the young priest promised, "on your word that you will attack neither me nor my companions."

The firbolg growled at him.

"By my estimation, we have no quarrel with you, mighty giant," Cadderly went on, "and we want none. It may be that I can aid you in your struggle."

The growling stopped, replaced by an honestly perplexed expression.

"Aid it?" Ivan bellowed from behind the shielding door. "Ye didn't say nothing about aiding any stupid giant!" Before Cadderly could react, the dwarf stormed around the barn door, axe in hand, Pikel rushing in from the other side to join him.

"Ivan!" Cadderly started, but Pikel's sincere, "Oo oi!" and the look of amazement on Ivan's face stopped the young priest.

"Let him up," Ivan snapped at Cadderly, giving the man a push. "Ye got no cause to keep one o' his kind in the dirt!"

"Well met, good dwarves," the giant said unexpectedly.

Danica and Cadderly exchanged stunned stares and helpless shrugs, Danica blowing away a lock of her hair and blinking.

"Let him up, I say!" Ivan demanded, pushing Cadderly once more. "Can't ye see the flames of his beard?"

Cadderly mouthed the words silently as he regarded the prone giant, wondering what the red color of its beard had to do with Ivan's apparent approval of the monster. Cadderly had seen Ivan and Pikel go after giants with wild abandon in Shilmista Forest. What made this one so different?

"He ain't no giant," Ivan explained.

"He looks pretty big to me," the disbelieving Danica remarked.

"He's a firbolg," Ivan answered impatiently, "a friend o' the land—and a friend o' the elves. We'll forgive him that, since firbolgs and dwarves get on well, too."

Ivan seemed to be winding up for a long dissertation on the subject of firbolgs, and would have continued, but Cadderly motioned for him to stop, needing nothing further. The aura of the strange giant made perfect sense to Cadderly, and he understood, too, beyond any doubts, why one of that being's honorable weal would be in league with that malignant wretch.

The giant was a prisoner.

A wave of Cadderly's hand removed the magical blades. The firbolg growled at the indignity of it all, took up his huge sword, and got to his feet. For a moment, it seemed to Cadderly and Danica that the monster would attack, but Ivan and Pikel, nodding and smiling, walked right into the barn and struck up a conversation—in a voluminous, grumbling language that sounded like the roll of boulders down a rocky mountainside.

The giant, talking with the dwarves, kept his sword up in front of him and seemed even more nervous when Cadderly and Danica joined their companions.

"He's not to trusting us," Ivan whispered to Cadderly. Then, louder, he announced, "His name's Vander."

"If we had wanted you dead, I would have lowered the blades," Cadderly reasoned.

Vander's thick lips curled back, his giant teeth showing white through the red tresses of his beard.

"Don't ye insult the thing!" Ivan warned harshly. "Don't ye ever tell a firbolg that ye could've beaten it unless ye've already beaten it!"

"Where are my associates?" Vander demanded, his huge sword hovering in the air only a few short strides from the companions. Cadderly realized then that the firbolg could probably take one great step forward and cut him in half before he even began to form a defense—and what defense could Cadderly put up against so monstrous a beast, anyway?

"They're all dead, except for one," Cadderly answered as firmly as he could, determined to show no signs of weakness, though he was less confident of how the giant would take the news.

Vander nodded, seeming none too upset.

It was a good sign, Cadderly noted, a piece of the puzzle that fit exactly.

"I came here to find you," the young priest explained, "to speak with you about our common enemy."

There, he had put things out in the open. His three friends stared at him, still not in the know about Cadderly's revelations.

"Ghost," Vander replied. "His name is Ghost."

Danica and the dwarves looked at each other and shrugged.

"Together we can beat him," Cadderly promised.

Vander snickered, a curious sound indeed, coming from the giant. "You know little of him, Cadderly," he replied.

"I'm still alive," Cadderly argued, not surprised at all that the giant had figured out his identity. "Can the same be said for most of Ghost's associates?"

"You know little of him," Vander said again.

"Then tell me."

Cadderly bade his friends to clean up the yard and set a watch from the house. The companions, particularly Danica, didn't seem anxious to leave their friend beside a dangerous giant, but Vander said something to the dwarves in some mountain dialect, and Ivan immediately took hold of Danica's arm.

"He gave me his word," Ivan explained. "A firbolg never breaks his word." Cadderly's nod further assured his concerned lover, and she left with the dwarves, looking back over her shoulder every step of the way.

"You should be wary," Vander said as soon as the others had left.

Cadderly looked at him curiously, wondering if the giant had just threatened him.

"I will not go against what I have promised," Vander assured him, "but Ghost can take my body when he chooses, and you would be an easy kill if your guard was down."

"Then we must act quickly," Cadderly replied, no tremble in his voice. "I know Ghost took your body and left you in his boots when we had cornered him in the inn. And I know, too, that the possession can be blocked."

Vander shook his head doubtfully.

"Danica, the woman you just met, blocked him," Cadderly replied. "Together, you and I can do the same. I have spells, and this." He held up the amulet he had taken from Rufo in Shilmista Forest, the imp's amulet that Cadderly had claimed as his own, that allowed the young priest to easily contact the mind of another. "The amulet will allow me to join with you in your struggle."

Vander eyed him suspiciously, but Cadderly could see he had at least intrigued the beleaguered giant.

They talked for a short while longer then went to the farmhouse to coordinate the defenses with the others. They found the dwarves hard at work freeing the captured Night Mask from the broken window.

The man at last slipped back to the kitchen floor, shakily finding his feet. He would have offered no resistance, so obviously outnumbered, except that he spotted Vander out of the corner of his eye, standing beside the outside door. With a jerk, the man pulled free of Ivan's halfhearted hold, punched the surprised dwarf in the eye, and rushed for the door.

"Master!" he cried hopefully.

"That one's going to be trouble," Ivan muttered.

There came a great *swoosh* as Vander's sword cut the air—and the man's torso—cleanly in half.

"Nope," Pikel said to Ivan, both of the tough dwarves wincing at the gruesome sight.

Vander shrugged against the stunned stares that lingered on him from every direction. "If you knew him as well as I," the firbolg explained, his tone casual, "you would have killed him long before now."

"Not like that," Ivan protested, "not when me and me brother got to clean the mess up!"

Cadderly closed his eyes and fell back out of the room, back to the relative clean of the wider yard. He wondered if he would ever get as accustomed to such violence as his sturdy, battle-hardened companions.

He hoped he would not.

C

Vander took the companions to the graves of the murdered farm family, explaining grimly that he had, at least, forced the assassins to properly bury the victims.

Danica looked quizzically at Cadderly, and the young priest knew she was wondering if he meant to go straight after the spirits of the departed, to resurrect the family.

Cadderly shook his head, more a gesture for himself than to Danica. Such actions were not so simple, he knew, and he didn't have time to make an attempt. Also, Cadderly, still bone-weary from his exhausting use of magic over the previous two days, was determined to save what little power remained in him. Confident that he would soon be tested again, the young priest decided to open himself to the song only when absolutely necessary.

Besides, the horrible memories of the shadowy things pulling the assassins' doomed souls to eternal torment were too fresh in Cadderly's mind for him to want a return trip to the edges of the Fugue Plane.

That afternoon, the farm was quiet once more, showing no sign that any trouble had occurred.

Watching the fast-westering sun, Cadderly led the firbolg back to the barn. If Ghost was coming for Vander, telepathically or physically, it might well happen soon.

Cadderly set his spindle-disks spinning, letting their crystalline center catch the lamplight and disperse it into a myriad of dancing shapes and flickers. The willing giant slipped into the hold of the mesmerizing crystal and let Cadderly into his thoughts. Vander put a hand into his pocket and clutched at the amulet Cadderly had given him, as though the closer contact would improve the joining of their minds.

A short while later, Cadderly sat quiet, out of sight, in one of the stalls in the barn, enjoying the majestic images playing in his mind at the firbolg's mental recounting of his frosty, rugged homeland.

TWENTY-FOUR

LAYERS OF TREACHERY

Q

The call drifted on the silent winds of the dimension where dwelled only the mind. It drifted inexorably toward the farm on the outskirts of Carradoon and the firbolg that had served for so long as the caller's waiting vessel.

Cadderly sensed the fear in the unseen giant, and knew that Ghost had come a-calling.

Stand easy, the young priest imparted telepathically to Vander. *Do not let your fear or your anger block me from our joining.*

Cadderly knew that the profound fear, far beyond what he would have expected from a mighty and proud giant, had not diminished, but Vander mentally reached back to him, strengthening their bond.

Ghost's call meandered in, and Cadderly drove it away.

Vander? the distant assassin questioned.

Like a mirror, Cadderly offered no response other than to turn the telepathic question back on the winds.

Vander!

Anger. Cadderly felt that above all else. The young priest smiled in spite of the importance of his task, pleased by the confirmation that he had at least unnerved the little assassin.

Then the call was no more, but Cadderly, suspecting the killer who had been so dogged in pursuing him would not give up that important link so easily, didn't let his guard down.

Vander hissed. Cadderly heard it distinctly.

"Fight!" the young priest cried, both aloud and mentally.

Ivan and Pikel moved to the stall door, weapons ready, as Cadderly had instructed. If the assassin found his way into Vander's identity, the dwarves would set upon him before he could sort out his surroundings.

But Cadderly had no intention of letting Ghost in, not while the trickster had his body as an open escape route, safely away in Carradoon. The young priest conjured an image of the spinning spindle-disks, shared it with Vander, and together they studied the hypnotic dance, remembered the specific defensive chants Cadderly had taught the giant.

Other, more evil sensations assaulted them, cluttered their space with the anger of another will. Cadderly prayed that Ghost wouldn't realize that Vander had an ally beside him.

Cadderly watched and chanted, and the firbolg, though his anger rose dangerously, managed to keep Cadderly in his mind.

Together, they drove the would-be possessor away.

Q

"You defy me?" Ghost asked in the dark alleyway. Above anything else, the assassin, vulnerable without Vander, knew such defiance could not be tolerated. Vander was his out, his escape from any situation. He couldn't allow the firbolg to somehow, somewhere, find the strength to turn his distant intrusions away.

Somehow? Somewhere?

The little assassin breathed a deep sigh. What was going on at the farm? he wondered. He feared that Cadderly might be involved, but how could that be? Certainly Vander, if an attack had come, would have called out to Ghost? Might Cadderly and his friends have taken the farm so quickly that the firbolg never got the chance?

Ghost dismissed the thought. Vander was still alive. Ghost had recognized the receptacle at the other end of his telepathic call. He told himself he was being paranoid, a dangerous state of mind for a killer living on the edge of artistry and disaster. Vander had denied him before, after all, from a distance, where the *Ghearufu's* power was not quite the same.

In a few hours, Ghost could call upon the firbolg again and get back in. Vander would not be able to keep up his mental defenses for very long. A twisted grin spread across the wicked man's face as he considered the boundless possibilities for punishment.

The smile did not last long. Ghost's mind was clouded by doubt. Something was wrong, and there was simply too much at stake for Ghost to readily accept that Vander had found a moment of strength to keep him out. The assassin had not located Cadderly and the young priest's friends in some time.

"To the farm," the assassin decided. He would go there, punish Vander, and regroup his forces.

He slipped out of the alleyway and approached an armed man sitting comfortably on a fine horse.

"Your pardon, gentle sir," Ghost said meekly to the city guardsman.

The assassin was wearing his mismatched gloves. No need to take chances.

Q

Up on the farmhouse roof, wearing the black-and-silver domino mask and nondescript clothes of a Night Mask, with the cowl of a black cloak pulled low, Danica watched the riders—two men on one horse—moving steadily down the road. The monk leveled her crossbow when the two entered the farmyard. She recognized the man on the back as the same assassin they had found at the Dragon's Codpiece. Danica's instincts prompted her to shoot the man from the horse, but Cadderly had warned her that the man might not be what he seemed.

Another factor urged Danica to hold her shot: the man in control of the horse wore the uniform of a Carradoon guardsman.

"He is a friend," the assassin on the back of the horse called out, seeing Danica atop the roof.

Danica smiled under the cowl, glad that her disguise had apparently fooled the pair.

"Friend," the guardsman said. He brought the horse into the yard, said something to the other man Danica couldn't hear, and dismounted, heading straight for the barn.

Danica was confused and worried. Cadderly had expected the weakling assassin to come in and confront Vander, not bring a city guardsman. She still held tight to her crossbow, still wanted to put a quarrel into the evil little man's androgynous face.

To her further surprise, the guardsman didn't go into the barn. Instead he moved to the gutter along one corner and began to scale it. He was halfway up the tall structure before the man on the horse took serious note of him, and Danica thought his reaction—wide-eyed and pale—a curious thing.

"What in the Nine Hells is going on?" the young woman whispered.

She looked around the yard to see if Ivan or Pikel had slipped out of the barn, to try to discern if anyone inside had any idea about the strange events in the yard.

The guardsman made the edge of the roof. Danica looked up to see him, and she pulled her cowl tighter, fearing that the man had climbed only to give him a better view of her position—a better view of her.

He paid her little heed, though. He wore mismatched gloves and stood on the edge, looking down at his companion, who, by that time, had dismounted.

"You have outlived your usefulness," the guardsman explained. He laughed wildly, clapped his hands, and dived headlong off the roof.

His laughter turned to a shriek then a groan then silence.

Danica breathed hard, not beginning to understand what had just occurred. She looked down to the man standing beside the dead guard, saw that it was he who wore the strange gloves. He looked up at her, shrugged, and bolted for the barn door. By the time he got there, the gloves were gone.

Q

"You resisted my call," Ghost said to Vander. "We have discussed this matter before."

"This kill is . . . ugly," Vander stammered in reply, obviously nervous in facing the man who had been his tormentor for so long. The firbolg gnawed his thick lips under his bushy red beard, wishing that his new-found allies would rush out and end that taunting nightmare.

"I am not speaking of young Cadderly," Ghost retorted. "He will be dealt with in time, do not doubt. I have come here to speak only with you, the one who dared to resist my call."

"I did not—"

"Silence!" Ghost commanded. "You know that to resist is to be punished. I cannot complete my task with an unwilling associate out here, safely separated from the town."

Unwilling *vessel*, Vander corrected, but he wisely held the thought to himself.

Ghost took a few steps across the barn floor, peering out through a crack in the side boards. "Do you remember your brother?" he teased, referring to the firbolg he had killed when Vander had run away from him, had run all the way back to the distant Spine of the World Mountains.

The wicked little assassin turned, smiling even more widely when he noticed Vander's great hands clenched in helpless rage at the giant's side.

C

Ivan peeked through a crack in the stall's wall, then looked back, concerned, at Cadderly and Pikel.

The young priest, intent on his telepathic connection

with the firbolg, didn't notice the dwarf at all. He felt Vander's mounting rage, a blocking emotion that diminished their bond. Things had gone pretty much as Cadderly had expected, but he was no longer certain of how he should react. Even across the miles from Carradoon, Ghost's intrusion had been difficult to fend off. How would he and Vander fare with the sneaky assassin standing just a few feet in front of the firbolg?

Calm, he imparted to the firbolg. *You must remain calm.*

Q

"Punishment," Ghost purred, putting one finger to his pursed lips. He fingered something in his other hand, something round and gold, though Cadderly couldn't tell exactly what it might be.

"I never told you this before," the assassin went on, "but I did more to your son, poor boy, than take his arm."

Vander's eyes widened. His great hands twitched, trembled, and his roar shook the walls of the wooden barn.

"Time to go?" Ivan dared to ask aloud under the cover of that prolonged growl.

Cadderly's mind was filled with a wall of red, the manifestation of Vander's uncontrollable rage. The young priest was out of contact with the firbolg, he knew, and he knew, too, that by the time he managed to contact his ally once more, the disaster might well be complete. He uncoiled his legs beneath him and accepted Pikel's arm to hoist him to his feet. Neither his spindle-disks nor his enchanted walking stick offered him much hope in defeating a giant, so he clenched his

337

hand, the hand with the enchanted ring, and reached inside his cloak for the wand.

"No!" he cried out, leading the dwarves into the main area of the barn. Cadderly calmed immediately, though, as did Ivan and Pikel behind him, when he regarded the scene, a scene that Vander apparently had well in control.

The firbolg, panting and growling, held the puny assassin in the air by the throat, shaking him hard, though the man was obviously already dead.

"Vander," Cadderly said quietly to calm the giant's rage.

The firbolg paid him no heed. With another roar of outrage, he folded the assassin in half, backward, and hurled him against the barn wall.

"He will return!" the giant wailed. "Always, he comes back for me! There can be no escape!"

"Like a damned troll," Ivan remarked from beside the firbolg, his voice reflecting sympathy for the beleaguered giant.

"Troll?" Cadderly whispered, the word inspiring an idea.

The young priest held his clenched fist out before him, barked the word, *"Fete!"* and sent a line of fire at the corpse.

He kept his concentration firm, determined to burn whatever regenerative powers he could from the wretch, determined that Vander would at last be free. He glanced sidelong at the firbolg, took note of Vander's satisfied expression then noticed, curiously, that Vander wore a golden ring.

Curious indeed, Cadderly thought as he turned back to the charred body, for he was just thinking of looking for such an item on Ghost's blackened form.

Cadderly searched his memory in an instant. Vander had worn no rings.

Aura.

"Ivan!" Cadderly cried, ending his flames and spinning around. The giant moved as well, whipping out his huge sword, with Ivan standing unsuspecting right beside it.

Cadderly proved the quicker. *"Mas illu!"* he screamed as he drew the wand. A burst of colors exploded in the firbolg's face. Blinded, the giant continued his swing, aiming for where Ivan had been.

The dwarf, warned and blinded by the blast, fell back. He heard the tremendous rush of air as the sword passed, taking off his helmet and clipping him enough to send him into a roll.

"I knew I'd get me chance!" the stubborn dwarf growled when he at last righted himself. Never shying from a fight, Ivan took up his axe and charged back in.

Danica slipped into the barn, discerned immediately what was going on, and fired a quarrel into the firbolg's belly.

The giant howled in pain but was not deterred from parrying Pikel's powerful charge, deflecting the over-balanced dwarf to the side, where he collided with a beam.

The giant feigned a sword thrust then kicked out instead, sweeping Ivan aside once more.

Another quarrel caught him in the shoulder, but again he seemed to hardly take note of it.

Danica was back at the door, Ivan and Pikel off to the sides, leaving Cadderly as the closest target. The young priest's first instinct told him to use his ring, to drive the beast back with a line of flame until his friends could regroup.

He realized the grim consequences for Vander, though, for the poor, proud firbolg who had been trapped in the weakling body and tossed aside like so much garbage. The magical ring had no power to restore burned flesh, and if his body was charred, like the assassin's corpse across the room, the firbolg could never reclaim it.

The giant lurched, popped in the back of the knee by Pikel's rebounding charge. With a grunt, the beast reached around and grabbed the green-bearded dwarf, hoisting him up into the air.

Pikel stared into the outraged giant's bloodshot eyes then promptly stuffed his foot up the beast's flaring nostril and waggled his gnarly and smelly dwarf toes.

Half-sneezing, half-coughing, the disgusted giant hurled Pikel into the far wall and wiped his arm across his face. When he looked back at Cadderly, he found himself staring down the end of that slender wand. Thinking another attack forthcoming, Ghost snapped his eyes shut.

"Illu," Cadderly said calmly, and the whole barn lit up with the brightness of a midday sun in an open field. Cadderly's aim had been perfect, though, and soon the glow of his wand's magic restricted itself to the firbolg's face, particularly to the giant's eyes.

Q

Whiteness? When Ghost opened his eyes, he saw only whiteness, glaring and blinding. The whole damned world had gone white! Or perhaps, Ghost wondered, more curious than afraid, he had been transported to some other world.

Another stinging crossbow bolt dived into his belly, driving that notion away.

His roar shook the walls once more, and the light-blind giant charged ahead, toward the unseen bowman, flailing his sword wildly. He slammed into the edge of the open barn door, dislodged the thing, and continued out.

Another quarrel sliced into the giant, and lured him ahead.

Ghost felt a club slam the back of his knee again, slipping through his great legs and tripping him as he tried to spin and react. Down the giant sprawled, shattering a water trough with his face and arms.

Something heavy and sharp, an axe, perhaps, sliced into his ankle, and a crossbow quarrel entered his shoulder, clicking off his huge collarbone.

Somehow the stubborn wretch managed to stand and stagger forward. His already wounded ankle took a hit from the heavy club.

He turned, sword leading, but the dwarf was already out of reach and the mighty weapon smacked hard against a small tree, uprooting it. Growling with rage, Ghost heard scuffling feet as the enemy continued to flank him, to encircle him.

He tried to call for the *Ghearufu*, even though he knew his own body was inaccessible, and knew that, even if he managed to hold enough concentration to summon the thing, Cadderly would somehow follow his spirit's movements. He couldn't get to it anyway. The hits were coming too fast, from every direction.

He jerked about, one way and another, leading with his low-cutting sword each time. Fury became his only defense, and he was confident that he was swift enough to keep his enemies at bay. Only weariness would slow him, and he hoped he could continue the blind assault until the infernal whiteness left his eyes.

Another quarrel whistled in, taking the giant in the lung, and Ghost heard the wheeze of his life's breath spurting out through a bloody hole.

He swung again and again, frantic and dizzy. He overbalanced, roaring and wheezing. He tried to step forward, but his badly gashed ankle would no longer support him, and he lurched ahead, bending low.

Right in line for the waiting Ivan.

The axe chopped into the firbolg's backbone. Ghost felt the burning flash then felt nothing at all below his waist. His momentum carried him one more long step forward, an awkward gait on stiff, unsupporting legs, and he tumbled and turned, crashing hard into the base of the huge elm at the side of the house.

There was only whiteness, pain, numbness.

Ghost heard the three friends shuffle near him but had not the strength to lift his sword in defense. Above all else, he heard the bloody wheeze at his side.

Ç

"Got him," Ivan remarked as Cadderly rushed up to join his friends. "Ye wanting us to tie him down afore ye talk with him?"

The young priest, stone-faced, did not reply, understanding that the loss of a physical body didn't end the threat of Ghost. He walked to the side of the helpless giant, took his spindle-disks in hand, and hurled them with all his strength right into the firbolg's temple.

The battered monster jerked once then slipped to the ground at the side of the tree.

Danica, holding her crossbow low, gaped open-mouthed at her lover's uncharacteristic lack of mercy.

"Take out your bolts," Cadderly instructed her, "but do not remove his ring!"

The last image the young priest saw was that of his friends exchanging confused glances, but he had no time to explain.

Spirits were waiting for him.

Q

Cadderly followed the flow of Deneir's song into the netherworld without hesitation. The material world blurred to him, and his friends appeared as indistinct gray blobs. As he had expected, the young priest saw the spirit of Ghost sitting near the fallen giant's body—on one of the lower limbs of the elm, actually—the spirit's head resting in its translucent palm, waiting patiently for the magical ring to open the receptacle for its return.

Cadderly knew then that he had two choices: go back and remove the giant's ring, or go and find the rightful owner of the soon-to-be-restored body. He willed himself to the barn, leaving his corporeal body standing impassively beside his friends.

Vander's spirit crouched inside the barn, terribly afraid and uncertain.

You also? came his thoughts to Cadderly.

I am not dead, Cadderly explained, and he beckoned for the firbolg to follow him, showed his lost friend what he must do.

Together, the two spirits set upon Ghost with a

vengeance. They could do no real damage to the assassin's ghost, but they mentally pushed him away, combined their wills to create a spirit wind that increased the distance between the evil spirit and the recovering body.

You'll not stop me, the wretch's spirit told them, its thoughts burning into their minds.

Cadderly looked back and saw a glowing ring form beside the firbolg's massive form. *Go,* he bade Vander.

The giant's spirit rushed away, but Ghost's spirit followed quickly.

Cadderly held up a hand. *No,* he commanded, and Ghost slowed almost to a stop as he passed the young priest's mental barrier. Cadderly's spirit arms wrapped around him, further delaying him. The young priest, in both his corporeal and spirit forms, smiled as Vander's spirit narrowed like a flying arrow and slipped through the glowing ring, entering the waiting giant form.

You are lost, Cadderly told the assassin, releasing his mental hold.

Ghost didn't hesitate; he rushed for the only other waiting, spiritless receptacle.

C

"Shave me if this one ain't alive again!" Ivan growled, lifting his axe dangerously above the firbolg's head. "He lifts one o' them big arms, and I'm gonna give him such a headache. . . ."

Danica grabbed the dwarf's arm to quiet him, explaining that the firbolg, alive or not, was in no position to threaten anyone. The reassurance sent Pikel skittering up beside the giant's head, the curious dwarf bending low to watch the reawakening.

A strange mewing sound from Cadderly turned all of them around. The young priest's body trembled, one eye twitched wildly, and his mouth contorted as if he were trying to say something but couldn't control himself.

Ghost had gotten there first, had slipped into Cadderly's waiting shell. Cadderly rushed in right behind, felt the burning pain of rematerializing, and felt, too, that he was not alone.

"Get out!" he finally managed to shout, aloud and telepathically.

Ghost did not respond, other than to push at Cadderly's spirit. The young priest felt the burn begin again and knew it signified that he was slipping back out of his form.

But to be pushed out then was to lose himself forever. Cadderly called on his recollections of mental battle, of his experience with the imp, Druzil, back in the forest, and called, too, upon the song of Deneir, hoping to find in its notes some clue that would give him an edge.

But Ghost, too, had experiences to call upon—three lifetimes of exchanging spirits with unwilling victims.

What it came down to was a test of willpower, a test of mental strength.

Ghost didn't have a chance.

"Out!" Cadderly screamed. He saw his friends clearly for a moment then slipped back to the spirit world and saw Ghost's stunned form floating helplessly away.

You have not won, came the defiant assassin's promise.

Your connections are gone now, Cadderly argued. *You have no magical ring upon a corpse to give you a hold in the material world.*

I have the Ghearufu, the sinister spirit retorted. *You*

cannot know its strength! There will be other victims about, foolish priest, weaklings who will lose out to me. And I will come again for you! Know that I will come again for you!

The threat weighed heavily on Cadderly, but he didn't believe Ghost's promises were likely. A black spot appeared on the ground, accompanied by a growl, confirming Cadderly's suspicions.

Your connections to the Prime Material Plane are gone now, Cadderly reiterated, seeing the other spirit's confusion.

What is it? Ghost cried to Cadderly, his panic showing clearly.

A black hand shot up from the ground, grabbed the evil spirit's ankle, and held it fast. Frantic, Ghost struggled to pull away, the effort tripping him to a sitting position.

Black hands grabbed his wrists, and growling shadows rose all around him.

Q

Cadderly blinked his eyes open to see his concerned friends, Danica and Ivan holding him by the arms, and Pikel studying his face. He felt unsteady, thoroughly drained, and was glad for the support.

"Eh?" the green-bearded dwarf piped curiously.

"I'm all right," Cadderly assured them, though his shaky voice weakened his claim considerably. He looked at Danica, and she smiled, knowing beyond doubt that it was indeed Cadderly standing before her.

"The giant's alive again," Ivan said with wonder.

"It is truly Vander," Cadderly assured them. "He returned through the power of the ring."

He drew a deep breath to stop the world from

swimming in front of his eyes. His head throbbed more painfully than he ever remembered.

"To the barn," he instructed, and he stepped out of Danica and Ivan's grasp and took a step forward.

And pitched sideways to the dirt.

Q

It took the young priest some time to orient himself when he again found consciousness. He was in the barn—the stench of burned flesh told him that more than the blurry images dancing before his half-opened eyes.

Cadderly blinked and rubbed his bleary orbs. His three friends were with him, and he realized he hadn't been unconscious for very long.

"They just appeared," Danica explained to him, leading his gaze to the items—a small, gold-edged mirror and mismatched gloves adorning the charred and broken corpse by the wall.

"*Ghearufu*," Cadderly said, remembering the name Ghost had given the thing. The young priest stared closely at the item and felt a sensation of brooding, hungry evil. He looked around to his friends, concerned. "Have any of you handled it?"

Danica shook her head. "Not as yet," she replied. "We've decided that the best course of action would be to bring the item to the Edificant Library for further study."

Cadderly thought differently, but he nodded, deciding it best not to argue. "Has the firbolg awakened?" he asked.

"That one'll be out for days," Ivan answered.

Again, Cadderly thought differently. He understood

the regenerative powers of the magical ring and was not surprised, a moment later, when Vander, hearing the discussion, walked into the barn.

"Shave me," Ivan whispered under his breath.

"Oo oi," Pikel agreed.

"Welcome back," Cadderly greeted the giant. "You are free from Ghost—you know that—and you're free, too, to go your way. We shall escort you as far as the Snowflakes—"

"You should not make such an offer so easily," the firbolg's resonant voice interrupted, and Cadderly wondered if he had misjudged the giant, if perhaps Vander was not so innocent after all.

The others were apparently thinking the same thing, for Ivan and Pikel put their hands to their weapons, preparing for another fight.

Vander smiled at them all and made no move toward the greatsword belted at his side. "I know where lies Castle Trinity, your true enemy," the firbolg explained, "and I pay my debts."

EPILOGUE

Q

The temple priests regarded Cadderly and his three companions curiously as they made their bouncing way to the guest rooms.

Rufo heard the racket and opened his door to see what was going on.

"Hello to yerself, too," Ivan growled at him, putting a hand on the man's chest and shoving him back into his small room.

The other three came in right after the dwarf, Danica closing the door behind her.

"Are you surprised to see me . . . alive?" Cadderly asked, sweeping his blue cape dramatically from his broad shoulders.

Rufo stammered the beginnings of several words, not really knowing where to begin. Dozens of questions and fears assaulted him, stealing his voice. How much did Cadderly know or suspect? he wondered. Where was the young wizard, or the rest of the Night Masks?

"The assassins are no more," Cadderly told him

confidently, as if reading Rufo's thoughts. "And the young wizard, too, is dead."

"Got that one good," Ivan whispered to his brother, and Pikel gave the great axe, strapped to Ivan's back, a respectful pat.

"Dead," Cadderly reiterated, letting the word hang in the air ominously, "like Avery."

Rufo's chalky, sharp-featured face paled even more. Again he started to reply, to concoct some lie about the headmaster's fate, some tale that would allow him an alibi for his crimes.

"We know," Danica assured him before he got the first words past his thin, dry lips.

"I did not expect this of you," Cadderly said, hooking his walking stick into the crook of his elbow. "Even after the events at the library and in Shilmista, I trusted that you would find a better path to tread."

Rufo ran his bony fingers through his matted black hair. His beady, dark eyes darted all around. "I don't know what you are referring to," he managed to say. "When Avery was found dead, I decided that I, too, would not be safe at the inn. I searched for you, but you were not to be found, so I came here, to be with my friends among the Ilmatari."

"You were afraid?" Danica asked, not hiding the sarcasm in her tone. "Did you fear your cohorts would cheat you?"

"I . . . I don't understand," Rufo stuttered.

Danica slapped him across the face, knocking him to a sitting position on his bed. The monk started forward, her expression an angry grimace, but Cadderly quickly intercepted her.

"Why else would you be afraid?" Cadderly asked

Rufo, to clarify Danica's last statement. "If not for your cohorts, then who would threaten you?"

"He knew we'd catch him," Ivan put in, grabbing Rufo's arm with an ironlike grasp.

"Y-you err!" Rufo stammered, desperate. All the world seemed to be closing in on him. Ivan's clenching hand felt like the jaws of a wolf trap. "I did—"

"Silence!" The command from Cadderly quieted the blustering man and turned his friends' incredulous stares to him.

Rufo slumped in his seat and lowered his eyes, thoroughly defeated.

"You led Avery to his death," Cadderly accused. "You betrayed me in the library, your friends in the forest, and now Avery. Do not expect forgiveness this time, Kierkan Rufo! The headmaster is dead—his blood is on your hands—and you have crossed into a realm from which there is no return."

Q

Images of those awful, growling shadows assaulted Cadderly. He closed his eyes and took a few deep breaths to steady himself but found himself imagining Rufo's impending fate, of the hungry, evil things that would drag the fallen priest down to eternal torment.

Cadderly shuddered and opened his eyes.

"Hold him," he instructed the dwarves.

"What are you doing?" Rufo demanded as Pikel grabbed the arm opposite the one Ivan held and the two locked him steady on the bed. "My friends will hear! They will not allow this!"

"Ilmater?" Ivan queried. "Ain't them the ones dedicated to suffering?"

"Yup," his brother answered.

"Well, with the hollering ye're about to do," Ivan snickered to Rufo, thoroughly enjoying the man's distress, "they're likely to build a statue to ye."

Rufo bit Pikel on the arm, but the tough dwarf just grimaced and didn't let go. Danica was around the bed in an instant. She grabbed Rufo's hair and jerked his head back viciously. Between that strong hold, and the dwarves at either side of him, Rufo could only watch and listen.

Cadderly chanted quietly, his hands moving through specific motions. He extended one finger to point at Rufo, its end glowing white with heat.

"No!" Rufo cried. "You must let me explain!"

"No more lies," Danica hissed from behind.

Rufo screamed and twisted helplessly as Cadderly's enchanted digit branded his forehead, burned the curse of Deneir—the likeness of a single, broken candle above a closed eye—into the man's skin.

Q

It was over in a heartbeat, and Danica and the dwarves let Rufo go. He slumped forward, whimpering, not so much for the continuing pain—there was little—but for the knowledge of what Cadderly had just done to him.

Branded. He smelled the foul odor and knew it would follow him, would magically ward people away from him, for the rest of his days.

"You must never hide your mark of shame," Cadderly said to him. "You are aware of the consequences."

Indeed, Kierkan Rufo was. To hide the lawful brand of Deneir caused the lingering magic to burn deeper into one's forehead, to burn to the brain, resulting in a horrible, agonizing death.

Rufo turned an angry gaze up at Cadderly. "How dare you?" he growled with every ounce of defiance he could muster. "You are no headmaster. You have no power—"

"I could have given you over to the city guard," Cadderly interrupted, the simple logic cutting Rufo short. "Even now I could tell them of your crimes and let them hang you in the street. Would that be preferable?"

Rufo looked away.

"If you doubt my ranking in the order," Cadderly continued, "doubt that I have the power to cast such judgment over you, then simply cover the brand. We will learn soon enough if you are correct." Cadderly removed his wide-brimmed hat and held it out to Rufo. "Let us see."

Rufo shoved the hat aside and staggered to his feet.

"Highest Painbearer," he said hopefully when his door opened and a thick-jowled, bald-headed priest, wearing the red skullcap denoting high rank in the Ilmatari order, peered in. Behind the man stood a dozen or more disciples of the temple, aroused by Rufo's agonized screams.

"They heared his yells and thought he joined their order," Ivan whispered to Danica and Pikel, and the three, despite the gravity of the situation, could not hide their chuckles.

The painbearer sniffed the air, his face twisting against the foul smell. He looked hard at Rufo, at the brand, then turned to Cadderly and asked, no anger in his tone, "What has transpired here?"

"They have betrayed me!" Rufo cried desperately. "They . . . he—" he pointed to Cadderly—"led Headmaster Avery Schell to his death! And now he tries to blame me, to divert attention from himself!"

Cadderly seemed to have no reaction to the ridiculous claim.

"Would Deneir have granted me the magical brand if that tale rang at all of truth?" he asked the Ilmatari.

"Is it authentic?" the lean priest asked, motioning to the wicked mark.

"Do you care to test it?" Cadderly asked Rufo, again extending his hat.

Rufo stared at it for a very long time, at the Deneirrath holy symbol set in its front center, knowing he had come to a critical point in his life. He could not accept the hat and put it on—to do so would bring about his death. But refusing strengthened Cadderly's claims, showed Rufo to be an honestly branded outcast. He paused for a long moment, trying to concoct yet another excuse.

His hesitation cost him any chance of explaining.

"Kierkan Rufo, you must be gone from here," the painbearer demanded. "Never again shall you be welcomed in any hall of Ilmater. Never again shall any priest of our order show you any kindness or respect."

The finality of the words sounded like a nail in Rufo's coffin. He knew there would be no point in arguing, that the decision was final. He turned, as if to move for his chest of belongings, but the painbearer would brook no delays.

"Now!" the man shouted. "Your possessions will be dumped into the alley. Be gone."

Ivan and Pikel, always ready to lend a hand, grabbed

Rufo by the arms and roughly heaved him forward. Of the many witnesses, not a single one offered a word of protest.

Branded priests had no allies.

Q

Cadderly had only one more task to complete before he would consider his business in Carradoon at its end, and he found assistance from a local cleric residing outside the lakeside city's high walls. The aged priest led Cadderly and his four companions—with Vander traveling in his magically reduced state, as a red-haired and red-bearded barbarian warrior—to a small grave in the churchyard.

Cadderly fell to his knees before the grave, not at all surprised, but filled with pity and grief.

"Poor dear," the gentle old priest explained. "She went out in search of her lost husband and found him, dead, on the side of the road. Alas for Jhanine and her children."

The priest waited a few moments then nodded to the companions and took his leave.

"You knew this man?" a perplexed Danica asked, crouching beside Cadderly.

Cadderly nodded slowly, hardly hearing her.

Danica took Cadderly's arm. "Will you go for him?" she asked, a bit sourly, but with all sympathy.

Cadderly turned to her, but his eyes were looking to the past, to his exchange on the road with the unfortunate leper. *Could you cure them all?* Nameless had asked him. *Are all the world's ills to fall before this young priest of Deneir?*

"This makes no sense, and borders on irreverence," Danica remarked, misconstruing Cadderly's silence.

"Where next after here? To the graves of the unfortunate farmers and the city guardsman?"

Cadderly closed his eyes and withdrew from Danica's stinging logic. He had already tried to resurrect the farmers, and the unfortunate guardsman, privately, before they had left the farm. The spirits of the farmers were not to be found, and the guardsman would not come to Cadderly's call. The effort had cost Cadderly dearly, exhausted him and taken, he knew, a little bit of his life energy forever.

"How many thousands will Cadderly recall to populate the world?" he heard Danica ask. He knew her sarcasm was not intended to be mean, only practical.

He knew Danica could not understand. The act of resurrection was not as simple as it had seemed when Cadderly had brought Brennan back from the dead. Cadderly had come to learn, painfully, that resurrection was a gods-given blessing, not a magical spell. Whatever powers the young priest possessed, he could not defeat ultimate fate. Many conditions had to be met before resurrection could be granted, and many more before the spirits of the dead would heed the call and return to the world they had departed. So many conditions, Cadderly couldn't even begin to sort through them, couldn't begin to question the divine decisions beyond his mortal understanding.

Wisely, he didn't ask it of Deneir again.

"My powers are for the living," he whispered, and Danica quieted, confident that he had come to understand what must be. He said a prayer for Nameless, a plea to whatever gods might be listening to judge the lost man fairly, to grant him the peace in death that had been so unfairly stolen from him in life.

Cadderly never did learn the beggar's real name and he preferred it that way. He and his friends went back to the priest who had shown them the grave, bearing a fair amount of gold they could spare for the deserving Jhanine, but it was Vander who threw in the largest gift: Aballister's purse of gold, the advance sum given the Night Masks for Cadderly's execution.

"Do you mean to cure the ills of the world?" Danica asked Cadderly again, after the companions had left the priest's small house beside the graveyard. She looked at him pleadingly, fearful for her love, fearful that the new weight of responsibility would break him.

"I will do what I can," Cadderly replied stubbornly. "It is the most that can be asked of us, and the least that any of us should be willing to give."

A chill breeze blew in from the west, a reminder that winter was not far away. Cadderly looked into it, sought the lines of trails on the distant Snowflake Mountains, the paths that led to the Edificant Library.

Maybe it was time to go home.

FORGOTTEN REALMS

ONE DROW • TWO SWORDS • TWENTY YEARS

A READER'S GUIDE TO

R.A. SALVATORE'S

THE LEGEND OF DRIZZT®

"There's a good reason
this saga is one of the most
popular—and beloved—
fantasy series of all time:
breakneck pacing, deeply
complex characters and
nonstop action. If you read
just one adventure fantasy saga
in your lifetime,
let it be this one."

—Paul Goat Allen,
B&N Explorations on
Streams of Silver.

Full color illustrations and maps
in a handsome keepsake edition.

FORGOTTEN REALMS, DUNGEONS & DRAGONS, WIZARDS OF THE COAST,
their respective logos and THE LEGEND OF DRIZZT are trademarks
of Wizards of the Coast LLC in the U.S.A. and other countries.
©2009 Wizards.

The New York Times BEST-SELLING AUTHOR

RICHARD BAKER

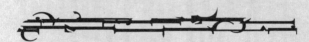

BLADES OF THE MOONSEA

"... it was so good that the bar has been raised.
Few other fantasy novels will hold up to it, I fear."
—Kevin Mathis, d20zines.com on *Forsaken House*

Book I	Book II	Book III
Swordmage	**Corsair**	**Avenger**
		March 2010

Enter the Year of the Ageless One!

A
DUNGEONS
& DRAGONS
NOVEL

FORGOTTEN REALMS, DUNGEONS & DRAGONS, WIZARDS OF THE COAST, and
their respective logos are trademarks of Wizards of the Coast LLC
in the U.S.A. and other countries. ©2009 Wizards.

TRACY HICKMAN

Presents

The Anvil of Time

The Sellsword
Cam Banks

The Survivors
Dan Willis

Renegade Wizards
Lucien Soulban

The Forest King
Paul B. Thompson
June 2009

The lost stories of Krynn's history are coming to light.

A DUNGEONS & DRAGONS NOVEL

DUNGEONS & DRAGONS, DRAGONLANCE, WIZARDS OF THE COAST, and their respective logos are trademarks of Wizards of the Coast LLC in the U.S.A. and other countries. ©2009 Wizards.

EBERRON

DRACONIC PROPHECIES

JAMES WYATT

From acclaimed author
and award-winning game
designer James Wyatt, an
adventure that will shake
the world of EBERRON®.

STORM DRAGON
AVAILABLE NOW IN PAPERBACK

DRAGON FORGE
AVAILABLE NOW IN PAPERBACK

DRAGON WAR
IN HARDCOVER AUGUST 2009

A
DUNGEONS
& DRAGONS
NOVEL

EBERRON, DUNGEONS & DRAGONS, WIZARDS OF THE COAST, and their
respective logos are trademarks of Wizards of the Coast LLC in
the U.S.A. and other countries. ©2009 Wizards.

39092 07562660 8

Everything you thought you knew
about MAGIC™ novels is changing...

From the mind of

ARI MARMELL

WHITE MOUNTAIN LIBRARY
SWEETWATER COUNTY LIBRARY
ROCK SPRINGS, WY

comes a tour de force of imagination.

AGENTS
OF ARTIFICE

APR 1 3 2010

White Mountain Library
2935 Sweetwater Drive
Rock Springs, WY 82901
307-362-2665

WM YA Fic Salv
39092075626608
Salvatore, R. A.
Night masks

MCO